The
Parlor
Game

The Parlor Game

ashtyn newbold

THREE LEAF
PUBLISHING

PROLOGUE

D*ear Lady Daventry,*

Your presence is requested at Birch House of Lockhart Square for a house party, beginning on the twenty-eighth day of August and ending on the sixteenth day of September.

Your attendance will present many priceless opportunities, the nature of which will be explained to you upon your arrival. Prepare for twenty days of games, entertainment, and exquisite dining at the most impressive manor in all of London, with the finest men and women of my acquaintance. As your hostess, I would be honored to have your company.

Sincerely,
   Lady Tottenham

CHAPTER 1

ANNE

August 28th, 1818

I t was five minutes past midnight when the second note of the evening was slipped underneath my bedchamber door at Birch House. It skittered across the floor, coming to a halt just inches away from my discarded boots.

"What on earth?" I muttered, jolting up straight on my bed. Had someone seen light coming from my room? I should have blown out my candle. I stared at the door, half-expecting the handle to jostle as the shadows of two feet finally dispersed down the corridor. I exhaled a slow breath, pressing one hand to my chest.

The first note had come less than an hour before, preventing my sleep due to its strange nature. I had known my hostess was a bit...peculiar, but I hadn't expected the first night of her house party to consist of such odd invitations.

The first note still rested on the table beside my bed, and its contents had been playing through my mind since I had first opened it.

Dear Lady Daventry,

You have been selected from amongst my guests to participate in this evening's secret parlor game. Please meet in the parlor at midnight for a night of frivolity you shall never forget. Be sure to bring your wit, imagination, and daring nature. I look forward to your attendance.

Your hostess,
Lady Tottenham

I clutched the sides of my nightdress and crept toward to the new letter on the floor. I swiped it up. The smudged ink was still damp. How could I sleep at all for the next week in this house if I was to expect mysterious letters under my door every hour?

Lady Daventry,

I must insist upon your attendance. Please make haste. We wait upon your arrival in the parlor.

Lady T

I cast my gaze upward with a sigh, glaring at the plaster-work on the ceiling. It would seem there was no escaping this 'game' without disrespecting my hostess. My mind raced with what 'secret parlor game' could entail. I would put nothing past Lady Tottenham and her love of theatrics.

And breaking rules.

I was a widow just as she was, but she seemed to think that her widowhood came with permission to ignore all the regulations of polite society. She was nearing the age of sixty, and she had no desire to marry again. She attracted friends from all over Town with her extravagant parties and peculiar soirees. The first day I met Lady Tottenham at a ball in Town, she invited me to a dinner party at which she served a dessert topped with dried crickets. She thrived on shocking people.

I suspected she liked me so much because I was easily shocked.

She had money, a title, and connections—and she was fearless about losing the latter. She had once told me that all she required to be happy were her gowns, her elaborate meals, and the memories of her late husband.

That was, perhaps, where we differed the most. She loved her late husband. I would eat a pile of dried crickets if it meant I could forget mine.

The invitation to Lady Tottenham's house party had come at the most opportune time. I had accepted it with one purpose: a place to live in London for the next twenty days. With my finances depleting steadily, I depended on her hospitality. I had received a different letter a month before, and it had become all I breathed for. I read it daily. The memorized words lived inside my mind.

Dearest Anne,

I am not certain this letter will reach you before I return from

India, but it is my hope that you receive it well. The months have been long without you. My time abroad has given me time to reflect on my future, and the dream I have of spending it with you. Forgive me if I am too bold in declaring my intentions in a letter after all these years, but I couldn't bear to wait another moment. All that I have done has been for you, for that dream, to secure a financial state that might make your life comfortable. When I learned that you were widowed, I already had plans to go to India. I was afraid my feelings might not have been returned. Now that I am here, I regret my decision to leave. I am coming back to London. I plan to arrive no later than the middle of September of this year in the hopes that we might soon marry. I hope to find you there.

With all of my heart,
Miles

The letter had been delivered to the dower house of my late husband's estate where I had spent the last year watching helplessly as the baron's land suffered. The letter summarized my dreams.

Miles Holland, the only man I had ever loved, was returning to London after two years, and he wanted to marry me.

The thought still flooded my heart with giddiness. He was my only source of hope. In a few short weeks, we would be reunited. Lady Tottenham's house party had seemed the perfect distraction and place of financial respite, though her strange notes were making me question my decision.

My eyes stung, begging for sleep, but I didn't have a choice. I groaned and reached for the bell pull.

The speed at which my maid arrived at my door was highly suspicious. Had she been waiting in the corridor? Jane gave a curtsy as she advanced into the room to help me back into my rigid lilac gown. She was the most petite woman I had ever seen, likely not older than sixteen, with rosy cheeks and dark curls like my own. She looked particularly miniature standing beside me in the looking glass as she laced my stays. The top of her head barely reached my shoulder.

I caught her gaze in the reflection. "Do you...happen to know anything about this secret parlor game?" My voice was a scratchy whisper. I didn't dare speak any louder.

Her eyes flitted to the floor. Her lips pressed together, and I could tell there was a lie hiding behind them. "I've never 'eard of such a thing." She unraveled my braid in silence and began pinning up the strands.

My stomach formed a knot. I swallowed hard against the worry rising in my throat.

She arranged my hair in a simple coiffure before taking her leave. Her rushed movements must have been due to Lady Tottenham's instruction.

My heart thudded as I sneaked out into the corridor behind Jane. But she was already gone, vanished somewhere between the pockets of candlelight. The sconces flickered on the dark paneled walls, and the intricate faces carved in the wood stared back at me. I gulped.

As I approached the staircase leading down to the ground floor, the sound of chattering voices and laughter drifted up from the parlor. The tension in my shoulders relaxed slightly. Had all of the guests been invited? It would come as a relief if I knew I hadn't been singled out.

A creaking sound came from my left, cutting through the

7

faint voices from below. I jumped, my hand flying to the bannister. I gripped it tightly as I noticed the open door that had caused the sound.

I nearly stumbled down the first stair when I noticed what was *beyond* the open door.

A man stood with one hand on the frame, the other on the brass doorknob. His dark hair was mussed, a shadow of stubble covering the lower half of his face. He blinked in confusion, as if he had just been jostled awake. All he wore was a pair of dark knee breeches slung low across his hips, his chest and abdomen fully displayed in the candle light. *What on earth?* Were all of Lady Tottenham's guests as improper as she was?

I averted my gaze, my neck growing hot. Whoever that man was, I hadn't seen him amongst the other twelve people at dinner. Of course his surprising state of undress had pulled my attention away from his face, but I didn't dare take another look.

I rushed to turn around, fully intent on pretending I hadn't seen him. The secret parlor game was suddenly far more inviting.

"Am I missing a party?" The man's voice echoed in the corridor.

My feet froze. I kept my gaze fixed on the stairs ahead. "No."

He was silent for a few seconds.

One particularly loud laugh drifted up from the parlor and betrayed me.

"There are people downstairs and you are about to join them," he said with a hint of accusation. "Obviously I am missing something."

"Yes, you are." I glanced back at his face, unable to hide my dismay. "Your shirt."

The dazed look cleared from his eyes as they met mine. He looked down at his chest. Had he only just realized he wasn't fully clothed? Half his mouth quirked upward. "Forgive me. I didn't think there would be a lady sneaking about the corridor at this hour." He shielded himself with the door, leaving just his head and one shoulder peeking through. Somehow, he didn't seem embarrassed at all. His smile persisted.

My gloved fingers held tight to the bannister. "Did you not receive a letter under your door this evening?"

He took a step back and examined the floor. "No."

"Then it would seem Lady Tottenham did not invite you."

He frowned. "That isn't very...hospitable."

His face was somewhat familiar now, though I couldn't place it. His features each paid a compliment to the other, creating a harmonious face that anyone would call handsome. Dark eyes, dark brows, tousled dark waves. He looked younger than most of the men at the house party—perhaps even younger than me by a small number of years. At twenty-nine, I wasn't a youthful blossom anymore. I was an aged widow for all of society to pity.

Awkwardness hung in the air as he continued standing in the doorway, curious eyes fixed on me. My best guess was that he had arrived late and missed the events and introductions from earlier in the evening. We should not have been speaking without an introduction, but I had quickly discovered that entering Lady Tottenham's house was like entering a cage where the rules of society no longer existed. It was surreal and disquieting to say the least.

"Are you permitted to bring a guest with you?" The man

9

asked. There was an edge of flirtation in his voice that made my shoulder blades tighten.

I turned around to face the stairs. "No. And you are fortunate to have been excluded from the invitation. I envy you. I would much rather be confined to my room sleeping."

"Perhaps I should accompany you and request entrance to this secret party."

His voice had grown closer, which told me he had stepped away from the door. He must have trusted that I wouldn't turn around to see his exposed upper-body again—or he didn't care.

Or he wanted me to.

All were very plausible intentions.

"What are you doing?" My voice was panicked. It would not serve my reputation at the house well to have a shirtless man following me at midnight.

"I wish to come."

"You cannot," I said in a harsh whisper. "You were not given a letter."

"If it will make you more comfortable, I will put on a shirt. Even a waistcoat if you insist upon it." His flirtatious tone caused a scowl to crease my forehead.

I kept my gaze fixed on the stairs ahead, eager to rush down them and escape his determined questioning. If I could invent something that might make the effort of attending too troublesome, he might leave me alone. I searched my mind for an idea. "A shirt and waistcoat will not be enough," I said in a stern voice. "In Lady Tottenham's letter, she insisted that gentlemen come dressed in their most fashionable riding attire. She specified a need for white leather knee breeches, two waistcoats, a wool frock coat, and a neck cloth of the French affectation. As for footwear...only hessians will be tolerable. For headwear, she favors a tricorn hat."

The man was silent for several seconds before he gave a laugh of disbelief. "All of that for the parlor?"

"Yes. As you see, it is not worth the effort, and not worth displeasing Lady Tottenham. Please excuse me." I didn't wait for a response. With the bannister as my guide, I hurried down the dark staircase. I only dared to look back once I was safely on the ground floor. Part of me had expected him to follow me, but I was relieved to find the staircase empty.

I wrapped my arms around myself with a deep breath, rubbing my elbows. I couldn't be seen until I was composed. I straightened my posture outside the parlor, listening to the voices within. Had they started their game without me?

Just as the thought crossed my mind, the door swung open wide.

I jumped. Lady Tottenham faced me, her hand still clutching the doorknob. "Ah! Lady Daventry, I was just about to send someone to break down your door." She chuckled deep in her throat before her expression snapped into solemnity. "Make haste. We have been waiting far too long for you."

My eyes adjusted to the bright candlelight, bringing Lady Tottenham into clearer view. She wore a taffeta evening gown, the ribbons and trims an assortment of orange, red, and pink. Her hair, only slightly less orange, was piled atop her head in a cone shape, mimicking a flame. Curls spilled out from the arrangement and framed the sharp, playful features of her face: green eyes, a pointed nose, and lips smeared with dark rouge.

"What are these secret parlor games?" I whispered as I took her extended elbow.

"You shall soon find out." She practically shook me off her

arm, depositing me on a settee beside a gentleman. I glanced at my surroundings. There had been thirteen total guests at dinner, not including the shirtless new arrival. I had been introduced to all of them, but now their names escaped me. In total, there were only eight guests seated around the parlor. Four women, and four men.

Lady Tottenham drifted away to the center of the room, taking a graceful seat in her striped silk chair. "Ladies and gentlemen, I believe all the participants have now arrived." She grinned, revealing a smudge of rouge on her front tooth. "Let the games begin." She crossed her hands in front of her, glancing at each of the guests in turn. I followed her gaze around the room.

There was Mrs. Fitzgibbon, also a young widow, who was seated beside her cousins, Miss Morton and Miss Rowley. The poor young girls likely hadn't realized how a house party hosted by Lady Tottenham might risk their reputations. Mrs. Fitzgibbon was a naive chaperone to have approved her cousins' attendance. For a moment, Mrs. Fitzgibbon's eyes met mine, ablaze with excitement. She was either oblivious, or just as wild as Lady Tottenham.

The gentlemen in the room consisted of Mr. Amesbury, Mr. Barnwall, Mr. St. Vincent, and Lord Kirkham. Lady Tottenham had made it clear at dinner that all the guests in attendance were single, unattached, and ripe for the picking.

She had used those precise words.

I was not ripe, nor was I looking to be picked. Not when Miles was so close to returning. To my friends and family, I had pretended to have cared less for him than I did. But in truth, I had never forgotten him, nor my feelings for him. I had never forgotten the painful circumstances that had prevented us from marrying. I had never stopped loving him or waiting for him, even if it made me a pitiful, boring widow in the eyes of society.

"Good evening, my lady." The gentleman beside me interrupted my thoughts. His large forehead gleamed with perspiration. The thinning dark hair that remained on his head was combed to one side.

"Good evening, Mr. Barnwall."

During dinner I had learned that his wife had died two years before, leaving him the sole parent of six young children. He had a fortune vast enough to employ nannies and governesses to watch over them while he enjoyed parties like this in London. From what I understood, he was only at home a few weeks each year. I was not particularly fond of Mr. Barnwall already.

My father had shown a similar disinterest in my sister and me, and so I found such views on parenthood entirely detestable. According to Lady Tottenham, Mr. Barnwall had come here to secure a new mother for his children. By the way he was looking at me, it was clear that his eager eyes were searching for signs that I might qualify. As a widow on the shelf, he would assume I had few options to choose from.

Mr. Amesbury sat across from me, legs crossed, hands fidgeting nervously. He had blond curls, a friendly face, and from what I had learned, a small fortune and modest country estate to boast of. He appeared to be the youngest of the gentlemen, likely in his late twenties.

Mr. St. Vincent was rather stoic, with large side whiskers and black hair. All I knew was that his favorite pastimes consisted of gambling and drinking.

Last of all, there was Lord Kirkham, a baron from

Lancashire. I had never seen a man with such a rectangular face. The width of his jaw and forehead matched perfectly, and his thick, short neck led to a pair of hefty shoulders. He smiled in anticipation. Those teeth...he had proudly told the story at dinner—the story of how they had been chipped and broken in a match of fisticuffs. Working toward the center, one tooth was completely missing, the next was halfway broken, and the last was chipped at the bottom. It looked like a staircase.

Lady Tottenham spoke to the group again. "You may wonder why I have chosen you to participate this evening."

I tapped my foot on the rug. *Yes, please do enlighten me.*

"I consider you my friends, and at one point or another, you have all expressed to me your desire to marry and be well-matched."

I narrowed my eyes. I couldn't recall such a conversation. Lady Tottenham had expressed *her* wishes for me to marry and be well-matched, but I had never agreed with her. I had never told her about Miles. My stomach spiraled with nerves as she continued her introduction.

"Since the death of my dear husband decades ago, I have come to thoroughly enjoy the art of matchmaking. I find that giving a friend the opportunity of a love like the one I experienced is the greatest gift I could ever provide." Her smile grew impossibly wider. "It is now my honor to act as your matchmaker. During the remainder of your stay at my house, you will be given opportunities such as this one to meet others in the party in a more...intimate setting...with whom you might be compatible."

I caught myself shaking my head. I stopped, clenching my jaw instead. What on earth was she thinking? Only Lady

Tottenham would be so unabashedly public about her intentions.

Escape was still possible. I could pretend to faint, or claim illness. I had never been tempted to do something so ridiculous and ungraceful, but the alternative was far worse. My mind spun as I glanced around the room again. Which one of these men did she have in mind for me? If she had chosen only a select number of guests to attend the midnight game, she must have given some thought to the idea of who among us might be most compatible. I exchanged a glance with Miss Morton, who looked just as appalled as I was.

Lady Tottenham continued with that ever-widening smile. "If even just one match can be made in the duration of my party, I will be quite overjoyed. Now, who's it to be?" She cast her gaze at each of us in turn.

It most certainly wouldn't be me.

The ladies in the room were all pale, but the men all sat a little straighter. I felt their eyes grazing over me. I felt like a mouse in a field, waiting to be plucked up against my will. No one dared interrupt Lady Tottenham's speech, or decline their participation. She was clever. Rather merciless, too. Opting out of her 'games' would likely result in being snubbed for the rest of the house party.

Or sent away.

I couldn't do anything to upset her. I had to remain in London long enough to see Miles. I could participate in a few harmless games, but that didn't mean I had to meet my match among her guests. I told myself to relax, and my pulse finally started to slow. The tension in my shoulders loosened.

Candlelight gleamed off the whites of Lady Tottenham's eyes as she paced back to her chair. "The first game will be a variation of bullet pudding." She snapped her fingers, and the parlor door opened. A footman brought in a silver tray holding a perfectly shaped and compressed mound of flour. He placed it on the tea table, then placed a bullet on top of it.

Mrs. Fitzgibbon gave a nervous laugh. "Is this not a Christmas game, my lady? It's August."

"I am aware that it's August," Lady Tottenham snapped. "That's why we will *not* be playing it the traditional way."

Mrs. Fitzgibbon sat back, pressing her lips together. The excitement I had seen in her eyes had faded since Lady Tottenham's announcement about her matchmaking scheme. I didn't know the story behind Mrs. Fitzgibbon's widowhood, but no matter how or why someone became a widow, it usually gave that person reservations about marrying a second time. There were several widows who had been invited to the party. Lady Tottenham seemed to favor us, intent to take us under her wing. Besides Mrs. Fitzgibbon, there was myself, and a woman named Mrs. Pike.

It took me a moment to register the surprise on Lady Tottenham's face.

"Mr. Holland? I didn't expect you downstairs this evening." Her eyes were fixed on the door.

Mr. Holland? I must have imagined her words. My heart thudded in my chest. Surely Miles wasn't here. He wasn't due to arrive in Town for at least a month, and there was no reason he would have been invited to her house party.

Lady Tottenham's mouth was agape. "And what on earth are you wearing?"

I shook the fog from my head and turned around.

The man in the doorway was the same one I had seen upstairs. But now, he wore white leather knee breeches, two waistcoats, a wool coat, and a neck cloth of the French affectation. My throat dried up like a leaf as I noticed the tassels on his hessians and the tricorn hat atop his head. He looked like he was prepared to go on a lengthy horseback ride in December.

But it was, indeed, August.

I had not expected him to own all of those articles of clothing, but with autumn coming, it was reasonable that he would have brought a wool coat. Perhaps I had underestimated the depth of his traveling trunk.

I found his face beneath the shadow of his hat. He took a visual sweep of the room, his expression twisting in confusion. Then his gaze found me, and realization crept over his face. His eyes declared a war of sorts.

I wanted to disappear into the settee cushions.

Mr....*Holland?*

I stared at him, and in an instant, his features clicked together like a puzzle in my mind. A fourteen-year-old boy, mischievous and ill-mannered, sent off to boarding school by his parents. I remembered that summer. I had been fifteen, and Miles had been eighteen. It was the summer I discovered my feelings for him. I had spent so much time focused on Miles that I had hardly noticed anything else.

The person in front of me now...I couldn't blame myself for not recognizing him. It had been another fourteen years since I had seen his face. He had doubled in age since then. He had grown up. He was no longer a boy.

He was Alexander Holland—Miles's unscrupulous younger brother.

CHAPTER 2

ALEXANDER

I stared at the face of the woman who had tricked me into digging through my traveling trunks to find my tricorn hat.

It was a beautiful face. The most beautiful in the room by far.

I shook myself of my admiration. No amount of beauty could make up for the undeserved sham she had just pulled on me. Her eyes were a fascinating shade of hazel, her hair dark and glossy. Her straight posture made her seem unfettered by my sudden appearance in the room, but her features betrayed her. A look of panic crossed her face before she looked down at her lap.

Very well. It would seem that she had no intention of owning up to her actions. I would have to explain the situation myself.

Our hostess had the audacity to ask *what on earth* I was

wearing, when she, in fact, was wearing the most ridiculous gown I had ever seen. Besides that, she had rouge on her teeth.

I needed to act like I belonged, or she might send me back to my bedchamber. I had no intention of missing a single event this house party had to offer. It was how I would endure the weeks before my brother's return from India. He had something of mine, and I intended to get it back.

"I heard voices from the parlor," I said to Lady Tottenham before drifting into the room. "So I clothed myself in my finest attire before coming to investigate. My suspicions proved correct. The lot of you have dared to have a party without me." I smiled before taking a seat beside the wicked, dark-haired woman.

She shifted a few inches away.

Lady Tottenham's sharp brows lifted. "I must confess, the coat is an interesting choice."

"If it offends you, even in the slightest, I shall take it off." I removed my outer layer.

Lady Tottenham applauded with a laugh. "Please, do not stop there." The flirtatious tone in her voice was unsettling, considering she was twice my age.

A gentleman in the corner grumbled under his breath as I unbuttoned one of my two waistcoats. Lady Tottenham would regret not inviting me to her midnight parties once she discovered how lively I could be. When I had walked into the room, there had been a grimness in the air. I planned to change that. Once my outer waistcoat was removed, I stood to hand my spare layers to the footman.

Lady Tottenham pouted in dismay. "Is that all?"

"I don't wish to upset any of your delicate guests." I glanced at the woman on the sofa beside me before reclaiming my seat. She resisted my gaze, keeping it fixed straight ahead. "The sight of me without my shirt is quite offensive."

Lady Tottenham chuckled. "I doubt that."

I turned to the woman beside me again. I was determined to pull her striking hazel eyes back to my face. I had never seen such a rigid posture as hers. Her jaw was tight, and I could sense the embarrassment she was hiding.

Lady Tottenham spoke again, demanding my attention. "Well, Mr. Holland, if you hadn't made such a delightful entrance, I might have sent you out. I suppose I will allow you to stay for the game."

I cast my gaze around the room. The bright colors of the chairs and settees clashed with the nervous expressions of the people sitting on them. "What exactly is this game?" I asked.

"Each evening after midnight, I will host a parlor game by invitation only," Lady Tottenham said. "My invitations must not, under any circumstances, be declined. Nothing vexes me more greatly. It is my ambition to give ample opportunity to my many single, unattached guests for flirtation and romance. I hope to make a match or two from amongst you."

My brows lifted. That was certainly unconventional. I hardly knew how to respond, so I simply nodded. Lady Tottenham and I had been acquainted only a short time, through a dinner party I attended the year before. I hadn't known what to expect when accepting her invitation. I certainly hadn't expected a trap like this. With the state of my finances, marriage was not at the forefront of my mind. With two elder brothers, I was far from being the heir to our family fortune and estate. Two years before, I had finally qualified to become a barrister. I had worked hard to repay my debts and begin saving money for my future.

And then all of it had been taken away.

Lady Tottenham's house party was nothing more than a method of living without expenses for twenty days. Most of my success in my profession had been in York, which was less competitive than London for a new barrister. But I had come back to London with a purpose: To ambush my thieving brother when he returned from India. I hadn't come to be thrown into a matchmaking scheme. But if I hoped to remain in Lady Tottenham's good graces, I would have to play along.

I cleared my throat, hiding my surprise behind a nod of approval. "Flirtation and romance are two of my favorite things. When do we begin?"

"You have come to the right place. We shall begin straight away, but first, let us all become acquainted." She gestured in my direction. "This is Mr. Alexander Holland. He arrived late this evening and was unable to join us at dinner." She proceeded to introduce me to the other guests in the room, ending the circle at the mysterious woman beside me.

"Lady Daventry."

Ah. A *lady*. It was no wonder she felt the need to be so condescending.

Her eyes finally met mine, but they flickered away in an instant. She gave a nod in greeting.

My accusatory smile seemed to make her uncomfortable. All the more reason to keep it. "A pleasure to make your acquaintance, my lady." When Lady Tottenham walked away, I whispered, "why the tricorn hat?"

Her voice was barely audible. "I'm sorry."

"Do you find them attractive? Is that why you asked me to wear one?"

Her jaw tightened. "They are only attractive on officers."

"Thank you for the compliment."

Her eyes shot to my face with surprise. I was not actually an officer, but it was worth the look on her face. I grinned, noticing the mound of flour on the tea table for the first time. A bullet sat on top, and a small butter knife rested on the tray beside it.

Lady Tottenham began speaking. "To begin, I shall assign each of you a partner." She surveyed the room. "Miss Morton and Mr. Amesbury. Miss Rowley and Mr. St. Vincent. Mrs. Fitzgibbon and Mr. Barnwall. Lady Daventry and..." her voice trailed off. "We shall have a trio, I suppose." Her gaze darted between Lady Daventry and me. "Lady Daventry, Lord Kirkham, and Mr. Holland."

Lady Daventry did not seem pleased with the arrangement. Her features were stiff, her skin pale.

"The objective of the game is to cut a slice of flour without causing the bullet to drop," Lady Tottenham said. "Each partnership will take a turn, alternating which partner takes the risk of making the slice. Please move to sit beside your partner, and we will begin with Miss Morton and Mr. Amesbury."

I shifted closer to Lady Daventry. Lord Kirkham replaced Mr. Barnwall to her right. The settee creaked under his weight. He pushed his hair back from his square forehead as he made a thorough study of Lady Daventry. He smiled, apparently pleased with what he saw. How could he not be? I sensed her discomfort with his attention, yet she still gave him a smile that was warmer than what I had received.

"Good evening, my lord."

"Good evening, my lady." He leaned forward, eyeing me with a challenge. "Mr. Holland." His voice was curt.

We might have been partners, but he seemed to view me as

competition for Lady Daventry's attention. I didn't wish to raise any sort of competition with a man who was obviously well-acquainted with violence. I eyed his chipped teeth and the scar that ran down the side of his forehead.

Miss Morton made the first cut in the flour, and the pattern continued as all the women in the partnerships took the first, and least risky slices, around the outskirts of the mound of flour. On the second round, Lord Kirkham bravely volunteered, leaving me to take the greatest risk on the third round. The mound of flour was significantly smaller now. The bullet hung off the edge of one side. I took a careful slice, leaving the pile in one piece.

Somehow, all the partnerships took another turn, leaving all the ladies safe from being the one to drop the bullet.

When it was Lord Kirkham's turn again, his hand shook as he held the knife. It looked minuscule in his sausage-like fingers. The knife cut through the very edge of the flour, and the entire pile collapsed.

Delighted gasps filled the room as the other partnerships celebrated their victory. Lady Daventry adjusted her gloves, nervousness taking over her expression.

I leaned forward with a whisper. "Our team may have lost, but Lord Kirkham will have to retrieve the bullet with his mouth. That's the traditional way, at least." I was eager to see any pompous lord make a fool of himself. It would make the entire game worthwhile.

"This is Lady Tottenham's game," she whispered. "It will be anything but traditional."

I followed her gaze to our hostess, who applauded and rose to her feet. She stepped forward to examine the pile of flour.

From where I sat, I had a clear view. The bullet had sunk to the bottom.

"Well, my lord, it would seem you are unlucky tonight." She winked. "You must now retrieve the bullet using only your mouth."

Lord Kirkham rolled up his sleeves, even though he would not be needing his arms. He cast a glance at Lady Daventry before kneeling in front of the pile of flour. Did he hope to impress her with his performance?

Lady Tottenham raised three fingers in the air. "On the count of three. One, two, three!"

Lord Kirkham dove into the flour like it was a Christmas goose. Seconds later, he came up with the bullet clamped between his chipped teeth. Flour had somehow coated his eyebrows and eyelashes, as well as his entire nose and mouth. He roared in victory, inhaling enough flour to set him into a coughing fit.

I watched in horrified fascination as he coughed up the flour, sending puffs of it into the air. He wiped at the spittle on his chin, and it rolled into a ball of dough that resembled a tiny loaf. If it were baked into bread, I was fairly certain not even a starving mouse would eat it.

I nudged Lady Daventry's arm. "You're safe from humiliation, even if you enjoy humiliating others." I removed my tricorn hat, placing it on my lap just within her view.

She glanced at it. Candlelight flickered across her scowl, deepening the furrows. "I didn't think you would actually come downstairs. I apologize. I was trying to deter you."

I laughed. "Something you must know about me is that I am not easily deterred."

"Perhaps you should be."

"Is determination not an admirable quality?"

Her eyes flashed with vexation. "I would call it pride if you aren't wise enough to listen to the advice of someone who is only trying to help you."

Our conversation was lost under Lady Tottenham's voice.

"Now that you have retrieved the bullet, my lord, you must grant it to your partner. Well, *one* of your partners. To whom will you bestow the honor?"

Lord Kirkham spit the bullet into his palm and wiped it on the side of his trousers. Lady Daventry's nose twitched. Lord Kirkham's eyes watered with tears from his coughing fit, and two ravines had formed through the flour on his cheeks. That tiny loaf of dough still rested on his chin. "I shall bestow it to Lady Daventry, of course."

He strode forward with a proud grin, his flour dusted lips cracking. He presented the bullet to her as if it were a bouquet of flowers.

She received it in her palm with enough grace to make me forget this was a ridiculous game. "Thank you, my lord."

"Very good," Lady Tottenham said as she observed the exchange. "However, lest you forget, your team *did* lose the game."

Lady Daventry's hand fell slack, and she nearly dropped the bullet. Her eyes blinked in anticipation.

"It is only fair that your team is penalized. By bestowing the bullet to you, Lady Daventry, Lord Kirkham has unwittingly chosen you to pay a forfeit."

A wave of delighted whispers came from the ladies across the room. I leaned my elbows on my knees, eager to catch more than just the profile of Lady Daventry's face. A forfeit in a parlor game usually consisted of an embarrassing or difficult task performed in front of all the other players. An unwelcome surge of sympathy enveloped me, but I pushed it away. It was only a game. She seemed to be a strong woman, though apparently a bit shy and uncomfortable with being the center of attention.

Lady Tottenham snapped her fingers, and a footman strode forward with a glass bowl filled with pieces of parchment. "Now, please draw one slip from the bowl and present it to me. Some options are more favorable than others, so it will be the luck of the draw."

The guests fell silent as Lady Daventry rose to her feet and joined our hostess at the center of the room. She lifted her chin and reached her gloved fingers inside the bowl. She released an audible breath as she unfolded her selection and read the words silently. Her face fell. Lady Tottenham snatched the paper from her hand.

Lady Daventry's skin paled. Her terrified gaze met mine before dropping to the floor.

What the devil was written on that parchment? I shifted to the edge of my seat in anticipation.

Clearing her throat, Lady Tottenham read the penalty aloud.

"Kiss your partner."

CHAPTER 3

ANNE

My vision lost focus, and the floor tilted up toward me. She could *not* be serious. I blinked fast, bringing Lady Tottenham's ginger curls back into view, followed by her round, eager eyes.

She was mad.

How had I not realized this before? I had always called her 'eccentric,' but not insane. Kissing games were for the rebellious young debutantes, not the respectable widows and gentlemen that were here in the parlor. My heart pounded, and my hands sweat through my gloves. I knew I shouldn't have come down to the parlor. But if I hadn't, I would have been sent home. I had no choice but to follow the rules.

"In this case, you may choose *one* of your partners to kiss." Lady Tottenham's voice echoed in my ears.

Whispers erupted in the room. I accidentally glanced at Alexander.

He sat forward, brows lifted. Half his mouth curved upward. That smile was far too confident. He must have assumed he was the obvious choice, and there was something about that smug assumption that made my skin crawl.

In truth, discovering that he was Miles's brother was the only thing making my decision difficult.

Yes, Alexander was vexing, but at least he didn't have flour caked across his mouth.

Lord Kirkham dusted off his face discreetly, eyes gleaming in my direction.

My hands shook. Everyone watched me, awaiting my decision. Alexander's gaze burned against my already blushing cheeks. I gritted my teeth, urging myself to be composed. *I never blush.* It was only a kiss. My heart hammered.

The last man I had kissed had been my late husband. I had never understood why people enjoyed it so much. Because of him, I was not a stranger to kissing someone out of obligation.

Choosing Alexander was not a possibility. Miles and I had never even kissed in the years of our friendship, nor in the weeks of our courtship before it was halted. He had always been a gentleman. How could I ever tell Miles that I had kissed his brother? I couldn't.

My choice was already made.

"Well, who do you choose?" Lady Tottenham asked.

I swallowed, my breath lodging in my lungs. "Lord Kirkham."

I didn't dare look at his resulting smile, but I did check Alexander's face. His dark eyes glinted with surprise, then amusement. Hopefully my decision would lower his opinion of himself just a little.

I strode toward Lord Kirkham with as much confidence as

I could manage. He stood to meet me. I had to appear like I owned my decision, not that I was deeply regretting it. The other guests didn't bother to hide their surprise. Miss Rowley giggled, crossing the room to whisper something in Miss Morton's ear. They both laughed.

I would have to have a word with Lady Tottenham in the morning, but for now, all I could do was kiss the brute in front of me.

Lord Kirkham chuckled, deep in his throat. "I don't consider this a loss in the slightest. You and I are the true winners of the game."

You and I? I gulped. I planned to initiate the kiss, the lightest of pecks, but Lord Kirkham swooped in before I could prepare. His mouth covered mine, and all I could taste was the raw bread dough I had sneaked from the kitchen as a child. I wrenched myself free after what felt like an eternity, though I knew it had only been seconds.

I swiped at my mouth with my glove as soon as my back was turned. It came away dusted with flour.

I returned to my seat, my cheeks blazing.

"You have something just there." Alexander gestured at my face, just to the right of my mouth. I swiped angrily at it.

His smile grew. I wanted to throw my fist at it. He seemed quite pleased to have had his revenge by seeing me humiliated. A tricorn hat and coat was nothing compared to this. I swiped at my mouth again, checking my glove for flour. Tears welled up in my eyes, and the reason was difficult to pinpoint. I blinked them away fast.

Memories surged through my mind. My late husband, the baron, was much like Lord Kirkham. He had been boorish and arrogant. His kisses were just as unwelcome. He hadn't been kind. He hadn't thought of anyone but himself. My legs shook beneath my skirts as I crossed my ankles. A tremor had started through my entire body, and I didn't know how to stop it. I prayed no one noticed.

Lady Tottenham was speaking again, but I couldn't comprehend her. I was fighting hard to hold my tears at bay.

"Here," Alexander's whisper caught my attention. My anger nearly prevented me from looking at him. I squared my shoulders, jerking my gaze in his direction.

He slid a white handkerchief into my hand.

Had he seen my tears? My humiliation intensified.

"For the flour," he whispered. "There's some on your nose." For a moment, I thought he was offering a kindness, but then his lip twitched.

He was still laughing at me.

All the stories Miles had told me about Alexander and the trouble he had caused their parents made sense. It made sense completely. I could easily understand why Miles didn't like him, and why they hadn't seen eye to eye over the years. Who could get along with such an impertinent tease?

He and Miles couldn't be more different, and not just in character. Seeing Alexander's face now, there was very little similarity in his and Miles's features. If I didn't know better, I would have never assumed they were brothers. Miles's face was warm and inviting. Alexander's features were much darker, his countenance brimming with mischief.

"I hope I have provided you all with enough entertainment and romance for this evening," Lady Tottenham said. "You may all be excused to your bedchambers. Sleep well, for the games have only just begun."

I was the first one to stand. I forced myself to stand tall as I tried to escape the heat of the room. Lady Tottenham stopped me at the door, her wrinkled fingers wrapping around my forearm. "Please do not ignore my invitations in the future. I take my games quite seriously, as should you."

I nodded, shocked by her foreboding tone. "Forgive me. It will not happen again."

She released my arm, and I slipped into the corridor. The fresh air cooled my skin as I put as much distance between myself and the other guests as possible. My feet carried me fast, though I refused to ever run in public.

Quick footfalls bounded up the stairs behind me. "My lady."

Drat it all. I had almost made it to the top. The deep voice was already familiar enough to recognize. I didn't want to turn around, so after a pause, I continued walking.

"Are you all right?" Alexander's voice came again.

"Yes." I glanced over my shoulder. "Goodnight, Mr. Holland."

He stood with one foot on the stair above him, hand on the bannister. The concern on his brow was unexpected. Had my emotions really been so obvious? It was a silly game, that was all. The kiss didn't matter. As mortifying as it was, no one would remember it tomorrow.

I hurried to my bedchamber and shut myself behind the door. When I glanced at the looking glass, I flinched.

At least Alexander hadn't lied. There was indeed flour on my nose.

A few minutes later, I stared at the dark ceiling, struggling to fall asleep. Lady Tottenham's words would haunt me all night.

Sleep well, for the games have only just begun.

♟♟♟

Kiss your partner.
Kiss your partner.

I tore another slip of paper from the bowl, then another. All of them read the same.

Kiss your partner.
Kiss your partner.
Kiss your partner.

I dropped the slips into the bowl with a frustrated sigh. "That conniving woman," I whispered to myself.

Despite the events of the evening before, I still hadn't been able to sleep later than sunrise. Lady Tottenham had encouraged all her guests to wander and explore Birch house, so I had taken the opportunity to sneak into the parlor before breakfast. The bowl of forfeits had been left on the sideboard.

So I wasn't as unlucky as I thought.

It wouldn't have mattered which slip of parchment I chose. Lady Tottenham had ensured that whoever drew out of that bowl would have to kiss their partner. It had been her plan all along—all part of her matchmaking scheme.

I shuddered at the thought of that kiss. I pushed the bowl back to the position I had found it in. The longcase clock in the corner chimed seven times as I sat on the edge of a black velvet chaise. Three large windows let in the grey morning light, washing out the vibrant hues of the green and pink wallpaper. The lofty ceiling displayed plasterwork, an intricate painting, and a stunning chandelier. The entire house was a display of wealth and status.

My widowhood hadn't granted me the same security Lady Tottenham's had. The late baron's house was in Wiltshire. After he had died, his land and property were passed almost entirely to his brother, with just a small sum provided to me annually based upon the success of the land. I had lived in the dower house periodically ever since the baron's death, but it didn't feel like home. Nothing did. My annual sum was growing slimmer. The income of the land was deteriorating, as were the contents of my reticule. I could not obtain a loan, nor could I obtain a lease. Soon, I feared I would be destitute.

I hadn't breathed a word of it to anyone.

My sister, Henrietta, and her husband, Charlie had financial struggles of their own. They had married for love, even when Charlie desperately needed a fortune. If I grew desperate enough, I could call upon my friends, Timothy and Nora, the Duke and Duchess of Heywood, but that was a last resort.

Perhaps I had been a fool not to try to marry again sooner. I had been widowed at the age of twenty-five, and I had allowed four years to pass by, waiting, hoping. Waiting for Miles was all my heart allowed me to do. I felt imprisoned by the beautiful memories of love and security that I had felt with him. There were few men of wealth in London who would choose to marry a destitute widow of twenty-nine. The promises in Miles's letter were the only thing that could save me.

I hadn't known if he forgave me for marrying the baron. The emotions in his letters were difficult to interpret, and he had run off to the East India Company without a proper farewell. But now he had made his feelings known.

My stomach fluttered with a mixture of nerves and excitement. I stood and walked to one of the three large windows of the parlor. All I had to do was make it through the next three weeks at this untamed house party. Miles would laugh if he knew I was trapped in the company of his younger brother. I was sure he would also tell me Alexander was not to be trusted.

I squinted out the window, catching sight of movement in the courtyard. A man in a long black jacket and top hat made his way to a waiting carriage, valise in hand. I glimpsed the side of his face. He wore spectacles. Grey side whiskers peeked out from the collar of his jacket.

I hid halfway behind the drapes as he stepped into the carriage. Who could he be? A secret lover of Lady Totten-ham's? Nothing would surprise me in regard to her. She could have secret visitors, spies in France, anything was possible. I shook my head in bewilderment.

I still had nineteen days to go. That was far too many.

"Are you enjoying yourself?"

I jumped, throwing the drapes over the window.

Standing in the doorway, one arm resting on the frame, was Lord Kirkham.

CHAPTER 4

ANNE

I hardly recognized him without flour on his face.

My heart picked up speed. It was early, most guests were still in bed, and Lord Kirkham had cornered me in an empty room. If we were seen together, especially after the events of the night before...I could only imagine the rumors.

"My lord, you startled me." The muscles in my neck tensed as he took a step into the room.

"My apologies. I thought I would find this room unoccupied." He strode closer. "But I am glad to have found you here."

"I cannot understand why." I gave a hard laugh, moving to the right. "A morning of quiet solitude is the best sort. I don't possess the talent for providing enjoyable conversation before ten o'clock."

Lord Kirkham chuckled. His grinning face was the shape of the portrait behind him. Not of the subject, but of the frame itself. "I don't care for conversation either. We might sit together a while? Perhaps read a book?"

"Actually, I was about to leave." I clasped my hands together, skirting closer to the door. "My hair is not to my liking, so I must have my maid arrange it again before breakfast."

He scoffed. "That's absurd. Your hair looks ravishing." His eyes trailed down my entire figure before returning to my face.

The door was in sight, but Lord Kirkham stepped in front of me. "My lady, please, don't leave. Take a walk outside with me." His gaze drifted to my lips. My stomach lurched. It was easy to lower defenses at a secluded party like this. Lines were blurred, and rules became suggestions. Gentlemen became oafs.

"I don't enjoy walking," I blurted. I cleared my throat. "Out of doors, that is. The air is far too chilled in the morning."

"Come now, it's August."

My chest tightened with frustration. "Good day, my lord." I rushed past him and into the corridor. I didn't stop until I was safely in my bedchamber again. I slumped against the back of the door, taking a deep breath to calm my nerves. I had hoped Lord Kirkham would forget the kiss, but it seemed he had not. I groaned. He might have assumed I liked him since I had chosen to kiss him over Alexander. How could I remedy the situation? Lady Tottenham was likely proud of her work from the night before, and she might have even seen a potential match brewing.

She had chosen the partners. She must have wanted me to court Lord Kirkham.

Why on earth would she want that?

Perhaps I could tell Lady Tottenham about Miles. If she knew I was already in love, she might exclude me from her matchmaking schemes. It was also possible that she would send me home, deeming me unable to contribute to her objectives. I bit one fingernail in thought.

I delayed going downstairs for as long as I could. Jane delivered a schedule for the events of the day, and I read it before heading to the breakfast room.

Nine o'clock:
Breakfast
Ten o'clock:
Gather in the hexagon room
Afternoon:
Luncheon
Various activities of nine pins, embroidery, and music
Tea
Six o'clock:
Dinner
Cards and music

I scowled at the space at the bottom of the page. It should have read: **Midnight:** *await a dreaded invitation under your door.*

The breakfast room was crowded when I stepped inside.

The air smelled of eggs and ham. My stomach grumbled. The sideboard was covered in pyramids of various fruits as well —nectarines, peaches, berries, and grapes. As I walked closer, I saw several tartlets, loaves of French bread, brioche, honey cake, and plum cake, all surrounded by an array of spreads and marmalades. Pots of hot chocolate, tea, and lemonade finished the display. After the elaborate meal that had been served the night before, I shouldn't have expected anything less. I gaped at the assortment. I hardly knew where to begin.

In addition to one long table, another round table had been brought in to accommodate the many guests. In total, there were fifteen chairs, with Lady Tottenham at the head. I thought of the guests she had invited...an even number of men and women. Seven of each. It all made sense. Birch House was a chess board. We were Lady Tottenham's pawns, bishops, knights, and rooks. She hoped to spend the next month moving us strategically as she pleased.

She glanced up as I entered the room. Her hair was piled atop her head in tight curls. Pins with gems and pearls were nestled throughout, along with a plume of feathers. Her dress was a vibrant pink.

I had captured her attention the night before. That was not a good position to be in.

Hers was not the worst attention I had captured, though.

Lord Kirkham's eyes followed me toward the sideboard. He missed his bite of ham. It fell from his fork onto his plate.

I filled my plate with a small bit of everything before turning back to the tables. There were several seats available at the long table, but the round one was more appealing since that's where Lord Kirkham was *not*.

I took one step, then halted. Alexander was at the round table.

Still, it was the better option. Lady Tottenham *and* Lord Kirkham were a worse combination.

Mr. Amesbury swooped in and took a chair at the round table, leaving just one available seat directly beside Alexander. I stayed firm on my decision, making my way to the table. There was no reason we couldn't be cordial. He was potentially my future brother-in-law, after all, though I had no intention of telling him that.

He didn't seem to recognize me. I was under the cover of my married name. If he had paid attention in his childhood to my family or me at all, he would have known me as Anne, or Miss Dixon—not Lady Daventry.

I set my plate down beside him, sweeping gracefully into my chair. "Good morning," I said, more to my plum cake than to anyone at the table.

"Good morning, my lady."

A spatter of grape juice hit me in the face.

Alexander raised the grape he had just speared with a fork. His dark waves were more tame today. His teasing smile was not. "I thought you would have chosen a seat by a certain baron."

I wiped firmly at the juice on my cheek, throwing him a scowl. "I would like to avoid him at all costs, actually." I spoke in a quiet voice, glancing at the others at the table. A pretty young lady, Miss Octavia Colborne, was seated between Mr. Amesbury and a man named Mr. Hatcher. They were engaged in their own conversation.

"That didn't seem to be your intention last night," Alexander said around a chuckle.

My jaw tightened, and I bit too harshly into my plum cake. I took my time chewing and swallowing before addressing him again. "I was trying to avoid the alternative."

"Me?"

"Yes, you."

He took a sip from his teacup, brows drawing together. A man like him must have been unaccustomed to rejection from women. I hated to compliment him, even in my mind, but he was obviously the most handsome man of the party. Seeing him in the daylight, with his sharp jawline and intense brown eyes, I was even more baffled at how he was Miles's relation. Miles had light brown hair and blue eyes.

Alexander sat back in his chair and crossed his arms. "Is it because he's a lord?"

"What?"

He lowered his voice. "Did you choose him because he's a lord?"

I sighed. "Please forget what occurred yesterday. I'm trying to forget it myself."

"Well, I'm trying to understand what compelled you to kiss him instead of me. He's a great deal older than you."

"Well, *you* are younger than me."

His brow furrowed. "How do you know that?"

I shook my head fast, realizing my mistake. "I assumed." The difference between our ages was only one year—not noticeable enough to be assumed in most instances.

Thankfully, he seemed more focused on my rejection. "Besides being old, he had flour all over his face. What made him a more attractive option?" His tone was light, but he seemed genuinely curious. I had wounded his pride.

Good.

I gave a dismissive shrug. "The tricorn hat didn't suit you. I couldn't forget it."

He shook his head with a grin. "You said they're attractive on officers."

I eyed him carefully, searching my mind for anything Miles had mentioned about him. We hadn't spoken of his family since our courtship before I married the baron. It had been four years since I had heard anything about Alexander's life. He had finished at Oxford, and then...

My memory leaped in triumph.

He had been seeking a profession in the church. I eyed him. Why was that so surprising?

"You are *not* an officer."

He raised one eyebrow. "That is a bold assumption."

"Well, I have no evidence that you wouldn't lie to me."

"All the evidence you need is in how dashing I look in a tricorn hat." He leaned closer. "You are the one who lied about the required clothing for the parlor game. I should be doubting every word you say. It is you who cannot be trusted."

I shot a glance at Miss Colborne and Mr. Hatcher. Did they know about the midnight games? Surely they would by the end of the day. Gossip was sure to spread in this house faster than butter on a hot piece of toast. "I simply don't think you seem like the sort of man to be an officer," I said. "Perhaps you would choose a profession in the church." I never would have guessed it on my own.

He speared another grape, his brow pinching. "That was my plan, actually. But I changed my course." His dark eyes met mine, matching the steaming cup of chocolate beside my plate. "I became a barrister. The law suited me more than a profession in the church."

"That's not surprising." I pressed my lips together, shocked at my own words. I was not usually so outspoken.

He leaned one elbow on the table. "You have known me less than twenty-four hours, yet you seem determined to think badly of me."

I set down my fork with a look of surrender. "That isn't

true. *You* are still offended that I didn't choose you during the game."

"I'm not offended." He scoffed.

"But your pride is wounded."

He didn't deny it, shaking his head in vexation.

I took a bite of nectarine, storing it in my cheek as a smile broke over my lips.

He studied my face for a long moment. I quickly swallowed, wiping a droplet of nectarine juice from the corner of my mouth with my serviette. What was he looking at?

"How old are you?" he asked suddenly.

I hesitated. "Why do you ask?"

He gave a nonchalant shrug. "I can't imagine why you haven't been married off by now."

There were multiple widows in the party, so I was surprised he hadn't made the connection yet. "I was married for a short time. He died." The words came out blunt.

"I'm sorry."

I nodded, shifting in my chair. Guilt wrapped around my heart as it always did. The fact that I had never truly mourned my husband made me feel like a wicked person, yet there was nothing I could do to feel anything but relief. His premature death hadn't been deserved, but neither had his treatment of me. Awkwardness hung in the air, so I hurried to resolve Alexander's previous question.

"I'm twenty-nine."

He gave a slow nod. "One year my senior. But you already knew that. How did you know?"

"I guessed."

He rubbed the scruff on his jaw, reading every feature of my face. His voice dropped, deep and quiet. "If you are lying to me again, my lady, I will go to Lord Kirkham right now and tell him you have been longing for another kiss."

I gasped under my breath. "You wouldn't."

"I think you underestimate me."

I crossed my arms, no longer hungry. My stomach twisted with nerves. Did Alexander even know about my closeness to Miles and our previous attachment? The two brothers didn't seem to be on good terms. I doubted they communicated about matters of the heart. What was the harm of Alexander knowing that we had once been neighbors? It was harmless, and it might even ease the contention between us.

I took a deep breath. "Very well." I looked him straight in the eye. "I recognized your name. I have known your family my entire life, though you and I have remained near strangers until now." I lifted my chin. "You would have known me as Anne Dixon."

CHAPTER 5

ALEXANDER

*A*nne Dixon?

The familiarity of her features was vague, but it grew clearer as the seconds passed. She must have been fifteen the last time I had seen her. She and Miles had shared a close friendship that troubled my parents, though he could do little wrong in their eyes.

Lady Daventry—*Anne*—stared at my face, as if searching for a reaction. I was frozen, held captive by this new realization.

Miles had spoken of Anne before he left for the London season. I remembered those months well, and the mess he had left behind. The details about Anne were muddled in my head. Miles had continued to maintain little direction for his profession, so his intentions for the Season were to find and woo an heiress. It was clear he had feelings for Anne, and was weighing the possibility of marrying her instead. Our parents had discouraged it, but he had gone to London with an open mind.

It was after his departure that his true nature had surfaced, and I had suffered greatly for it.

Anne was a widow, so she had obviously married someone else. Did Miles know she had been widowed? At that very moment, he was on a ship bound for England. I was here in London to confront him upon his return. Was Anne here to do the same? Her intentions were likely not as hostile as mine. She couldn't possibly...still have feelings for him?

I wiped my mouth with my serviette. "I remember how often my brother spoke of you."

Her eyes rounded. "You remember me? He...spoke of me often?"

I nodded.

Her gaze dropped to her plate, and she seemed to struggle to gather her thoughts. Her rosy lips parted, but no words came out.

"Is his return from India what brings you to London?" My question seemed to further aggravate her. "Have you still been writing to him?"

She looked up. "Yes."

I leaned back in my chair, too astonished to sit straight. How had Miles managed to woo *her*? She was...beautiful. Regal. Her emotions were obviously guarded. Perhaps they hadn't always been that way. I crossed my arms. Hot frustration tingled under my skin. Why did a woman like Lady Daventry, the widow of a baron, think Miles was worth waiting for? Had he promised her money? Had he manipulated her like he had so many others? I couldn't imagine why any woman would want to marry my brother, but that was only because I knew better than anyone what he was capable of.

I bit the inside of my cheek, debating the best way to proceed. Anne was obviously uncomfortable. I glanced at her downcast expression as she stared at her plate in silence. It was a weakness of mine to ask too many questions, but I couldn't help myself.

"Are you in love with him?"

Her features hardened. "That is none of your concern."

"You are." I scoffed in disbelief, running my hand over my hair. "You really think you're in love with Miles?"

A blaze of anger crossed her face. "I don't 'think' I'm in love with him. I am. Why is that so appalling?"

I leaned toward her. Our whispered conversation couldn't last much longer. Mr. Hatcher seemed to have noticed the tension, and I could practically see his ears perking up to eavesdrop. "He isn't the man you think he is. I can promise you that."

She cast her gaze heavenward, shaking her head. "Do you truly expect me to believe you? Miles told me all about your antics at home, and the gambling debts, and the general... mischief you caused."

"General mischief?" I laughed, but my insides boiled. Miles had blamed everything on me his entire life. It was his greatest talent—making others appear worse to elevate his own character, stealing trust with charm rather than earning it with his actions. I took a drink of water to cool the anger simmering inside me. "I would love to hear what else Miles has said about me. It seems you are credulous enough to believe every word out of his mouth."

She glared at me. "His ill words about you are growing more plausible by the minute."

"You may think of me however you please."

49

She stabbed at a piece of ham on her plate. "Perhaps I shall not think of you at all."

"Even better."

My breakfast was growing cold, but I didn't care. My stomach was in knots. Had Miles made it his objective to turn everyone in his life against me? Anger surged under my skin. I felt near to bursting. I clamped my mouth shut, glowering at the table. There was nothing I could say to make Anne see sense. Miles had captured her loyalty, just as he had my entire family's. He created a pedestal for himself by standing on the backs of the people he diminished. He had been standing on me for far too long. Anne would be next if she wasn't careful.

The rest of the meal passed in tense silence, and for once I was grateful to hear Lady Tottenham's voice.

"Ladies and gentlemen, good morning." She stood at the foot of the long table, circling to look at each of her guests. "We will now gather in the Hexagon room for a bit of entertainment."

I exchanged a glance with Anne. She seemed to remember that she was angry with me, snapping her gaze away from mine. She stood quickly, rushing off to stand near Mrs. Fitzgibbon. I remained in my chair. I couldn't look away from her, even as she made her swift escape from me. I studied the sheen on her curls, her dark, fierce eyes, her tall, curved figure. I tore my gaze away. How had I gone from vexation to admiration in seconds? It was rather pathetic.

I watched as Miss Morton whispered in Miss Rowley's ear. They both laughed, slipping past Anne and pulling Mrs. Fitzgibbon along with them.

Anne remained behind, snubbed by all three women. They

had seen what had happened in the parlor the night before, and I suspected the entire party would know about it soon enough.

Lord Kirkham weaved through the crowd at the door, stopping directly beside Anne. His eyes traced her figure from behind, the action so obvious that I could see it from across the room. Admittedly, I had been guilty of a similar thing, but at least I was discreet.

The moment she noticed him, his eyes snapped up to her face. He smiled with those chipped teeth. The panic in her features was obvious as he extended his arm.

I sighed. She had given me no reason to rescue her, but a true gentleman didn't need a reason.

I strode across the room, touching Anne's shoulder just as she was about to take Lord Kirkham's arm. "My lady, you promised to finish telling me the riveting story you started at our table."

Her brow twitched in confusion.

I extended my arm at her opposite side, giving an obvious nod toward it. "I would be delighted if you would walk with me to the hexagon room so we may finish our conversation."

Lord Kirkham's nostrils flared. He seemed the sort of man to make enemies at every turn, but seeing Anne's discomfort had taken away any of my concern on the matter of potentially having my teeth knocked out.

Anne's eyes narrowed with suspicion, but this time, I seemed to be the better option. She took my arm with a light touch, and I led her into the corridor, leaving Lord Kirkham stewing in our wake.

We walked in silence for several seconds. Finally, she glanced up at me. "Thank you." The word sounded painful, like the entirety of her pride had just been laid on a sacrificial altar.

I raised my eyebrows. "Are you admitting that you prefer my company over his?"

"You already know that I chose to sit by you at breakfast in order to avoid him."

I grinned. "I wanted to hear you admit it again."

She sighed. "It's only because I know you aren't trying to woo or court me." She paused. "Especially now that you know of my attachment to Miles."

My jaw tightened involuntarily. The moment we reached the hexagon room on the second floor, she released my arm.

The room lived up to its name. Six walls stretched up to a lofty ceiling, at the center of which was a large window facing the sky. The room had been cleared of all furnishings besides a sofa and a circle of brown velvet chairs.

"Another game?" I whispered, casting a sideways glance at Anne.

She grimaced, her hazel eyes connecting with mine. "It would appear so."

I counted the chairs in front of us. Thirteen. That was enough for all but one guest.

How many games would be played at this house party? To play games after dinner in the evening was one thing, but to arrange morning games and midnight games was excessive. It was fitting, I supposed. Lady Tottenham's entire being was nothing if not excessive. Her fashion, her wealth, her furnishings, her food, her personality. I should have known what I was agreeing to when I accepted her invitation.

Once all the guests had arrived in the hexagon room, Lady Tottenham moved to stand at the head of the circle of chairs.

"My dear friends, welcome to the hexagon room. This has long been one of my favorite rooms of the house. It usually serves as a ballroom, but in this case, it will serve as a game room." She gestured at the walls. "You will see many portraits of my late husband's ancestors, to whom I owe my deepest gratitude and respect. You will also see many of my husband's hunting prizes."

Glass cases with small, stuffed creatures of all kinds lined one of the six walls. On another, nine large animal heads were mounted on the wall. I made eye contact with a deer.

"My husband had a deep love for games, prizes, and tests," Lady Tottenham continued. "He found enjoyment in the way they challenged his mind and bolstered his spirits." She gave a wistful smile as she gazed at the largest portrait above the fireplace.

The man in the portrait must have been Lord Tottenham, frozen in his youthful likeness. He had a warm disposition, large blue eyes, and a long nose. He looked intelligent, cheerful, with just enough eccentricity to be compatible with his wife. She stared at his portrait for a long moment before coughing into her elbow. She drew a rattling breath. "To honor him, I have gone to great lengths to arrange a series of games to take place during the next month. These games are not what you might expect from a London house party. In my invitation, I stated that rules must be followed. If you are not prepared to play my games as they are intended to be played in my husband's honor, you may choose to leave." She took a step closer to the line of guests. Her skirts rustled in the silence. "If you break the rules, you will be *forced* to leave." Her sharp eyes danced over every face in the room. "As the weeks progress, the games will become more difficult. The stakes will be higher.

You must keep your eyes open at all times—for the entire house party itself is a game." Her lips curled into a smile. "Search for clues at every turn, for at the end, there will be a prize."

A ripple of whispers flooded the room. Her cryptic words hung in the air. Those who had been invited to the midnight game the night before were under the impression that the house party was a matchmaking scheme. Perhaps it still was. The gathering seemed to have multiple purposes, and keeping them straight was going to prove difficult. The entire house party was a game? What the devil could she mean by that?

There were two reactions amongst the guests. Concern and delight. Miss Octavia Colborne, one of the twin sisters in attendance, wore an alarming grin. Her sister's expression was more reserved.

I glanced at Anne. Her cheeks were pale.

"The game we will be playing today is my variation of buffy gruffy." Lady Tottenham gestured at the circle of chairs. "In an orderly fashion, please come take a seat."

Lady Tottenham's *variation* could never be a good thing. I recalled that there were only thirteen chairs, yet there were fourteen guests. Anne seemed to have noticed the same thing, because she rushed toward the circle. Before I knew what had happened, she was already in a chair. I hurried forward and claimed one on the other side.

The last person standing was Miss Octavia. She looked nearly identical to her twin sister Miss Victoria. Both young ladies had blonde curls, icy blue eyes, and slightly upturned noses. The only differences that set them apart were the color choices of their wardrobes and jewelry. Octavia dressed in an extravagant manner that was similar to Lady Tottenham, which already seemed to have won her favor.

"Miss Octavia." Lady Tottenham beamed. "You have failed to obtain a seat in the circle. That means you will be the first to play the game."

Octavia covered her mouth with her gloved fingers and laughed. "Oh, dear." She blinked innocently. Mrs. Pike, her widowed aunt and chaperone, wore a look of concern. It wouldn't have surprised me if Octavia had found herself in the center of the circle on purpose.

Lady Tottenham stepped up behind Octavia and draped a yellow blindfold over her eyes. She secured it with a knot in the back. With one hand on her shoulder, she spoke the rules close to her ear, but loud enough for all to hear. "Those in the circle will move when I clap my hands together. When I clap again, they must stop and sit in the nearest chair. Miss Octavia will stop in front of a chair of her choice without knowing who occupies it. She may ask three questions in an attempt to discern the person's identity, with the exception of asking their name. The person in the chair may disguise their voice, but they must answer the questions honestly. She may also touch the person in an attempt to discover their identity. If she guesses correctly, she may ask for one of three rewards. She may ask for a kiss, a secret, or a flattery, after which, the player will replace her at the center of the circle."

From behind the blindfold, Miss Octavia's face lit up with a grin.

I met Anne's gaze from across the circle. Would every game at this party involve kissing? I nearly laughed when I noticed that Lord Kirkham had managed to plant himself in the seat beside her. I had to admire his determination.

Lady Tottenham clapped, the sound echoing off the six walls of the room. We all stood, rearranging ourselves until Lady Tottenham clapped again.

Octavia staggered forward, walking in a diagonal line until she collided with my knee. Instinctively, I reached out to steady her. Her hands clasped onto my forearms, and her grin widened. "Who might this be?" she asked amidst a giggle. "Certainly a gentleman."

Her hands traced up my arms, squeezing periodically. "A strong one."

Several ladies in the room giggled along with her. I held perfectly still, staring at the plasterwork on the ceiling. I had never had a conversation with Octavia, so I trusted she wouldn't recognize my voice. I doubted she knew enough about me to learn anything from the answers to her questions. I held my breath as she ran her fingers over my hair. There were several balding men in the circle, so she had just eliminated at least half.

"Is your hair dark or light, sir?" she asked.

"Dark." It was clever to ask questions based on the person's appearance. She would have me narrowed down quickly if she continued. Her hands shifted down to my face. She ran her hands over the overgrown scruff on my jaw and cheeks.

Mrs. Pike sat on the edge of her chair, eyes round with mortification.

"How old are you, sir?" Octavia's grin told me she was already close to discovering my identity.

"Twenty-eight."

"Are you wearing a blue waistcoat?"

I glanced down at my chest. How had she already noted the color I was wearing? I cleared my throat. "Yes."

She squealed with delight. "This is Mr. Holland."

Lady Tottenham applauded, as did the other guests in the circle. "You're correct, Miss Octavia! You are a clever girl." Octavia removed her blindfold. Her icy blue eyes settled on my face with triumph. I gave her a congratulatory smile, though my nerves were on edge.

Lady Tottenham motioned toward me, addressing Octavia again. "You may now ask Mr. Holland for a kiss, a secret, or a flattery. Which will it be?"

She tapped her chin. "Lud, I would like all three if I could have them." Her sister let out a giggle from across the circle. Octavia's eyes gleamed with excitement. "But if I must choose...I should like a kiss."

CHAPTER 6

ANNE

M rs. Pike looked ill. She shook her head at Octavia, but the girl had eyes only for Alexander. I crossed my ankles under my skirts, wringing my hands together in my lap. Alexander must have been pleased with her choice. He did seem like a shameless flirt, and Miss Octavia was quite pretty. She had a significant dowry too—she and her sister had already made that clear during the dinner conversation the night before. Alexander would be wise to woo her, and from the way Octavia was looking at him, I didn't imagine it would be very difficult.

I squeezed my fingers so hard they turned white. Alexander stood, taking a step closer to Octavia. He interlocked his hands behind his back, leaned forward, and pressed a kiss to her cheek.

Was that allowed? I jerked my gaze to Lady Tottenham. I

didn't expect she would be content with a kiss on the cheek, but to my surprise, she didn't object. Octavia certainly did. As she turned around to take his chair, I caught the hint of disappointment on her features.

Lady Tottenham waved Alexander forward and began tying the blindfold over his eyes.

His words against Miles had been stoking a flame in my chest since we left the breakfast room. Why was he trying to poison my image of Miles? My hope for Miles was all I had. It made my heart ache that the two brothers were not fond of each other, but I had always believed their enmity to have been caused by Alexander. Miles was far too sweet, gentle, and kind to be deceitful. Alexander was bitter, that was all. I couldn't allow him to burrow his lies inside my head.

Lady Tottenham clapped her hands. In my distraction, I had forgotten what it meant. I jumped to my feet, selecting a new chair across the circle. Lady Tottenham clapped again, and we all fell silent.

Alexander rotated where he stood. My stomach fluttered with dread when he stopped. He faced me.

I held to one side of my chair, keeping my breathing quiet as he began walking forward. *Move to the left,* I urged him in my mind. Unfortunately he couldn't hear me. He continued with cautious steps in my direction until his boot kicked against my skirts. He reached forward, and I resisted the urge to duck. His hand touched my sleeve, then lifted to the side of my face. His touch on my cheek was light, but it sent a string of shivers down my neck. I clenched my jaw. That was not acceptable.

My stomach lurched with nervousness as his fingers traced

over my curls. Would he know it was me? Surely not by touch alone. Once he asked his questions though, my identity would be clear. We had spoken enough now to make my voice recognizable. The effort of disguising it would be more embarrassing than it was worth.

"This is a lady, there is no question," Alexander said. Both his hands held my face now, and I could hardly inhale for fear of being discovered. My heart pounded fast.

I stared up at him. The blindfold covered the entire top half of his face, but his grin was still visible. Why was he smiling like that? Surely he didn't already know it was me. His thumb traced the curve of my cheek before his hands lowered from my face. I released the breath in my lungs.

"There are a number of widows amongst the guests here," he said. "Are you one of them?"

I nodded before remembering he couldn't see me. *Drat it all.* He would recognize my voice. "Yes." My voice was a quiet squeak.

"What are your plans for your time in London after this house party is over?"

I gritted my teeth. "I plan to socialize." It was a vague enough answer.

"With whom do you plan to *socialize*? Anyone in particular?"

I wanted to reach up and tighten the knot on his cravat until he could no longer speak. The other guests would wonder why he was asking such strange questions. A wave of heat rose to my cheeks. "No." I had broken the rules of the game by being dishonest, but Alexander already knew the answer. He was simply taunting me.

Lady Tottenham stepped up beside him. I had never been more grateful to see her. "That is all your questions, Mr. Holland. You may now guess the person's identity." She wore a mischievous grin.

He didn't hesitate. "This is Lady Daventry."

She clapped, as did the rest of the guests. I didn't dare look around. My face was still on fire.

Lady Tottenham untied his blindfold, and I made sure to prepare a cutting glare for him when his eyes settled on my face. I squared my shoulders.

He was completely unfettered by my formidable stance. If anything, he looked even more amused.

"Mr. Holland, would you like to ask Lady Daventry for a kiss, a secret, or a flattery?"

I held his gaze, injecting as much venom into my eyes as possible. If he dared ask for a kiss, I would sooner kick him across the room and be sent back to Wiltshire. I was in a losing position no matter what. The other two options didn't sound pleasant either.

"Hmm." His dark eyes bored into mine, and he tipped his head to one side. My heart raced at the probability of a kiss. He had been vexed all morning that I had chosen Lord Kirkham over him the night before. Would this be his way of repairing the wound to his pride? I could hardly breathe as I awaited his choice.

He broke the suspenseful silence after several seconds. "From Lady Daventry, I must ask for a secret."

The tension in my shoulders relaxed, and his smile grew as he gazed down at me. He must have known how horrified I was. I searched my mind for any secret I might tell, but found nothing I was willing to share. If I could think of something witty and slightly offensive, it would be enough to qualify as a secret.

An idea came to mind, but I hesitated. The seconds ticked by.

"Well?" Lady Tottenham raised her thin brows. "What is your secret, Lady Daventry."

"I have far too many to choose from," I said with a laugh, standing from my chair. I stared straight at Alexander's smirking face. I paused for a long moment, feigning deep thought. "I may be remiss to tell this secret in the presence of our hostess." I paused, giving a nervous laugh. "But I must confess that I am not fond of parlor games at all. I despise them."

Alexander's mouth curled in a slow smile. His eyes darted over his shoulder at Lady Tottenham. The guests in the circle gasped with amusement and shock. Some laughed. I stood as confidently as I could manage.

Lady Tottenham stared at me for a long moment. I couldn't tell if she was dismayed or amused, but then a laugh burst out of her chest. "We are all entitled to our opinion, I suppose." Her green eyes gave me a critical sweep before a smirk tugged on her lips. "But you came to the wrong house party, my dear."

That had been made quite apparent already. I gave a humble laugh, hoping Lady Tottenham would forgive my bluntness. She didn't seem ruffled by it at all. Whether I liked her games or not, she would still force me to play them. She waved me forward, lifting the blindfold.

Alexander sauntered past, taking the chair I had left

behind. How he had managed to choose me from amongst all the other guests was baffling. The only explanation I could think of was that he had cheated, which would quickly have him sent home. If I could find a way to prove it, I wouldn't have to endure his company for the rest of the house party. I was tempted to accuse him of cheating at that very moment, but I held my tongue.

Lady Tottenham draped the blindfold over my eyes, tying it securely at the back of my head. My eyes adjusted to the dim light behind the fabric. Faint details of the hexagon room came into view—the various animal heads on the wall, the small animals in the glass case, and finally the outline of Alexander's face. His features were shadowed, but still recognizable.

I touched the side of the blindfold to ensure it was properly in place. There was nothing wrong with the way it was positioned.

I could see straight through it.

Lady Tottenham clapped, and everyone circled to a new chair. My jaw was slack. Was this what Lady Tottenham had intended? A semi-transparent blindfold was the perfect way for her to see who each player would choose to steal a kiss or secret from, and the perfect way for players to flirt while appearing innocent.

That meant Miss Octavia had chosen Alexander intentionally.

And he had chosen me.

My mind flashed to the way his thumb had caressed my cheek unnecessarily, and how his fingers had brushed through my hair. I clenched my jaw. He had seen my face the entire time.

Lady Tottenham clapped again, stopping the rotation. I

pivoted, debating over what might be the best way to proceed. Choosing one of the women would be the best course of action, especially if she was more reserved than Miss Octavia. Mrs. Pike or Mrs. Fitzgibbon could be trusted to avoid choosing Lord Kirkham. That was my sole objective at the moment—ensuring he did not end up at the center of the circle.

I chose Mrs. Pike and guessed correctly after my three questions. I asked for a flattery, only to give her the least amount of distress possible. She paid a compliment to the pink lace on my dress before taking her place at the center of the circle.

The game continued for three more rounds, and to my relief, Lord Kirkham was never chosen. Each time I glanced at Alexander, he maintained his wicked smile. He wasn't ashamed in the slightest, even knowing that I was aware of the transparency of the blindfold.

What was he trying to do? Was he trying to steal my attention away from Miles, or just infuriate me? The first would never work, and the second was working all too well.

During the afternoon activities, I tried to stay close to the other women of the party. In the garden, we watched as the men played nine pins with Miss Victoria and Miss Octavia. Mrs. Pike stood nearby, quietly scolding Octavia when she came too close to Alexander. Ever since the game of buffy gruffy, she had become infatuated with him. She cheered each time he knocked down a pin, clinging to his arm with squeals and delighted giggles. He didn't seem to mind the attention. From my place at the nearby table, I narrowed my eyes at his back as he threw the ball again.

The hot sun beat down on my parasol. I sipped at my cup of lemonade. White roses grew on a bush beside me, as well as a patch of purple foxglove, which was attracting several bees. Mrs. Fitzgibbon kept one eye on the creatures as she bit into a vanilla glazed cake. Her cousins, Miss Morton and Miss Rowley sat beside her. It had been excruciating trying to engage them in conversation. It was clear that they had judged me for my decision to kiss Lord Kirkham the night before.

I leaned forward, desperate for a subject that might intrigue them. "Do you think there will be another midnight parlor game tonight?"

The three women exchanged a glance. "I hope so," Miss Morton said.

Miss Rowley pursed her lips, brushing a strand of chestnut hair from her eyes to better see the nine pin players. "I hope Miss Octavia isn't invited."

"She makes me want to claw my eyes out," Miss Morton said in agreement. Both young ladies peeked at Miss Octavia out on the lawn. "Yesterday she said she liked Mr. Hatcher, but now she has obviously changed her mind."

"Mr. Holland is the most handsome man here," Miss Rowley said with a disgruntled sigh. "And Miss Octavia is the prettiest girl here. It is entirely unfair."

"Victoria is pretty too. She looks exactly like Octavia." Miss Morton flicked a bee off the rim of her teacup.

Mrs. Fitzgibbon shrieked, jumping up from the table and walking a safe distance away from the flowers.

"Yes, but Octavia is a flirt," Miss Morton said in a casual voice. "She will always win against her sister. It doesn't matter, though. Victoria seems to have set her attentions elsewhere."

I followed her gaze to Victoria, who stood off to the side of the lawn with Mr. Hatcher. I shook my head in amazement. Would Lady Tottenham successfully create matches at her party? It was only the second day and attachments were already forming. Time would tell if they were one-sided.

"And you." Miss Rowley's golden irises met mine. "You seem to have a liking for Lord Kirkham."

Miss Morton snickered behind her glove.

I shook my head fast. "I assure you, I don't."

Miss Rowley scoffed. "I refuse to believe it. You chose to kiss *him* instead of Mr. Holland."

"We were shocked," Miss Morton said with a nod.

"Mortified."

I sighed, closing my eyes for a moment to block out the bright sun. "I pitied Lord Kirkham for having to retrieve the bullet. I felt it was the polite decision to make."

They exchanged a glance. "He does have money and a title. We will not judge you if you pursue him for those reasons alone."

"I am *not* pursuing him," I said, my voice too defensive.

Miss Morton shrugged. "Very well." She took a sip of lemonade, her eyes sliding to her cousin. Neither one of them believed me. There was nothing I could say that would make my decision logical to their minds. Meanwhile, Alexander had already managed to charm them without even trying.

"Whether you pursue him or not, it is obvious that Lady Tottenham intends Lord Kirkham for you. We figured it out." Miss Rowley held up her fingers. "There are seven intended matches at this party. From the partnerships at the game last night—you and Lord Kirkham, myself and Mr. St. Vincent," she gestured at Miss Morton, "Kate and Mr. Amesbury, and Mr. Barnwall is intended for Lydia." She gestured at her cousin and chaperone, Mrs. Fitzgibbon. "Mr. Holland, of course, was not actually invited to the games last night, so his intended match could not have been among us."

I nodded, glancing at the rest of the guests out on the lawn. "Do you have theories for the others?"

Miss Rowley nodded. "We suspect Octavia and Mr. Holland, Victoria and Mr. Hatcher, and Mrs. Pike and Mr. Lymington."

That did make sense. Mr. Lymington was close to Mrs. Pike's age, and both seemed to be equally appalled by the impropriety exhibited by the younger guests.

"I wish my match wasn't Mr. Amesbury," Miss Morton said with a groan. "He is handsome, I suppose, but not like Mr. Holland."

"At least you haven't been chosen for Mr. St. Vincent." Miss Rowley's nose wrinkled. "He is far too old. I would much rather compete for Mr. Holland."

Both girls gazed out at the lawn. Miss Rowley picked up her fan, fluttering it vigorously at her face. "He looks so handsome with his shirtsleeves rolled up." She burst into laughter.

Miss Morton threw her head back with a giggle. Her blonde curls stuck to her forehead with perspiration. She leaned forward with a devious grin. "How are we going to steal him from Octavia?"

At this point, I was simply an observer of their conversation. I sat back, nibbling at a cake as they plotted and planned. I would keep the fact that I had seen Alexander shirtless to myself. I couldn't have them swooning face-first into the pitcher of lemonade.

Out on the lawn, Alexander knocked over all nine pins. Octavia leaped toward him, squeezing his arm in celebration. A slow smile climbed my face when I noted his discomfort with the situation. He tugged his arm away gently, but his eyebrows were pinched with concern. It would seem he had an unwanted admirer as well. He was no longer at liberty to tease me about Lord Kirkham without retaliation.

My attention focused back on the conversation between Miss Morton and Miss Rowley. Mrs. Fitzgibbon had dared to return to the table, keeping her fan poised to swat away any bees.

"What could Lady Tottenham have meant when she said the entire party is a game?" Miss Morton asked with a quizzical look. "I wonder what the prize could be."

Miss Rowley raised her eyebrows. "Clearly the prize is Mr. Holland."

They both laughed.

In truth, I had been wondering the same thing. Knowing Lady Tottenham, the prize would be something no one would expect, and likely something no one actually wanted. She had a collection of strange curiosities from her travels that could be easily handed out to a winner. There could be some cryptic, intangible prize like 'true love' or the promise to host the wedding of the match that became engaged by the end of the party. The possibilities were endless.

The prattle at the table fell silent. Lady Tottenham approached from the right, a glass of lemonade in hand. Her maid strained her arm to hold the parasol above Lady Tottenham's hair arrangement, beads of perspiration running down from her cap.

"Good afternoon, ladies." Lady Tottenham took a sip of lemonade, her rouge leaving behind a mark on the rim of the glass. She sat down in the chair beside me. A second maid appeared from behind the rose bush with a fan, waving it continuously at the side of Lady Tottenham's face.

She rotated toward me in her chair, one eyebrow raised. "Is nine pins yet another game that you despise?"

I nearly choked on my lemonade. I set down my cup. It clattered against the saucer. "No, my lady. I decided I would rather stay in the shade."

"I see." She released a dramatic sigh. "However, I don't understand why you wish to remain here at the table instead of in the company of all the gentlemen."

I glanced at the other three ladies at the table. The attack seemed to only be directed at me and my decision not to play the game.

"I have been enjoying my conversation with these women," I said. "I find men to be far too competitive at lawn games."

"I would argue that ladies are more competitive." Lady Tottenham's eyes shifted toward Miss Rowley and Miss Morton, then to Octavia, where she still flirted relentlessly with Alexander. Had Lady Tottenham overheard our conversation? My stomach twisted with dread. If she hadn't, her maid certainly had. It made sense that Lady Tottenham would have spies positioned all over the house and grounds.

"*I* should like to go play," Miss Rowley said, pushing away from the table.

"As would I." Miss Morton joined her, giving a curtsy before rushing off toward the lawn. Mrs. Fitzgibbon took a tea cake with her as she joined them, leaving me alone at the table with Lady Tottenham. I couldn't allow her to scare me away. She was a headstrong woman. Perhaps she would appreciate my willingness to hold my ground.

She eyed me with pursed lips, creating an array of wrinkles around her mouth. "You still insist on sitting out?"

I gave a polite smile. "Unless you insist that I play. If it is required of me as your guest, I will."

She gave a hooting laugh in the back of her throat. "You are a peculiar one, Lady Daventry."

I tipped my head to one side. "Am I?"

"Do you think I am not aware of your financial situation? I investigated each of my guests thoroughly before inviting them here."

I swallowed, interlocking my fingers in my lap. "Did you?" My voice was weak.

"Open your eyes." She looked like she wanted to reach forward and shake me. "I am presenting you with an opportunity. Multiple opportunities. You are nine and twenty, a widow of nearly four years, and on the brink of destitution. Your time to make a respectable match is running out." She instructed her maid to fan faster before addressing me again. "You and I both know you must marry again, and I have invited you here to give you that chance."

I felt equally honored and horrified. She truly cared about my future, even though we had only been briefly acquainted. Her investigation into my life was disconcerting, but it showed her dedication.

"If you are such an advocate for marriage, why do you not marry again, my lady?" I asked. "Why haven't you married in the decades since your husband's death?"

Her green eyes gleamed with mirth. "You are a bold one."

"Forgive me. I am simply curious." I gave a bashful smile.

She drew a breath, and it rattled in her chest. She coughed, blinking away the resulting moisture from her eyes. "I have no reason to. I have money. I have this house. I have my husband's memory to hold close to my heart. I loved him, and I have no desire to love anyone else." She studied my face. "Now it is my turn to ask a bold question."

A jolt of nerves hit my stomach. "Very well."

"Did *you* love your husband?"

Her question hung in the air. A bee buzzed past my ear, a welcome distraction. I swatted it away before sitting up taller. "No. I did not. Nor did he love me." I adjusted my gloves. "So you must forgive my resistance to marry again, my lady."

Her sharp eyes didn't leave my face. "I will forgive your resistance, but I will still advise against it. For the sake of your future comfort, it would seem that you don't have any choice but to marry, and marry soon."

My throat was dry, no matter how much lemonade I drank. Lady Tottenham had spoken aloud the deepest fears in my heart, leaving me completely vulnerable. There was nothing to argue with. She was right. I didn't dare tell her about Miles, so I kept my response vague. "My only hope is that if I do choose to marry, it will be for love this time."

"My sincerest wish is the same." She smiled, and a hint of sadness crossed her eyes before she blinked it away. "Faster," she barked at the maid.

The young woman supported her arm with her other hand as she waved the fan even harder.

"However, if you find that love still evades you, and another loveless marriage is not appealing, then you may find that other opportunities await you here."

"Other opportunities?"

Lady Tottenham shrugged. "If you are willing to play my games."

I tried to hide my confusion as I took another sip from my cup.

"Do consider the gentlemen here at my party," Lady Tottenham added in a stern voice. "Do not be so stubborn as to allow a good thing to pass you by." She arched one eyebrow.

"Of course." I smiled, turning my attention back to the lawn. *Not,* I added in my mind.

Sometimes, stubbornness wasn't a choice. My heart hadn't been swayed in fourteen years. I wouldn't be swayed now.

CHAPTER 7

ALEXANDER

I snapped my financial ledger closed with a sigh, taking two handfuls of my hair.

I rested my elbows on the writing desk in my bedchamber and closed my eyes. I felt the absence of the two hundred pounds Miles owed me more keenly than ever. If I wanted to travel back to York and build my client relationships there, I would need more money to secure a place to live.

I had only learned that Miles was on his way back to England by speaking with my eldest brother. Miles hadn't answered any of my letters, which didn't surprise me in the slightest. I hated to hope that Miles had become rich in India, but if he had spent the money he stole from me and made no profit with which to repay it, I would be in dire straits. And so would he. Surely Anne wouldn't want to court him if I made his teeth resemble Lord Kirkham's.

I let out a frustrated sigh. My expectations associated with being a barrister had never been foolish. All I wanted was to build a list of clients who could trust me, gain a reputation I could be proud of, and earn enough money to make a comfortable and modest living. I dreamed of purchasing my own small house, my own horses, and providing a home for a wife and children. My aspirations weren't driven by greed. My heart whispered what it wanted, and I listened. Those humble requests weren't out of reach if I could make my way back to York with the two hundred pounds Miles had stolen. At the moment, I hadn't a sixpence to scratch with.

I stood and stretched my back. It was too early for breakfast. My stomach rumbled. Lady Tottenham's party was already training my body to expect more food. I had been accustomed to living off much smaller portions, so I would enjoy it while I could.

Exploring the house in the early morning seemed like a better way to pass the time than agonizing over my finances. I adjusted my cravat in the mirror before stepping out into the corridor. The staircase was just outside the door to my room, the polished wood of the bannister gleaming in the morning light. A maid stood at the base of the staircase, dusting every inch of it.

I made my way to the ground floor, passing by the dreaded parlor. Memories from the night before flashed through my mind.

I had been officially invited to the second midnight parlor game. Those in attendance had consisted of myself, Mr. Hatcher, Mr. Lymington, and the twin Colborne sisters, Octavia and Victoria. We had played Lady Tottenham's version of the game "rhymes with rose." Each of us had been required to write a flattering poem for our partner using only words that rhymed with rose. It hadn't come as a surprise that Miss Octavia had been assigned to be my partner.

Since the game of buffy gruffy the day before, she hadn't left my side. During nine pins, during dinner, and then during the midnight game. I needed to convey the message that I was not at the party to find a match, but that was difficult when Lady Tottenham was observing my every move. Her words about sending people home if they broke the rules of the game had been troubling. I *had* to stay, but I couldn't entertain a budding attachment with Miss Octavia. It was a delicate situation. Kissing her on the cheek had been an obligation, but she had somehow taken it as a token of affection. Lady Tottenham seemed to have chosen Miss Octavia for me, and she would continue pushing us together at every opportunity.

From the corner of my eye, I caught a flash of white fabric. The nearby drawing room door creaked closed. I pivoted in that direction. What the devil was that?

I glanced down the corridor before walking slowly toward the door. I turned the knob, but was met by resistance from someone inside. I turned the knob harder. "Is someone there?"

I glanced down the corridor. Heavy footfalls came from the parlor, but the corridor was still empty.

Someone was behind the drawing room door. My curiosity overthrew my manners. I rattled the doorknob.

The footfalls down the corridor grew louder. Who else was awake? I watched for the person to come into view, but then the drawing room door swung open toward me.

Anne's eyes, wild with panic, met mine. She waved me forward before tugging the door closed behind me. I blinked against the sudden darkness. We were not in the drawing room. We were in the small space between the outside door and the inside door. With such thick walls, a space was afforded for servants to wait, unseen, before entering a room to wait upon the family. The space between the inside door and outside door was only the width of the doorway itself, with a maximum depth of three feet. A small amount of light filtered under the door from inside the drawing room, but the outside door led to the dim corridor.

I laughed in surprise, but Anne shushed me.

I wouldn't complain about being trapped with her in what was essentially a closet. I was simply surprised she wanted me there. My eyes adjusted to the dimness.

"I'm sorry!" she whispered. "I-I didn't want him to hear you."

Her features slowly came into view. Dark brows, panicked eyes, white gown. She looked terrified. My stomach clenched against another bout of laughter. "May I venture a guess who you're hiding from?"

Her brow contracted into a scowl. "This is not a laughing matter," she hissed.

"Would you rather I be serious?" I erased the smile from my face, drawing an inch or two closer. I studied each of her features in turn, ending with her lips. I had no choice but to flirt with her after she had tugged me into a dark closet.

She stepped back, coming in contact with the wall. "Stop!" she said in a harsh whisper. "We must be quiet. Lord Kirkham is in the corridor." She caught her breath. "He has been following me."

"Is the drawing room occupied? Please don't misunderstand, I would love to stay between the doors with you, but—"

"I don't know," she interrupted before I could finish. "The inside door is locked."

"So there is no escape until Lord Kirkham is gone." I smiled down at her, and she seemed unsure of where to look.

Her gaze settled on my cravat. "Unfortunately, yes."

"Unfortunately? You're the one who abducted me."

She scoffed. "I did not *abduct* you. You were about to reveal my hiding place."

"It's a bit obvious."

"Obvious?" She gave me a steely glance. "Just like how you cheated in the game yesterday."

A slow smile crept over my mouth. Buffy Gruffy. "You cannot blame me. I'm not the one who chose a transparent blindfold."

"But you chose me." She narrowed her eyes. "And then you asked such...specific questions about my time in London, knowing full well why I'm here."

"I know why you're here, but I don't understand it." My jaw tightened. "You are wasting your time."

Her eyes flashed with anger, and she opened her mouth to speak again. Before she could, we both froze. The footfalls in the corridor echoed closer. We stood perfectly still for several seconds. Thankfully, they passed, fading in the direction of the staircase.

Anne released an audible breath. "He must have assumed I went back to my room. Do you think he went upstairs?"

"It does sound that way."

Her shoulders relaxed, the panic fading from her expression.

"You do realize you owe me a favor," I said.

"For what?"

"Helping you hide."

She shook her head. "You didn't help me at all."

"That doesn't matter. We're hiding partners now. If the time comes that I need to hide from Octavia, you must be on my side."

Her brows shot upward. "You wish to hide from Octavia? You seem to enjoy her attention."

I cast her a skeptical look. "What could have given you that impression?"

She shrugged. "You remained by her side the entire day."

"*She* remained by *my* side. That doesn't mean I wanted her there."

Anne crossed her arms, raising her chin to meet my gaze. "Well, you didn't discourage her flirting."

"But I didn't flirt back." I leaned closer. "I would prefer to save such endeavors for you. You seem to enjoy my attention."

A laugh of disbelief burst out of her. "What could have given *you that* impression?"

"Lord Kirkham is long gone," I said in a quiet voice, "yet you have made no move to leave our hiding place."

I was momentarily distracted by her scent—flowers—and something sweet like molasses sugar. Her eyes were layered and deep as they searched mine. I drew a step closer to her, but she was already up against the wall.

Her dark lashes fluttered downward, hiding her eyes from view. She was silent for a heartbeat, but then she pushed against my chest with two fists. "Only because you're in my way." She slid past me and grabbed the doorknob of the outside door.

A flood of light came into the space between the doors, but not from the direction I expected.

Anne and I whirled around at the same moment. The inside door to the drawing room was wide open, and Lady Tottenham stood just beyond it. The blue ruffles of her dress climbed up her neck, devouring her chin in fabric. She blinked in surprise. Her serious expression shifted to a grin saturated with intrigue. "My, oh, my." She clucked her tongue. "What have I stumbled upon?"

I searched my mind for any excuse, but Anne stepped forward before I could speak.

"I was hiding," she said in a quick voice. "Mr. Holland—er —well, he found me."

Lady Tottenham stared blankly in her direction. "I was having a private meeting in the drawing room. Were you spying on me?"

I glanced beyond her shoulder where a gentleman with gray hair stood, spectacles on his nose. He wasn't one of the other guests—I had never seen him before.

"No, no, of course not," Anne said with an innocent smile. "I—I..." her voice trailed off. The flush on her cheeks was condemning her.

"We weren't aware that it was you in the drawing room, my lady," I said. "We didn't mean to interrupt your meeting."

Lady Tottenham's lips pursed into a circle. "It would seem I was the one who so rudely interrupted *your* meeting." Her eyes darted between us. The awe and excitement on her face was unsettling.

"No—" Anne and I said simultaneously.

We exchanged a glance. She cleared her throat. "It was an accident that we both..." she gestured at me, her words evading her.

"I found her when she didn't wish to be found." I pressed my lips together.

"Yes." She nodded.

Lady Tottenham didn't blink as she surveyed both our

faces. "There is no need to explain yourselves to me." Her mischievous grin persisted. "You have surprised me, that is all. I do enjoy being surprised."

I could practically see the protest rising up under Anne's skin. She looked near to bursting as she opened the outside door and walked into the corridor. Lady Tottenham and the gentleman with the spectacles walked past, but not before she threw a knowing glance in my direction.

I stood with my arms crossed, staring at the floor as Lady Tottenham led her guest around the corner toward the vestibule. As soon as she was out of sight, Anne pivoted toward me. In the light, she looked angelic. Her dark features contrasted with her white gown, and the additional blush on her cheeks was endearing. I hadn't known she could blush like that. She would likely scold me for smiling, but I couldn't help it.

Anne covered her face with both hands. "What might she be thinking? The...the *assumptions* she must be making...." She shook her head, uncovering her eyes. "She is going to send me home."

I stepped forward, keeping my voice quiet. "No, she isn't. Did you see how happy she was to find us there? This is what she wants from her house party. Nothing brings her greater joy that discovering romantic encounters happening in hidden alcoves."

"It was *not* a romantic encounter," she snapped, the red on her cheeks climbing higher.

I shrugged, tossing her a smile. "If you say so."

She cast her gaze heavenward, releasing an exasperated sigh. "I suppose you're right."

"That it was romantic?"

"*No.*" She shot me a glare. "Lady Tottenham is nothing but pleased with what she saw. She has no reason to send either of us away prematurely."

I tipped my head to one side, studying the desperation in her features. She disguised it well, but she seemed just as eager to complete the twenty days at Birch House as I was. "If you were sent away for any reason...where would you go?"

She tugged at a loose thread on the ribbon of her gown. "I don't know. I would like to stay in London until Miles returns, but I cannot afford a lease at the moment." She lifted her chin and met my gaze. "So I must remain in Lady Tottenham's favor and stay here." She paused. "Where would you go?"

"My situation is similar to yours. Unfortunately I can't afford to leave either. I too am eagerly awaiting Miles's return, but not for the same reasons you are."

She frowned. "What are your reasons?"

I bit the inside of my cheek, shaking my head. "You wouldn't believe me if I told you."

"I might."

"I already know of your inclination to trust him over me. I would rather not waste my breath."

She groaned, drawing a step closer. "Alexander!"

The sound of my name on her voice sent a wave of warmth through me. I stared at the gold streaks in her hazel eyes, the dark lashes surrounding them. She looked so sincere; I almost explained everything to her. But this was a woman who claimed to be *in love* with Miles. She was his ally, and therefore my enemy. I desperately needed to remember that, or I was in grave danger. If I wasn't careful, she would give me something to lose—and losing to Miles wasn't something I ever wanted to do again.

I looked down at the floor. "How you regard him is not my business. I won't say anything to poison your opinion of him."

"My opinion isn't as malleable as that." She laughed under her breath. "My opinion isn't formed by gossip or words alone. I formed an opinion of him through our interactions. It won't be swayed by what you say, though I am still curious."

I gave her a skeptical look. "You had an opinion of *me* before you even knew me."

"Yes, but—" her tone was defensive.

"Your entire opinion was formed off the opinion of someone else," I continued, walking close enough to see the light freckles on her cheekbones.

She held her ground, scowling up at me. "The facts were quite condemning."

"Facts." I gave a slow nod, anger welling up inside me. "I invite you to make your own investigation of my character."

She was silent for a long moment. She drew a deep breath, her brows pinching together. "Moving forward, I will disregard the things he has said about you." She looked down. "Likewise, I will disregard the things you say about him. During this house party, I shall remain...neutral. I hope the two of you will find a way to heal your animosity someday." She finally met my gaze again. A hint of doubt crossed her features, but then it was gone.

My frustration still lingered, but I nodded. Her loyalty to him would drive me mad. He had spun her into his web, and she was helpless to escape. She had just revealed the state of her finances to me. If she didn't have money, Miles would never pursue her. It would break her heart if I told her that, but eventually her heart would be broken either way.

"Let us make it a rule not to speak of Miles ever again." I extended my hand to her.

She eyed my hand with misgiving. "Why do I suspect that you have a habit of breaking rules?"

"Only if I disagree with them." I grinned. "But this rule is important to our friendship."

"Friendship?" Her brows shot up.

"We both need a friend in this household if we are to survive."

She hesitated to take my hand. "I have friends here."

"I saw the way Mrs. Fitzgibbon and her two cousins snubbed you. Mrs. Pike and the Colborne sisters don't seem to be your first choice. Unless you would rather call Lord Kirkham your friend."

She sighed, her lips fighting against a smile.

"Don't forget, we are hiding partners," I added. "Shake my hand, and we shall agree not to speak of Miles. You can make your decision later about the matter of our friendship."

A genuine smile lit up her face, and she gave a quiet laugh. "Very well." She took my outstretched hand.

I shook it, squeezing her fingers softly. Her eyes met mine, and she pulled her hand away fast, tucking it in a fold on the side of her skirts. "I ought to take my leave before Lady Tottenham finds us again. Let us hope she forgets what she saw."

"Our romantic meeting?"

Anne gave an exasperated sigh, pivoting away from me in one swift motion. "Good day, Alexander."

I didn't look away until she was around the corner.

CHAPTER 8

ANNE

That evening, I could still smell the port on Lord Kirkham's breath when I closed my bedchamber door behind me. I set down my candle, collapsing on my bed with a groan. He hadn't left my side. He had been sitting far too close to me on the sofa, and his leg had been pressed against mine all night. Each time I moved away, he moved closer. When Octavia finished her fourth singing performance of the night, I retired for the evening, no longer caring what Lady Tottenham thought of my decision to leave the drawing room festivities before anyone else.

Octavia had been just as attached to Alexander all day as Lord Kirkham had been to me. There were few things more entertaining than watching his failed attempts at avoiding her. During each of Octavia's performances, she had stared at Alexander's face through every word of the songs. His discomfort was what had made the evening bearable.

I smiled to myself. Now that it was all over, I was eager to escape my tight stays. I had only been filling my lungs halfway all night.

My gaze caught on a piece of parchment that had been tied around my bedpost with a thin pink ribbon. My heart pounded. I rolled over on my bed and cautiously tugged one end of the ribbon, releasing the parchment. Was it another note or invitation? I read the short message.

Love is blind, and lovers cannot see
The pretty follies that themselves commit
Open your eyes and see straight through
Find the heart meant for you.

"What on earth?" I muttered. Who had sneaked into my room and tied that to my bed? I hurried to the door to slide the lock into place before returning to the note.

I recognized the first two lines from Shakespeare's *The Merchant in Venice,* but the other two seemed to have been added on. What reason could someone have to tie that message to my bed? Was the person still here, lurking in a dark corner of the room?

I picked up the candle and cast it toward each wall. Whoever had put the note in my room must have done it while I was at dinner. The hour was now past eleven o'clock, and the noise from the drawing room had died down. The guests would all be retiring for the evening soon, which meant a number of us would be invited to a midnight parlor game. I had managed to avoid the game the night before. Was this hidden message part of the game for tonight?

I pinched the parchment between two fingers, setting it on

the table beside my bed. I tucked my knees to my chest, resting my back against the headboard. My mind was tired from the events of the day, and the worries that came with them.

Lady Tottenham had been watching me.

Ever since she had seen Alexander and me together between the doors, she had taken a special interest in observing my behavior. I felt her gaze on me almost constantly, and when it wasn't, she watched Alexander. I hadn't had a chance to speak with him since that morning. Between deterring Lord Kirkham and Octavia, we were always occupied.

The night before, I had started a sheet to mark off the days until the house party was over. So far, I only had three marks. There were still weeks to go. If my only purpose was to deter Lord Kirkham, I would lose my mind before the party was through. I needed to commit myself to another purpose in order to pass the time. My mind wandered to that morning when I had noticed yet another gentleman caller at an early morning meeting with Lady Tottenham. It hadn't been the same man as before, though they both wore spectacles. Lady Tottenham had offered no introduction to Alexander or to me as the man had walked by. It was certainly peculiar.

Solving that mystery could be a goal of mine. There was also the matter of the overarching 'game,' and the mysterious prize Lady Tottenham continued to refer to. My gaze slid to the message on the table. I read the cryptic note again, eyes narrowed in thought.

"Love is blind, and lovers cannot see..." I mumbled to myself. "Open your eyes, see straight through."

I sat up straight, my legs shooting out in front of me. The blindfold? Was this message a clue of some sort? Perhaps it had been tied to my bed since the day before and I hadn't noticed. I flopped to the other side of my bed to reach the writing desk. I searched the drawer for the invitation I had received to the first midnight parlor game. The writing looked the same. Both notes were written in Lady Tottenham's hand.

She seemed to have given me a clue—further invitation to participate in her game. Had everyone received the same clue? Or had she singled me out?

The questions raced through my mind as I sat on my bed. I debated tugging the bell-pull, but I wanted to wait until after midnight. Nothing sounded worse than freeing myself from my uncomfortable dress only to put it back on again.

The minutes rolled by, and the house fell silent. Occasional footsteps in the corridor caught my attention, but I excused them for the servants. I closed my eyes, drifting off for a moment, until a rustling sound caught my attention.

I sat up, catching sight of the letter just as it skittered under my door.

I leaped off the bed and snatched it up from the floor.

Lady Daventry,

You are invited to the parlor at midnight for a special game. You will not be permitted to leave until the game is complete.

Your benevolent hostess,
    Lady Tottenham

. . .

90

My heart picked up speed. I folded the note and placed it in the pile on my writing desk. I wouldn't be permitted to leave until the game was complete? Would I want to? A surge of dread came through my chest. If it was the same group as last time, that would mean that Lord Kirkham would be there again.

I watched the clock on the wall approach twelve. Since I had been late the first night, I didn't want to be late again. I opened my bedchamber door, sneaking out into the dark corridor. Would the other guests be emerging from their rooms at the same time? I glanced in all directions, noting candlelight under a few of the doors, but darkness under the others. I passed Alexander's door. Light seeped out from beneath it.

With one hand on the bannister, I hurried down the staircase and made my way to the parlor. A footman stood at attention, his white wig and the whites of his eyes glowing in the dimness. He opened the door, ushering me inside.

The room was flooded with soft candlelight. The furniture had been rearranged. I glanced around in confusion as my eyes adjusted to my new surroundings. At the center of the room, a small card table was covered with a tray of food and tea, a vase of red roses, and a chess board. Two chairs sat across from one another, the chess board between them.

I walked forward with cautious steps, catching my reflection in the silver cream pot. My pale green dress was distorted, my face elongated. The silence of the room was unsettling. A sudden chill raised bumps on my arms. I wrapped them around myself, studying the assortment of food on the tray. Tiny tartlets, rectangular cakes, and savory offerings were stacked on a platter. Steam escaped the tea pot, dancing upward until it disappeared. A few rose petals had been scattered around the chess board.

I had expected to find Lady Tottenham in attendance, but the room was empty. My thoughts wandered back to the riddle that I had found tied to my bed post. I shot a glance at the closed door before rushing over to the sideboard where I had found the bowl of forfeits.

"Found you," I whispered as I swiped up the blindfold from the day before. I examined both sides of it before holding it up in front of my eyes. I gasped.

There was a note inside the folds of the fabric. It hadn't been there before, I was sure of it. A few of the words came into focus, but the message was too close to my eyes to read the entire thing. I hurried to unfold it, keeping one eye on the door. No one else had arrived, so I pulled out the slip of parchment and read the words.

If you wish to pass the test
   You must stand out from all the rest
   Take part in my peculiar feast
   And eat no less than twenty-three

I folded the note and slipped it down the bodice of my gown, replacing the blindfold where I had found it. Had she written that clue just for me? Or had others received the same clue tied to their bed posts? I hadn't the slightest idea, but preventing other people from finding it must have been part of the game. If it was a race, I would have to be the fastest at solving the riddles.

I eyed the tray of small desserts and savories. Was that the 'peculiar feast?' I swallowed hard. My stomach was still full from dinner. Was I being tested to see if I could eat twenty-three of the items on the table? That was ridiculous.

I jumped when the parlor door opened, my heart leaping to my throat.

Alexander stood in the doorway. His dark gaze captured mine, a small smile lifting his lips. He gave a slight bow. "Anne."

I returned the gesture. "Alexander." My heart picked up speed, but I shushed it. He made me nervous, and I didn't like it one bit. I couldn't tell if his flirtations were genuine or made in an attempt to tease me. Either way, it was unacceptable.

His sly smile remained as he strode farther into the room. He wore the same clothes he had worn at dinner—a gold waistcoat, black jacket, and white cravat. The cravat was a little looser than it had been before. He rubbed his jaw as he studied the room in confusion just as I had.

Where was everyone else?

Just as the thought crossed my mind, the footman closed the door behind Alexander. We both glanced back when we heard a clicking sound.

Alexander frowned, testing the doorknob. His eyes widened. "He locked us in."

CHAPTER 9

ANNE

I rushed forward, testing the knob for myself. It didn't move.

We exchanged a glance.

Alexander's brow furrowed as he crossed the room to the card table and all that had been arranged on top of it. A deep chuckle rumbled from his chest. "Well, this is certainly unexpected."

I walked toward him with cautious steps. He glanced up as I approached. I felt his gaze on the side of my face as I inspected the chess board closer. I had played countless games of chess when I had been a companion to my friend Nora. To combat our boredom, we had become quite skilled at it. Under normal circumstances, I wouldn't have objected to a game of chess, but these circumstances weren't normal at all.

I was locked in a room with Miles's brother at midnight.

My invitation had said I wouldn't be permitted to leave until the game was complete.

My throat was dry. I could hardly swallow or breathe or think clearly. "We have to finish a game of chess," I said in a flat voice. "That is the only way to have the footman unlock the door."

Alexander gave a slow nod. "That's what I've gathered as well."

I pinched the pendant of my necklace, drawing a deep breath. "Lady Tottenham must have chosen us because of what she saw this morning."

"I have no doubt." He laughed. "It seems she has a new match in mind. She wanted us to be alone."

My eyes darted to his. I looked away fast. "She really needs to stop with her matchmaking."

"Why would she stop now? Her skill is improving." I could hear the teasing smile in his voice.

"No, it's not."

"Do you not agree that you and I would make a better match than you and Lord Kirkham, or Octavia and myself?" The depth of his gaze threatened to throw me off-balance.

"I don't agree. I think you and Miss Octavia would make a very handsome match."

"I'm glad to hear that you think I'm handsome." He walked closer, stopping at my chair to pull it out.

I sat down with a sigh. "You are insufferable."

He laughed as he sat across from me, resting his folded arms on the table. "Do you know how to play chess?"

I rested my chin on my hand, debating the best way to respond. If I led him to believe I rarely played, he would be more shocked when I took my victory. I shrugged. "I think I remember how to play. Do you know how?"

He tipped his head to one side. "I think so."

My gaze slid to the tray of tiny desserts and other pickings. What would Alexander think if I began stuffing my face with them? Did I really care what he thought? If the riddle told me I had to eat twenty-three, then I would have to eat quickly before Alexander could snatch too many of them. To start, I grabbed two miniature hot cross buns. I popped them in my mouth, one after the other.

I swallowed, picking up two almond cakes. "I'm hungry," I said with a laugh.

Alexander didn't look appalled as I had expected. His smile grew as he watched me fill my cheeks with both cakes at once. "That is completely understandable considering what little we were served for dinner."

I nearly inhaled the cake into my lungs. The dinner had been nothing short of a feast. Alexander must have thought I was a glutton now. I didn't know how I would prove that I had eaten all twenty-three as the riddle had specified, but I had to try. Lady Tottenham's game was underway, and I didn't want to ruin my chances now. "I cannot resist sweets," I said with a shrug.

"Do not stop on my account." Alexander pushed the plate toward me. He poured me a cup of tea.

"Thank you," I said, glancing up through my lashes as I took a sip. The tea burned my tongue. I sputtered, coughing out the hot liquid. My eyes watered.

He leaned his arms forward on the table. "The fastest way to victory is to wound your opponent."

I lowered the teacup with a glare. "Well, then. Shall we start the game?"

His expression didn't falter, amusement still gleaming behind his eyes. "A simple chess game sounds rather boring, does it not? I suggest we raise the stakes."

I raised one eyebrow. "Are you suggesting that I gamble?"

"No." He poured a splash of cream into my teacup before preparing his own. "I don't gamble."

According to Miles, gambling had been one of Alexander's worst habits. Hearing him deny that he ever gambled at all was difficult to believe. What reason could Miles have had to make Alexander out to be such a villain? It seemed more reasonable for Alexander to lie in order to paint himself in a good light than it was for Miles to lie in order to condemn his brother.

One of them was lying. How could I not assume it was the man across from me? I hardly knew him. I would sooner trust Lady Tottenham with my hair arrangement than I would trust Alexander's mischievous smile.

"What are you suggesting then?" I asked.

He picked up one of the roses from the vase, rolling the stem between two fingers. The rose spun, a blur of red velvet petals. "A bargain."

I raised my brows. "That is vague. What are the terms?"

"If you win the game, you may choose a woman from among the guests at the party for me to court. If I win the game, I will choose a gentleman for you to court."

I gaped at him, an astonished laugh escaping my chest. "You would allow me to choose *any* woman here for you to court? Even Mrs. Pike?" The woman was at least fifteen years his senior. Mrs. Fitzgibbon was at least five, and I was closest at one.

"Well, I do specialize with older women." His lips twisted in a smile as his eyes met mine.

I chose to ignore that remark. "Why do you want the opportunity to choose a gentleman for me?" I narrowed my eyes at him. "You know that I'm waiting for—" I stopped myself. We had agreed not to speak of Miles.

Alexander set the rose down in front of his teacup. "That's exactly why I want the opportunity. I want you to be sure that Miles is the man for you. If the man I choose doesn't win over your affections by the time Miles returns, then you will have proven me wrong." He took a sip from his teacup, setting it down firmly on the saucer. "I don't think Miles is your match, and I want the chance to prove it."

Our rule not to speak of Miles had already been broken, and it hadn't even been a day. A wave of frustration anchored me to my seat. I took a steadying breath. Proving Alexander wrong would be a pleasure, though I didn't want to be forced to court any of the men at the party. If I had to guess, he would probably choose Mr. Hatcher or Mr. Amesbury. I drummed my fingers on the table. If I won, I could have the pleasure of matching him with anyone I chose. He would regret suggesting the bargain at all. Miss Morton or Miss Rowley would love the opportunity to court Alexander, and it would hopefully serve to humble Miss Octavia as well.

Alexander wasn't aware of my hours upon hours of chess practice. He didn't know who he was competing with.

"Very well, we have a bargain," I said. I ate two more desserts from the plate, popping one in each cheek. My stomach protested, but I still had sixteen to go. I would have to spread them out over the course of the game.

Alexander looked far too pleased with my reply.

And too confident.

"Go on, make the first move." Alexander sat back in his chair, picking up a cherry tartlet from the plate. I kept my eyes fixed on the pastry. He took a bite, wiping a drop of jam from his lower lip with his thumb. I looked away fast. I had already forbade myself from finding him attractive, and looking at his lips would only make matters worse. *Focus, Anne.*

I moved my first pawn, sitting back while Alexander made his move. I snatched up another two pickings of my own from the plate. If he went on eating, my twenty-three would run out before the game was over.

His eyebrows lifted and his hand froze over the board as he watched me pick up another hot cross bun. "Ten," I whispered by accident. I chewed fast and took another sip of tea. Thirteen to go. I counted the items that remained on the plate. There were only sixteen remaining, which meant Alexander couldn't eat more than three. I would have to keep one eye on him the entire time. The footman in the corner of the room might have been watching to see how many I ate—to see if I deserved another clue in Lady Tottenham's game.

I moved another piece, and Alexander made his second move. His hand reached for the plate of sweets. I panicked and snatched up two more, moving them to my side of the table. I cast him an innocent smile.

After ten minutes of strategic play, I realized that Alexander was not as unfamiliar with the game as he had portrayed. He knew exactly what he was doing. After twenty minutes, he struggled to keep a serious expression as he watched me devour the plate of sweets. He was winning the game because I was too preoccupied with a different one. I didn't know where my desperation to obtain another clue had come from, but I could taste my victory along with almost twenty small pastries.

Alexander only reached for the tray twice, but that was enough to make panic rise up in my chest. I had been eating three times as fast as he was, but I still had four to go. Alexander had already eaten his allotment if I were to claim all twenty-three of mine. My stomach ached as I took my turn on the chess board.

I grimaced. I should have been more focused throughout the game. I had never been skilled at dividing my attention. I stuffed a miniature pear cake into my mouth.

Alexander's smile brought a surge of dread to my over-filled stomach. He reached for the plate, and I jumped to my feet. I nearly lunged across the table. "No!" I clutched the back of his wrist to stop him from taking one of my final three cakes.

His eyes rounded as he stared up at me. I released his hand, my face burning. I sat back in my chair. "I'm sorry," I mumbled. "I didn't realize I was so competitive."

His lip quivered with laughter. "Over sweets?"

"I—well..." my voice faded. "I found a clue to Lady Tottenham's game," I whispered.

"A clue?"

"Yes." I could hardly sit up straight. My stomach felt close to bursting. "Did you have a note tied to your bedpost today?"

He shook his head. His dark brows pinched together. "I haven't seen any clues."

"Did she only leave the clues for me?" I mused, more to myself than to him.

"What did she leave you?"

I eyed him with caution. "Perhaps I shouldn't tell you."

"Why not?"

I sighed. "One moment." I picked up the last items from the plate, finishing them in three bites. I drained my teacup, forcing myself to keep a proper posture. I had already been behaving like swine; I could at least maintain a shred of elegance. Alexander's wide eyes made a laugh bubble out of my mouth. I swallowed hard to keep anything else from coming up with it. "Now I can be sure you won't sabotage me."

"Please do explain," he said with a nervous smile. His eyes flickered to the trail of crumbs on the table.

"Close your eyes for a moment," I said.

He hesitated, but finally obeyed, his dark lashes fluttering closed. I reached in my bodice and withdrew the clue I had found in the blindfold. I unfolded the foolscap just as his eyes opened. I read it aloud.

"If you wish to pass the test
    You must stand out from all the rest
    Take part in my peculiar feast
    And eat no less than twenty-three."

His eyes widened. "Twenty-three of these?" He gestured at the plate.

I nodded, and my stomach lurched with dismay. "I have never eaten so much in my entire life."

A laugh burst out of him. "Why the devil would Lady Tottenham require you to do that?"

I shrugged. "Her games are never ordinary. She seems to enjoy watching her guests embarrass or torture themselves.

Don't forget that as we speak, we are locked in a room after midnight being forced to play a game of chess."

"That is true." His gaze settled on my face for a long moment, eyes narrowed in thought. "Are you determined to participate in her game, then?"

"If I have no choice but to stay at Birch House, then I see no reason not to. It will help pass the time. She obviously wants to see her guests enjoying their time here, embracing her ideas, and searching for her secret 'prize.'"

"She also wants her guests to fall in love with one another," Alexander added with a sideways smile. "Do you plan on participating in that?"

I took a sip of tea, meeting his gaze over the rim of the cup. "You already know that answer."

"You might not have a choice if I win this game." He grinned, lifting his next piece on the chess board.

"You are not going to w—"

My eyes blurred for a moment, my stomach roiling as I inspected the board. I had been far too distracted. "Drat it all," I muttered, gritting my teeth.

He had beat me in a smothered mate. That was even more embarrassing than an ordinary loss. How had I allowed myself to become so careless?

Alexander leaned back in his chair with an apologetic grimace. "Checkmate."

"You cannot be serious." I pressed a hand to my stomach. I had focused my attention on the wrong game. Those blasted pastries had seemed more important than Alexander's bargain.

"I won the game," he said. "And the bargain."

I laughed, my voice shaking. "Surely the bargain wasn't serious. There's only one man at the party who would even want to court me. You wouldn't be so cruel as to force me to court Lord Kirkham." I stood, cringing as I held my stomach. Had the footman unlocked the door yet? I took a few steps toward it.

I shrieked with surprise as Alexander rushed around me, blocking the path. His eyes danced with amusement as he took me by the shoulders and backed me toward the table again. "You can't escape until we discuss the terms of the bargain. Are you a woman of your word?"

"Yes," I snapped. I scowled up at him, my heart racing. His hands held my shoulders, crumpling my sleeves, but all of that was buried under the sensation of his thumb against the edge of my collarbone. A string of shivers ran down my arms and spine, which only infuriated me further.

He stopped walking when I was a safe distance from the door, but his hands still held me still, as if he thought I would make a dash for the corridor at any moment.

"Please don't make me court Lord Kirkham," I blurted.

Alexander laughed, and his hands slipped away from my shoulders. "If I had any confidence that he could steal your heart, I would, but you have made your feelings about him perfectly clear."

"I don't like any of the men here." I rounded my eyes with sincerity. "It would be a waste of time for me to encourage any of them. Not only that, but it would be unkind to pretend I was interested in one of them if I am not."

"Do you actually know any of them? Have you ever had a conversation with anyone but Lord Kirkham?"

"Yes. Mr. Barnwall." He was only in search of a mother for his six children, all of whom he rarely saw or interacted with. "I am not fond of him either."

Alexander bit his lower lip. The brown of his eyes appeared more golden in the candlelight as he searched my face. "Perhaps you're right. None of the other men here would suit you."

The tension in my chest relaxed, and I nodded my agreement. "They wouldn't."

"However, you still must uphold the bargain and court someone of my choosing."

I sighed. "Is that truly necessary? You just said—"

"You may rest assured that I haven't chosen one of them." His smile quirked upward, and dread filled what little space was left in my stomach.

"Who did you choose, then?" My voice cracked. I guessed his reply before it escaped his grinning lips.

"Myself."

CHAPTER 10

ALEXANDER

I only felt a small twinge of guilt as I watched the color drain from Anne's face.

"You?" she scoffed.

"Yes, me." I interlocked my hands behind my back. She had a pastry crumb above her upper lip, and I had been tempted to brush it away for the past ten minutes. I clenched my jaw against the laughter in my throat. The horror on her face at the prospect of me vying for her heart should have been offensive, but I took it as a compliment.

She must have thought I had the best chance at succeeding.

Her horrified eyes met mine. The green hues overpowered the brown, matching the pale green of her dress. "Are you trying to...steal me from Miles? Is this some sort of retribution?" The anger in her features only made her more attractive. I eyed the crumb on her lip again with a smile. No matter how threatening she tried to appear, she was nothing short of endearing.

Her concerns were valid. Courting Anne would be a delicate endeavor. If she thought the courtship was real, she would never agree to it. If I tried to poison her opinion of Miles, she would only put more distance between us. But I wanted to come to know her, to show her how she deserved to be treated —and that she was worth more than an occasional letter from the man who supposedly loved her. I stared down at her face.

Perhaps I did want to steal her from him.

"No," I said. "It's not retribution."

Her dark brows furrowed. "You said you wanted to prove that Miles wasn't the man for me."

I crossed my arms over my chest. "I want to show you what a real courtship should look like."

She exhaled sharply with frustration, tipping her head up to look at me. "You're going to try to woo me, and charm me, and win me over just to spite him. It isn't going to work."

"Is it not?" I took a step toward her, leaning down until my face was just inches away. She took a step back, running into the edge of the table. The teacups clattered, and the chess pieces slid off the board. I brushed my finger across the top of her lip, wiping away the pastry flake. "A crumb," I said in a low voice. I dropped my gaze to her mouth a moment longer. There was a faint line of freckles above her cupid's bow, and a crease at the center of her full lower lip. I met her gaze. Her beauty was everywhere, but her eyes were what made my stomach drop the furthest. The anger vanished from her expression, a hint of pink rising to her cheeks.

I leaned forward. She didn't move. She seemed to be frozen

there against the table, her gaze trapped in mine. Kissing her now would be premature, no matter how gladly I would do so. If she came to her senses, she would kick me across the room.

I reached around her at the last second to pick up my teacup from the table. I took a long sip, hiding my smile with the cup.

The color on her cheeks deepened, and she marched several paces away from me. "I will not court you, Alexander. I know we made a bargain, but I wasn't under the impression that you were a contender."

"I *am* a guest at this house party."

"Yes, but..." Her nostrils flared as she took a deep breath.

I regarded her seriously. "Are you afraid I might steal your heart?"

"*No.* That is the least of my concern." She paced the floor on the other side of the table. "Courting you would be entirely pointless."

"It wouldn't be pointless." I set my teacup down and gripped the back of my chair. She stopped walking, facing me across the table. "If it were known throughout Birch House that there was an attachment between us, there would be many positive consequences. Lord Kirkham would give up his pursuit, Miss Octavia would give up her pursuit, and Lady Tottenham would be pleased to see a match forming. She might even stop throwing both of us into matchmaking games with the other guests here." I paused. Anne still seemed guarded, but a little more open to the idea. "What I'm suggesting is a fake courtship."

Her eyes widened. "Fake?"

"Unless you would prefer a real one."

"No." She paced the floor in a loop again, hands on her hips. "It would be a relief not to have Lord Kirkham at my heels."

I nodded. "And I would like to kindly send the message to Octavia that I'm not planning to court her."

"She isn't the only one who would benefit from that message."

"What do you mean?"

"Miss Morton and Miss Rowley are infatuated with you as well." Anne cast her gaze heavenward, as if she couldn't begin to understand. I chose not to be offended. "They were gossiping about Miss Octavia with no small measure of envy."

I stood up a little straighter. "Well, then, you shall be the envy of the party."

"They'll all hate me!" Anne said with a laugh. "Octavia most of all."

"Do you think I'm fond of the idea of Lord Kirkham hating me? He could knock my teeth out."

Anne's broad smile was contagious. She covered her mouth to muffle her laughter. When it subsided, she shook her head. "I don't know. A fake courtship is madness."

I withdrew a rose from the vase. "I think it's brilliant. At any rate, you made a bargain." I walked around the table and extended the rose to Anne. "I won the game, so you don't have any choice but to accept me as your...counterfeit lover."

Her nose wrinkled as another laugh escaped her. "Never say that again."

"Your pretend beloved?"

She covered her face with both hands, peeking between her fingers. "I understand how a fake courtship could benefit us both, but how could I ever explain it to Miles?"

"You won't have to. At the conclusion of the party, we may go our separate ways. He doesn't need to know we were ever acquainted." The idea of Anne running back to Miles was enough to make me ill, but I ignored the dread in my stomach. I had plenty of time to show her that he was not worth her time and not worthy of her heart.

She released a long, shaky breath, taking the rose from my hand. She stared down at the petals. "If we're going to do this, we have to make a plan. If Lady Tottenham hears of any deceit, she will be sure to send us away. Neither of us can afford that."

"No." I rubbed one side of my jaw. "We will have to be convincing."

She blanched. "But not *too* convincing."

"The other guests have to believe that we're madly in love," I said with a grin. "There will need to be some acting involved."

Her features hardened, becoming more stern. "I will create a list of rules to ensure you don't...take your role too far."

"What do you mean by that?" I asked in an innocent voice.

"You know exactly what I mean." She pointed an accusatory finger at me. "I won't tolerate any flirting unless it's done in public to add credibility to our attachment."

"Very well." I gave a resolute nod. "You may create your list of rules if it makes you more comfortable."

"Good. I will share it with you in the morning." She rubbed her hands over her skirts. "Lady Tottenham obviously already believes there is something between us. It won't take a great deal to convince her of a deepened attachment." The soft glow of the candlelight on her skin, and the way her curls fell over her brow tossed my stomach like a ship in a storm. Anne was the one that would take the most convincing, but I was determined.

"So we begin tomorrow?" I asked.

"I suppose...but what do we plan to do at breakfast? How shall we make our attachment clear enough? I haven't the slightest idea of how to act."

I gave her a reassuring smile. "You may leave that to me."

CHAPTER 11

ANNE

F ake Courtship Rules
    1. Flirting is only allowed with an audience.
2. No speaking of a future engagement or marriage.
3. No kissing, even in parlor games.
4. Acting must be kept within the bounds of propriety.
5. No unnecessary proximity.
6. The ruse must end no later than the adjournment of the house party.

I set down my quill, blowing the ink dry. I was fully aware of what I had agreed to the night before, but still, my stomach squirmed. I rubbed my dry eyes, already feeling the pull of fatigue. Sleep had evaded me, and for good reason. My stomach had been upset with a mixture of twenty three bite-sized pastries and dread over my new role as Alexander's 'counterfeit lover.'

I folded the list of rules and tucked it under one of my stockings. Jane had already come to arrange my hair and help me dress in my favorite red gown. I chose an orange ribbon for the waist, a mauve shawl, and a simple necklace. I even put a touch of rouge on my lips and cheeks. My bold choices seemed to have surprised Jane, but if I hoped to win Lady Tottenham's favor, I could begin by dressing according to her preferences.

Since I had passed the test with the 'peculiar feast' the night before, I expected to find another clue in my bedchamber at some point that day. Before heading down to breakfast, I checked outside my door for any sign of another clue.

I found nothing.

I would have to check again later.

I had forgone my attempt at early morning reading since the last two had resulted in disaster. Staying in my room to write my list of rules had been much more productive, and had kept me safe from Lord Kirkham.

I paused outside the door. The voices within made a fresh surge of fear wash over me. *You can do this, Anne. Be bold.* I shook out my arms, desperate for even a drop of courage. Had I made a grave mistake? Pretending to court Alexander could have dangerous consequences. What if rumors escaped the house party? If Miles was greeted in London with gossip about our attachment, he would never see me again. I drew a deep breath, my heart racing. It was my weakness to make a disaster out of everything. The fake courtship could be entirely harmless. It could make the rest of the party bearable and entertaining, so long as Alexander kept my rules.

I reached for the door. My hand was shaking.

"Good morning." A deep voice reached my ears from behind. My shoulder blades relaxed as Alexander stepped up beside me. His hand reached around me from behind, steadying my fingers on the doorknob.

"Good morning," I managed. I glanced up at him.

His hair was combed away from his face. "Are you ready?" he asked. His voice was close to my ear, and I realized I wasn't ready at all. My heart hammered, and I ducked under his arm.

"I made the list," I blurted. I looked both ways down the corridor before reaching into my shoe to withdraw it.

Alexander's lips twitched as he took the wrinkled foolscap from me. His gaze flickered over the page. "No kissing, even in parlor games," he read aloud. His eyes met mine. "Are you determined to take all the enjoyment out of this arrangement?"

I hoped he was jesting, but I could never be certain. Not with him. He continued down the page. When he finished reading, he folded the list and gave it back to me. "I certainly see room for improvement."

I planted one hand on my hip. "How so?"

"I may require clarification as the days go on. There are some areas that are open to various interpretations." A slow smile tugged on his mouth, but he corrected the expression.

"Please take it seriously," I said with a frown.

"I am very serious." His eyes widened, his mouth firm.

I tucked the list back inside my shoe before straightening my posture. "I don't believe you. On which points do you disagree?"

He stepped closer and lowered his voice. "I would argue that proximity is necessary if we wish to be convincing."

My hands began sweating. I wiped them on the sides of my skirts. "Very well."

"Keeping our acting within the bounds of propriety is also a bit...unclear. Lady Tottenham's idea of propriety is obviously very different than the world outside of Birch House."

"Lady Tottenham's definition of propriety is not what I had in mind." I clamped my mouth shut when I heard a loud giggle from the adjacent corridor.

Mrs. Pike rounded the corner. She wore a white floral morning dress, her mushroom brown hair pulled tight into a knot atop her head. Miss Octavia and Miss Victoria followed closely behind, revealing the source of the giggling. Both young ladies' golden curls were perfectly shaped, both sets of identical blue eyes landing solidly on Alexander. Octavia's neckline was deep, the bright sapphire blue of her gown setting her apart from Victoria, who always dressed in pastels.

I exchanged a glance with Alexander. At first, I wasn't certain he would begin our ruse, but then I felt the weight of his hand on the small of my back. He applied just enough pressure to usher me forward as he opened the breakfast room door.

My pulse echoed in my ears, a flush already heating my cheeks. I had never been one for public displays of affection—especially when it was part of a ruse. Lady Tottenham had said it herself—the entire party was a game. A pretend romance was only fitting. I squared my shoulders, willing myself to be confident as we stepped into the room. Alexander leaned close to my ear from behind.

"Red looks lovely on you." His breath brushed my ear, and I chose to ignore the leap my heart took at his words. Was he referring to my dress or my blush? I would stab him with my fork if it was the latter. I tried to focus, but several guests were already looking in our direction. I brought a demure smile to my face. The blush on my cheeks couldn't be feigned, so I hoped it would add to the performance.

Immediately, Lady Tottenham glanced in our direction. Her mouth hung open, just inches away from her forkful of scrambled eggs. She lowered her hand, lips twisting into a victorious grin.

Alexander's hand fell away from my back, but it hadn't gone unnoticed. I cast him one more smile over my shoulder before walking toward the display of food on the sideboard. I felt his gaze on my back as I went, and then he was beside me again. We filled our plates as usual before choosing seats at the round table. He moved his chair closer to mine before sitting down.

I dared to take a look around the room. Miss Morton chewed on a piece of orange, a deep furrow in her brow as she whispered to her cousin. Lord Kirkham's short neck looked a little longer than usual as he strained to see over Mr. Amesbury.

"Are you hungry?" Alexander asked, his gaze focusing on my face. The admiration in his eyes shocked me. How was he so good at this? I felt like a circus animal with the attention we had drawn as we entered the room.

"Not at all. I ate plenty of food last night." I had only taken a small portion from the sideboard, but none of it tempted me. I would have been too nervous to eat even if I *had* been hungry. Mrs. Pike and the Colborne twins had finished filling their plates and Octavia was leading the way toward our table. She had never looked more determined.

Alexander took a slice of pear from his plate and lifted it toward my mouth. "Try it," he said in a light voice.

I cast him a warning glance. "What are you doing?" I whispered through gritted teeth.

"Try it."

"I am not going to eat from your fork," I hissed.

The pear came closer to my lips, so I finally opened my mouth at the last second. I bit my teeth into the fruit in the least graceful manner possible. Juice dribbled down to the white tablecloth just as Miss Octavia took the seat on Alexander's other side. Her icy blue eyes shot daggers at me. I nearly choked on the chunk of pear. I forced a giggle out of my throat, my stiff smile directed at Alexander as he ate the other half of the pear. It was all I could do to hide my astonishment.

His idea of propriety must have had no bounds at all.

If his intentions were to shock everyone in the room, he was succeeding.

I wiped at my chin with a serviette.

Octavia's nose twitched. Her pale brows drew together.

"You look well today, Mr. Holland," she said in a sugary sweet voice. She leaned toward him. Her gaze darted in my direction. Reading her stony features was difficult, but she did seem to perceive me as a threat. Her confidence wasn't as high as the day before.

If I wanted Alexander's help with deterring Lord Kirkham, I would have to play my part as well in helping to deter Octavia.

I swallowed my pride along with the bite of pear. "He always looks well," I said, gazing up at him. Unfortunately it wasn't a lie. I watched the sharp corner of his jaw as he ate another slice of pear.

His brow jolted with surprise. He rotated in his chair toward me, a smirk lifting one side of his mouth. Surely he knew I was acting. Perhaps he was surprised at my willingness to participate so fully in the ruse.

Octavia jabbed her fork into a piece of fruit. "I haven't known you to speak so freely, my lady. You have hardly said a word this entire party. I wasn't aware that you had an opinion of anything."

Alexander bit back a laugh as he took a bite from his plate. "Lady Daventry has many opinions."

Miss Octavia lifted her chin, which I noticed had a dent at the center of it. It made her more intimidating. "I would love to hear more of your opinions about Mr. Holland."

Alexander sat up straight, a teasing glint in his eye that was surely meant just for me. "I would love to hear as well." The edge of flirtation in his voice was just enough to deepen the crease between Octavia's eyebrows.

My heart thudded when Alexander's gaze landed on mine expectantly. I forced myself to focus on Octavia, since she was the one who had asked the question. I hardly knew what to say. My opinion of Alexander was as conflicted as it could possibly be. All the things Miles had told me about Alexander's past were horrible, but they didn't seem to match the man sitting beside me. Had he been reformed? Or had Miles lied to me? It didn't make sense.

You're an actress, I reminded myself. This wasn't a time for perfect honesty, yet I couldn't open my mouth. "I—I never wish to speak my opinion on a person unless it's clear to me. I thought I knew what to think of Mr. Holland, but now I'm not certain. He's a mystery that I'm still trying to solve." I pressed my lips together. I needed to end with something flirtatious. "I am fond of mysteries." I fluttered my lashes as I looked down at the table, feeling like a complete ninny.

Octavia laughed, a high-pitched sound that grated on me. "The only mystery about Mr. Holland is why he hasn't married yet."

Alexander smiled. "I do plan to marry when the time is right, and when I feel I can provide a woman and children with the comfortable life they deserve." His eyes met mine. "When I do marry, it will only be for love."

My heart beat a shallow rhythm. It would be counterproductive to our ruse to break the lock on our gazes, so I held perfectly still. His words were so genuine, I almost wondered if he meant it. Was he secretly a romantic? The contradictions in my head were far too confusing. Miles had always described him as a rake. Unfeeling, uncaring, and opposed to matrimony. Discerning which of his words were true and which were part of his act would be more difficult than I had expected.

Octavia's voice cut into my thoughts. "*You* have been married before, my lady. Did you marry for love, or for money?"

Her blunt questions made my skin prickle with vexation. Mrs. Pike and Victoria listened in silence, making no attempt to scold her.

"I married out of obligation," I said firmly. Alexander hadn't yet asked me such personal questions, though he must have been curious about why I hadn't waited for Miles the first time if I was so eager to see him now.

"How could you have been obligated to marry? Was it your parents who forced you? Were you not yet of age?"

I didn't plan to elaborate, but Octavia was relentless. She seemed intent on digging up my worst secrets in front of Alexander. "I don't wish to share the details, Miss Colborne, nor do I wish to speak of my late husband at all."

"How did he die?"

"Octavia." Mrs. Pike finally intervened, reaching around Victoria to grab her niece's wrist. "That is enough."

Octavia sighed, popping a grape in her mouth. Her eyes slid up to Alexander's face, a coy smirk on her lips. She didn't seem prepared to give up yet. In fact, she hardly seemed discouraged at all.

The muscles in my neck and shoulders were tense, and I realized how tightly I had been gripping my fork. Alexander's leg nudged mine under the table. I met his concerned gaze just as Lady Tottenham called the room to attention.

"Good morning, my dear friends. I trust you all slept well." I barely caught the fleeting glance she threw in my direction. She had robbed me of sleep with that chess game and those twenty-three pastries, and she knew it. She was happy about it, in fact. Her hair was a mixture of braids and curls, all piled together with violet flowers to form a bouquet. "After breakfast," she continued, "we are going to gather outside." A slow smile curved her lips. "I trust you are all familiar with the game of cricket?"

♟♟♟

"Is a storm coming?" Mrs. Fitzbibbon squinted up at the sky as the group walked outside to the rear of the house. I followed her gaze upward. The grey clouds slunk across the sky, headed in our direction. Lady Tottenham didn't seem concerned at all. Despite the lack of sunlight, she still had a parasol propped against her right shoulder.

I held Alexander's arm, keeping him close as we paraded

through the other guests. The brim of my bonnet shielded him from view, but I sensed him lean close to my ear. "Are you all right?"

I tipped my head up to look at him. "Yes," I lied. Octavia's questions had rattled me a little, and so had all the attention. Were my nerves so obvious?

The worry in Alexander's expression caught me off guard. He wrapped his opposite hand around my fingers at the crook of his elbow. The gesture was simple, but it sent a jolt of warmth through my chest. "You're doing well. Keep it going."

I nodded. I stiffened in panic when I caught Lord Kirkham's eye. He walked quickly, weaving around Mr. Hatcher and Julia in order to be closer to me.

Alexander's lips twisted in a sly smile. "Untie your bonnet."

"What?"

He tugged discreetly on one end of the ribbon, causing the bow to loosen. I tugged it the rest of the way until both ends hung loose in front of me.

Alexander's eyes found mine again beneath the brim of my bonnet. "Now pretend I said something extremely amusing, and tip your head back with a laugh. Ensure your bonnet falls to the grass."

"You already fed me a piece of fruit," I whispered. "That is quite enough for one day."

"Lord Kirkham is watching," he said through closed teeth.

That was reason enough. I threw my head back with a flirtatious laugh, putting one hand to my forehead. I nudged the bonnet off, sending it to the ground behind me. "Oh!" I exclaimed, pressing a hand to my curls. I held back a genuine laugh as Alexander scrambled to retrieve it, biting the inside of my cheek.

He scooped up the bonnet just as I had expected him to. He stood in front of me, straightening the tangled ribbons. I felt the gazes of several guests on us—hungry for fresh gossip, to be sure. Alexander drew a step closer, placing the bonnet on top of my head with a slow, gentle movement. His soft eyes traced over my face. "May I?" He held the ribbons in each hand.

I swallowed, forcing a demure smile to my lips. "Yes."

He tied the ribbons slowly, his knuckles grazing my neck. My body reacted to his touch, a shiver following each one. I cursed myself for noticing the sensation at all. A furrow marked the center of his brow as he finished the bow and met my gaze again. I thought he was finished, but then he traced the curve of my cheek with the back of his forefinger. "There. Beautiful, as always." His eyes bored into mine, warm and gentle.

I didn't know whether to laugh or smile or run away. He was far too good at this. His acting would convince anyone.

It would even convince me if I wasn't careful.

I drew a deep breath, tearing my gaze away from his adoring eyes. They reached all the way into my soul, prodding around in there and digging up emotions I wasn't familiar with. No one had ever looked at me the way Alexander was looking at me now, fake or not. It was completely unsettling.

A sound escaped me—a breathless giggle. "You are too kind, Mr. Holland." My strained smile made my cheeks ache. Contrary to Alexander's talent, I was not good at this at all. I wrapped my hand around his arm again, glancing at all the faces around us.

Lord Kirkham's mouth was a firm line, his venomous eyes fixed on Alexander. Octavia glared at me, though Victoria appeared amused. Mrs. Fitzgibbon was all shock, her gaze bobbing in every direction like a startled pigeon. Miss Morton and Miss Rowley shared their cousin's surprise, though Miss Morton stared at me like I was a thief who had just stolen the very dress off her back.

Lady Tottenham grinned.

We stopped walking when we reached the edge of the open lawn near the rose bushes and lemonade table. Cricket was generally a man's sport, and did not sound enjoyable in the slightest. I fully planned to sit at the table with the women, even knowing that I would either be snubbed or interrogated. Either one would be painfully awkward.

I studied the field. It was empty. Cricket was played with a bat and ball, with two sets of three wickets set up at each end of the pitch. The lawn was not set up for a game of cricket. Besides that, there weren't nearly enough guests to have proper teams, even if all of the ladies participated.

"This doesn't look like cricket," I said in a quiet voice.

Alexander looked just as confused as I was.

"Ladies and gentlemen, gather round." Lady Tottenham's loud voice faltered at the end, and she coughed into her arm. A maid rushed forward to give her a handkerchief. She cleared her throat, continuing in a softer voice. "I promised you a game of cricket, and that you shall have."

"I don't see a ball," Mr. Barnwall said with a frown.

"Or wickets," added Mr. St. Vincent.

Lady Tottenham laughed, throwing her head back in a similar fashion to what I had just done to drop my bonnet. The high-pitched laughter made three birds take flight out of a nearby tree. "There is no need for wickets or a ball," she said, wiping at the corner of her eye. "How silly of me. I should have explained." Her smile disappeared as she snapped her fingers. From behind the crowd, two footman stepped forward, each placing a covered silver tray on the table beside the rose bushes. Lady Tottenham's violet skirts rustled as she moved to stand beside the table. "I have my own version of the game of cricket."

"Of course she does," Alexander muttered.

With a flourish, Lady Tottenham lifted the lid that covered the first tray. A set of gasps came from the front row of guests —Mrs. Pike, Octavia, and Victoria.

I stood on the tips of my toes.

My stomach sank.

Of course. The moment I heard the word *cricket* I should have known Lady Tottenham's true intentions.

On the tray were dozens of dried crickets, spindly legs pointed toward the grey sky.

CHAPTER 12

ANNE

"I find it deucedly difficult to sleep at night at Birch House," Lady Tottenham said with a sigh. "The crickets are far too loud."

My hand tightened on Alexander's arm. Every time I thought Lady Tottenham's house party activities couldn't possibly become more shocking, I was proven wrong. At the one dinner party I had attended of hers, she had caused a stir by serving dessert topped with dried crickets. It was her speciality.

"Therefore, my groundskeeping staff catches them from the shrubs, bushes, and hedgerows for me," she continued. "I am not so cold-hearted as to allow them to go to waste." She smiled lovingly at the creatures on the tray. "Though a little peculiar, they make an excellent addition to any feast. All they need is a little salt or sugar."

Her words rang in my ears.

Peculiar...feast.

I closed my eyes against the sight of the crickets on the tray. "*Blast it* to Cumbria and back," I hissed under my breath.

Alexander seemed to have made the same realization I had, except he wasn't nearly as distressed. He smiled down at me, eyes gleaming with amusement. "You ate those twenty-three pastries for nothing."

"Not for nothing," I snapped. "They were delicious."

He laughed, his entire body shaking to suppress it. I squeezed his arm just hard enough to hurt. It only made his smile widen. "I hope you're hungry," he whispered.

My hairline was wet with perspiration. How on earth would I be able to eat twenty-three of those crunchy little creatures? I had a stronger stomach than most. I could do it. I had to. My efforts the night before to obtain the next clue had been wasted. I couldn't give up now, no matter how entertained Alexander would be. I shushed him as he tried to tease me again, straining my ears to hear Lady Tottenham's instructions.

"The game will be played in teams. I will ask a question or pose a riddle to be solved, and the first team to guess the answer correctly, will win five points. The losing team will have to select a player to go to the table and eat a cricket. The game will continue until all the crickets on your team's tray have been eaten. If a player chooses to eat more than one cricket, each additional cricket will count as a point toward their team's total score, bringing them closer to clearing their tray. As you can see, there are multiple ways to win." Lady Tottenham glanced up with a sigh. "Let us hope it doesn't rain. No one likes soggy crickets." She picked up a cricket from one tray and popped it in her mouth.

The crunching sound brought Mrs. Fitzgibbon to tears. She turned away from the table, rushing toward the back of the group. Mr. Lymington handed her his handkerchief, a grim expression on his face.

Miss Rowley's cheeks were pale, a hint of green under her skin. She pressed a hand to her stomach.

Octavia smiled, leaning forward to examine the trays more closely. "What do they taste like?" she asked with fascination.

Lady Tottenham pursed her lips. "They have a unique taste, but most akin to almonds, roasted legumes, or seeds."

"Hmm," Alexander said with a grin. "I like legumes." His gaze found mine. "Do you?"

I filled my lungs, squaring my shoulders. "I love them."

He chuckled, and the sound brought a laugh out of my own mouth. It was all so ridiculous, I could hardly believe it. The smiling creases at the corners of Alexander's eyes made the nerves in my stomach relax. This game didn't need to be dreadful. It could be as enjoyable as we made it. It felt good to laugh. The tension in my shoulders softened, and I breathed a little easier.

I made eye contact with one of the crickets on the tray, and my stomach turned sour. I closed my eyes. They were *legumes*. Not crickets. *Delicious little legumes*, I repeated in my mind. *With eyes and legs and antennae.*

Lady Tottenham divided us into two teams. I stood on one side of the grass with Mrs. Pike, Mr. Lymington, Miss Morton, Miss Rowley, Mr. St. Vincent, and Alexander. The other seven stood across from us.

"You must decide as a team if you prefer sweet or salted," Lady Tottenham said. "I have ensured the two trays have an equal number of crickets."

My team formed a circle facing one another.

"Shall we request salted?" Mr. St. Vincent asked. His gruff voice matched his exterior perfectly.

Mrs. Pike gulped. "Sweet sounds more tolerable to me."

"Are you actually going to eat crickets?" Mr. St. Vincent scoffed.

"I will in order to help my team," she said, though her pallor belied her words.

Mr. Lymington nodded. "As will I." He cast an admiring glance in Mrs. Pike's direction, to which she responded with a bashful smile. Another of Lady Tottenham's intended matches seemed to be forming.

"I would choose salted," Miss Morton said.

Miss Rowley scowled. "No! Sweet."

"Does it really matter?" Alexander asked, his deep voice silencing the circle. "They're still crickets either way."

Mrs. Pike raised an eyebrow in my direction. "Do you have a preference, Lady Daventry?"

The thought of sugar on a cricket made me ill. At any rate, I had eaten enough sweets the night before. "My choice would be salted."

Mr. St. Vincent took that as his answer, lifting his hand high in the air. "We would like them salted, my lady."

Octavia called out from the other side of the grass. "We would like them sweet."

The two footman stepped forward at Lady Tottenham's instruction, one with a salt shaker, and the other with what I assumed was sugar. They each sprinkled one tray.

A maid came to Lady Tottenham with a long piece of parchment rolled together like a scroll.

"Here is your first riddle, and it is an easy one." She unraveled it, reading from the top. "Create a word from the following phrases. 'Here the Queen her debutantes receives, there the navy sails across the seas.'"

Both groups fell silent as we contemplated the answer. Within seconds, my hand flew into the air. Lady Tottenham must have been a reader of Jane Austen. The answer was the same as one in the novel *Emma*, though the clues were different. Given her romantic nature, I wasn't surprised. "The word is courtship," I said in a quick voice. "The queen receives her debutantes in court. The navy sails in a ship."

"Well done, Lady Daventry." Lady Tottenham raised one eyebrow, half her mouth raising with it.

Alexander nudged me. "I'm impressed."

A surge of pride rose in my chest, but I pushed it away. I didn't need to impress anyone, especially not Alexander. "I have a way with riddles."

"Is that why you ate twenty-three pastries last night?" His eyes collided with mine, brimming with amusement.

I ignored him, watching as the other team selected the first person to eat a cricket. Octavia stepped up to the table, plucking one up from the tray. She popped it in her mouth without hesitation. Mrs. Fitzgibbon fanned herself with one hand.

"It tastes like a sugared almond," Octavia said with a giggle. She picked up a second one, then a third. My jaw lowered as she popped three more in her mouth, for a total of six. A hint of disgust crossed her features. She gagged. They weren't as delicious as she claimed. She swallowed. It looked painful. "How many points is that?"

"One eaten as a forfeit, and an additional five crickets makes for a total of five points," Lady Tottenham said with a grin. "You have tied the game."

Octavia popped one more cricket in her mouth, brushed the sugar off her fingers, and skipped back to her team. Mrs. Fitzgibbon cheered, though her face was still contorted with a grimace.

"Six points!" Lady Tottenham said. "You have taken the lead already."

Octavia beamed, her sharp blue eyes drifting over to me. Her proud smile transformed to a smirk.

Lady Tottenham turned her attention to the scroll once again. "Another word must be created from the following phrases. 'A cloudless sky creates this hue, the other lives within a lady's shoe.'"

Mr. Lymington's hand shot up seconds later. I hardly had time to think of an answer. Lady Tottenham gestured toward him. "Yes, Mr. Lymington? What is your answer?"

He rubbed his grey side whiskers, hesitating for a long moment. "A grey toe."

Miss Morton and Miss Rowley burst into obnoxious laughter.

"That is incorrect, Mr. Lymington." Lady Tottenham motioned toward the other team. "Do you have an answer to offer?"

A stone of dread settled in my stomach. The answer was obvious.

Mrs. Fitzgibbon raised her hand from across the grass. "The word is bluestocking, my lady."

"Very good!"

Mr. Lymington hung his head, glowering at the grass. Mrs. Pike rushed to reassure him, patting him on the back. "That was a difficult one," she whispered.

I took a deep breath. "I'll eat the crickets," I said.

Mr. St. Vincent nodded. No one rushed to volunteer in my place. I didn't dare look at Alexander's grin as I made my way to the table. I could end the game quickly if I did what had to be done. The only question was whether or not my stomach could bear it.

Legumes. Salty legumes, I reminded myself. *Delicious little legumes.* I chanted those words in my mind as I took the final steps across the grass.

Upon closer inspection, the tray was most certainly not covered with delicious little legumes.

My hand shook as I reached for the pile. If touching them was already this difficult, eating them would be much worse. I had done it before. I could do it again. Last time, however, they had been coated with custard sauce atop a pudding. I had tried not to notice they were there. Nothing disguised them now.

I felt a raindrop on my arm as I picked up the first cricket. Without thinking, I popped it into my mouth. Another raindrop splattered on my arm.

As Lady Tottenham had said, no one liked soggy crickets.

If I waited until my next turn to finish all twenty-three, I would dread it even more.

One at a time. That was the only way I would be able to bear it. Octavia had taken a mouthful, and that was when she had gagged.

Legumes, legumes, legumes, I repeated in my head as I ate each cricket.

Eight. Nine. Ten. Eleven.

I kept my focus on the tray, though I could hear my team cheering behind me. I thought I heard Alexander laughing, but I didn't glance back. My heart pounded, sending a thrill across my skin. I had never done something so bold. If Miles saw me now, he would think I had lost my mind. During the years I had known him, I had been reserved, proper, and would have never participated in such a ridiculous game. He had complimented my elegance and manners on many occasions. I had prided myself on it.

Now, I was feeling a surge of pride as I bit down on my nineteenth dried cricket.

They did taste like legumes. The salt was the prevailing flavor. I finished my final four crickets before dusting off my salty fingers over the tray. I turned around. I hadn't noticed the quaking in my legs before. Every muscle in my body was charged with energy, and a smile broke over my face. I gave a curtsy in Lady Tottenham's direction. "That makes twenty-three."

She held still for a long moment, those sharp green eyes appraising me. Then she lifted her hands and clapped, a slow applause that grew in intensity. A smile, just as slow, took over her expression. "You continue to surprise me, Lady Daventry. You have earned twenty-two points for your team."

My teammates burst into their own applause. Alexander shook his head as I approached. I brushed my hands off on my skirts. "You're next," I said with a jab at his upper arm.

"I think Mrs. Pike would rather volunteer," he said in a low voice. I followed his gaze to where she had been standing. She held a handkerchief to her lips, and her eyes watered with disgust. She gagged when she looked at me, so she jerked her gaze back to the grass beneath her feet.

I couldn't stop the laugh that burst out of me. Alexander's smile was contagious. He shook with laughter. My cheeks ached as I tried to keep my giggles contained. What had come over me?

A heavy droplet of rain landed on his cheek. I tore my gaze away from his face, looking up at the sky. The rain intensified, fat droplets wringing out from the clouds. After a few seconds, the light drizzle turned into a storm. My bonnet protected my head from the water, but Alexander's hair was soaked. The ladies on my team shrieked, raising their shawls above their heads. Soon enough, the crickets would be swimming.

Lady Tottenham held her parasol over her head. "Blast and botheration. I was just beginning to enjoy myself. We shall have to call this game complete; you may all return to the house. Lady Daventry's team has won."

The droplets made Alexander's dark lashes stick together. His hand wrapped around mine. I didn't pull it away, because the guests and Lady Tottenham were watching. *That is the only reason,* I told myself.

He tugged me toward the house. I laughed until my stomach ached, holding my bonnet in place as we ran. The elation I felt made my head light, as if I could float away at any moment. My feet barely touched the ground. My heart galloped with a sense of accomplishment.

I had earned my clue.

CHAPTER 13

ALEXANDER

"What could be the cause of that smile?" The gravely female voice could only belong to one person. I glanced to the right, catching Lady Tottenham's gaze as she stared down at me on the settee.

She drifted closer, taking a seat beside me. Her inquisitive eyes matched the peacock feathers in her hair.

"Was I smiling?" I asked.

"You were, indeed." She wouldn't allow me to escape without giving her an answer. The guests had all gathered in the drawing room before dinner, but Anne wasn't there yet. My mind had been wandering to the events of that morning, and the triumphant grin that Anne had displayed. I had never seen her smile or laugh so freely, and the image, and the sound, had been trapped in my mind all day. Her rain-soaked skin, vibrant eyes, rosy cheeks and lips smiling without reservation— I couldn't banish the sight from my head. I didn't want to.

I tapped my boot on the drawing room floor, recalling that Lady Tottenham had just asked me a question. "Would you like to play a game, my lady?" I asked.

She gave a hooting laugh. "Don't tempt me. You know I cannot resist a game." The wrinkles in her forehead deepened. "What is this game you wish to play?"

"If you are so curious about the source of my smile, guess what it might be and I'll tell you if you are correct." I wanted to know if Anne and I had been obvious enough about our attachment during the events of the day. *Fake* attachment, I corrected in my mind. It didn't feel that way, at least not to me. For the first time in my life, I understood my brother. In one regard, he wasn't a fool. Winning Anne's heart was an accomplishment I had to commend him for. However, he was an absolute blockhead to have left her behind.

Lady Tottenham chuckled. The sound was raspy and weak, as if she had spent too much time speaking or laughing that day. "There is only one reason you would be smiling like that. You're falling in love."

I hadn't expected those words exactly, but they struck me squarely in the chest. I laughed. "I suppose I am."

She kept her voice low, but her eyes were ripe with mischief. "Did you enjoy your game of chess?"

"Very much."

"I am glad to hear it." She opened a small blue fan, fluttering it toward her face. "Lady Daventry's heart is not easily won. She is reluctant to marry again given the circumstances with her first husband. You have a great task ahead of you, winning her trust, but I don't doubt your ability. You are quite charming, you know."

I wanted to ask about Anne's marriage to the baron, but I

kept my mouth closed. It wasn't Lady Tottenham's story to tell. I still didn't understand why Anne married someone else if she claimed to have been so in love with Miles. He had never proposed to her. Had she simply grown impatient? If she had, why was she awaiting his return so patiently now? It didn't make sense.

The drawing room door opened. Anne walked through it.

I sat up straighter. She wore a silver gown with a square neckline, her dark curls piled high atop her head. A simple pendant rested at the hollow of her throat. Her eyes met mine, pausing there for long enough to make my stomach flop like a stranded fish.

"I won't prevent her from sitting beside you," Lady Tottenham whispered before rising shakily to her feet. She groaned with the effort, stepping aside with a wink.

Anne crossed the room toward me, taking the cushion Lady Tottenham had just vacated. Had she only sat beside me because of our ruse? Or had she sat beside me because she wanted to? My sudden insecurities were unprecedented. I took a deep breath, scolding my heart for behaving so erratically.

"Anne," I greeted.

"Alexander." She gave a soft smile before her gaze drifted to the other guests in the room. She tugged at one glove, which was a habit I had picked up on. It meant she was nervous. "Everyone is looking at us," she whispered.

"In that case, you ought to sit closer."

She glanced at me, her lips suppressing a grin. "No unnecessary proximity, don't you recall?"

I shook my head. "It's necessary."

She laughed before reluctantly shifting closer to me on the settee. Her leg rested against mine, and her hands were tucked together in her lap. The shy side of Anne was just as endearing as the headstrong side. I couldn't help my smile as she glanced at me for approval. "Is this close enough?"

"I'll have to leave that up to you, because I would never object to unnecessary proximity."

She narrowed her eyes.

"We're in public," I said, leaning close to her ear. "I'm allowed to flirt, and you're not allowed to glare at me at the risk of revealing the ruse."

Her lips twisted into a frustrated smirk. When she finally looked at my face, a genuine smile broke through her expression. She laughed, shaking her head. "I never should have agreed to this."

"I still think it was a brilliant idea," I said in a quiet voice. "Lord Kirkham hasn't bothered you, Octavia is not hanging on my arm, and I am permitted to spend more time with you."

Her eyes connected with mine. She blinked fast, dropping her gaze to her skirts. "I found another clue," she said, changing the subject.

"Already?"

She gave an eager nod. "It was inside my glove when I dressed for dinner."

I frowned. "Is it not concerning how these clues *appear* in your bedchamber?"

"I suspect it's my maid, Jane, who delivers them for Lady Tottenham." Her eyes shifted to our hostess, who had joined a conversation with Mrs. Pike and her two nieces. "At any rate, I may need your help to decipher it."

I chuckled. "I thought you had a way with riddles?"

She exhaled sharply through her nose. "This one is proving to be more difficult."

"Surely I won't be any cleverer than you are," I said in a dismissive voice.

"Please." She begged with her eyes. "You're the only one here I can trust."

Lady Tottenham's words about winning Anne's trust echoed through my mind. I wanted her to trust me, but I didn't believe that she actually did. She had disregarded what I had said about Miles, but I doubted she had fully disregarded the things he had said about me. She couldn't trust one of us without distrusting the other. I was still in second place at the moment.

"Very well." I cleared my throat. "Of course I'm willing to try. But don't have your hopes too high."

Her brow furrowed. "Why do you doubt yourself? You're a barrister. You must be quite intelligent. Surely you're capable of more than you think."

Though spoken lightly, her words struck my heartstrings. No one had ever had such high expectations of me. No matter how hard I tried, I had never done anything right in the eyes of my parents. All I had ever done as a child was take blame quietly in the hopes of winning the favor of the one person who still seemed to need me. Miles.

I knew how Anne felt. Miles could make anyone feel wanted and needed, even loved in order to obtain his purposes. Anne's eyes gleamed with kindness in the candlelight, and I saw my own reflection in her dark irises. How deeply would her heart break when Miles returned to discover that she had no money to offer? If he had written to her with his intentions to court her upon his return, it was only because he was under the impression that her widowhood had brought her wealth of some kind from the late baron. He might have genuinely cared for her, but love or fondness was never enough for a man like Miles.

He thrived on strategy, logic, and greed.

All it took was one look at Anne's disposition to know that she thrived on the opposite—trust, empathy, and love. She was strong, but with a fragile heart. A fiercely loyal one.

I pushed aside my thoughts and the sudden emotions in my throat. "Well, then. Are you going to read me the clue?"

Anne shook her head, dark curls bouncing. "Not now. I don't want anyone else to see or hear it."

"Tomorrow?"

She pressed her lips together with a nod. "Before breakfast."

"In the space between the doors?" I asked with a grin.

"No." She shot me a subtle glare under her lashes. "We already know Lady Tottenham meets with the man with the spectacles in the drawing room in the early mornings. Hopefully Lord Kirkham won't be lurking in the corridors in search of me now that he sees the attachment between us. Shall we meet in the study on the second floor?"

I nodded. "Is there a specific time you have in mind?"

"I'll knock twice on your door in the morning," she said in a whisper. "Then you may follow me out."

I threw her a curious look. "Is a shirt required?"

She cast her gaze upward toward the chandelier. Her lips fought against a smile, the corners of her eyes twitching. "Yes, *and* a tricorn hat."

"That can be arranged."

All the guests filtered out of the drawing room into the dining room for dinner. The long table was set as usual, but when everyone took their seats, I noticed three empty chairs.

Lady Tottenham had assigned Anne and me two chairs beside each other, so I leaned toward her. "Did you notice..."

"The empty chairs." She glanced around the room. "Mrs. Fitzgibbon, Miss Rowley, and Miss Morton..."

I frowned. "Where could they be?"

The first course, a creamy orange soup of some sort, was brought to the table. Lady Tottenham raised her spoon, taking a delicate slurp.

"Is Mrs. Fitzgibbon unwell?" I asked in a casual voice. "I noticed she and her cousins are not at the table this evening."

Anne and I must have not been the only ones who were curious. All conversations fell silent in wait of Lady Tottenham's answer.

"Mrs. Fitzgibbon, Miss Rowley, and Miss Morton will not be here for the remainder of the house party." Lady Tottenham took a sip from her goblet.

Octavia and Victoria exchanged a glance. Mr. Amesbury dropped his spoon on the white tablecloth. He scrambled to pick it up, but not before it left a yellow stain.

I heard Anne's sharp intake of breath from beside me. I had never considered that Lady Tottenham might be serious about sending people home. It seemed to be a threat that she gave for dramatic effect, or to make her party more theatrical. I never thought she meant it. All *three* women could have broken a rule, but it was more likely that only one of them did, making it impossible for the others to stay. The two young women required a chaperone, so if one of them was sent home, all three would be.

My curiosity couldn't be helped. "What rule was broken?"

Lady Tottenham's stern features were shadowed by the sconces on the wall beside her. "They did not break a rule. Mrs.

Fitzgibbon took offense to my game of cricket, and decided to leave Birch House. Her sensibilities are too delicate, I suppose. I am vexed only because she took two of our finest young ladies with her. There are now less women at Birch house than there are men."

Most of the men here didn't seem overly competitive—besides Lord Kirkham. Mr. Amesbury seemed slightly disappointed with the loss of Miss Morton, but Mr. St. Vincent looked relieved. He smiled as he stirred his soup. Mr. Barnwall had obviously been intended for Mrs. Fitzgibbon, but his expression was difficult to read. He was stoic as always. Finding a mother for his six children would have to wait, and he would surely pass the time with his many other pursuits. Mrs. Fitzgibbon must not have been interested—perhaps she had even left in order to avoid him.

Lady Tottenham's gaze settled on Anne and me. "I am pleased to see at least some of my guests are forming attachments." She shot a glance toward Mrs. Pike and Mr. Lymington as well.

Anne's face darkened a shade as I met her gaze. If any of the guests had failed to notice our fake courtship by now, they were no longer in the dark. Lady Tottenham had just held a candle to our attachment, lighting it up for all to see.

When the ladies removed to the drawing room, I remained with the men at the table for port. Between the seven of us, Mr. Barnwall always drank the most, followed closely by Lord Kirkham. I typically enjoyed half a glass. I hadn't managed to befriend any of the men of the party yet, and I wasn't certain I wanted to. Of the six options, Mr. Amesbury seemed to be the most agreeable. He sipped slowly on his port, pale eyebrows peeking out over the cup. Mr. Hatcher, with his walnut brown hair and ready smile, reminded me a little of Miles. He was amiable enough, but a little too arrogant to make his company enjoyable.

Lord Kirkham's beady eyes lingered on my face as he finished his second glass. He had hardly said a word all evening. He wiped his mouth with the back of his hand. "I see you have taken a liking to Lady Daventry."

My cup rested against the table, but my fingers still gripped it tightly. "I have."

"All the ladies here seem to have taken a liking to you." His square jaw clenched. "You could have your choice of any of them, at least for the duration of the party. You might play with one or two while you can, and marry the one with the largest dowry when the party is over."

Mr. St. Vincent and Mr. Barnwall laughed.

I didn't flinch. "I don't treat women in such a vile way, nor do I treat love like a game."

"Lady Daventry is handsome, but she isn't as young or as pretty as Miss Colborne," Mr. St. Vincent said with a scoff. "I've heard rumors that the late Baron of Daventry's land isn't profitable at all. To be so attached to a penniless widow approaching the age of thirty....you must be toying with her."

"Yes," Lord Kirkham said, gulping down another cup of port. "Surely you are hoarding all the women here for your own pleasure. Give up Lady Daventry to a man who is better suited for her age. You may take one of the Colborne sisters."

"I did find her efforts with the crickets rather attractive," Mr. Hatcher mused, tracing the rim of his cup with one finger. "She is a determined one, to be sure."

Lord Kirkham sat up taller, flashing his chipped teeth.

"Well, I'm the only one she chose to kiss during the game the first night of the house party."

"I would fight you for Lady Daventry," Mr. Barnwall said with a nudge in Lord Kirkham's direction. "As a widow, she has experience being married, so I would expect her to grow accustomed to the role quickly and adapt to motherhood with ease. She would make a fine wife."

A surge of anger prickled in my chest. I filled my lungs with a deep breath, but it didn't help. I drained my glass, my neck growing hot with irritation.

Mr. Hatcher grinned. "You might stop by her chambers tonight to see just how fine of a wife she would make."

Mr. Barnwall gave a deep laugh. "I think I will. A woman like her must be rather desperate."

I slammed my glass down on the table. I stood, straightening my jacket. "If you do so, I will ensure that you leave Birch House with teeth like Lord Kirkham's."

Mr. Barnwall stood, face red with anger.

Lord Kirkham glared at me. "Don't pretend you haven't been plotting to take advantage of her desperation. You can't fool us."

"My intentions are honorable," I said. "I hope to marry her."

Lord Kirkham grunted.

Mr. Hatcher tipped his head back with a laugh. "Is that so?"

I set down my glass and stood, starting toward the door. I couldn't endure another second at the table. It took all my self-control not to burst into the drawing room. I steadied the anger coursing through me and opened the door without startling the women inside.

I found Anne sitting with an open book in her lap. Mrs. Pike played a lively tune on the pianoforte.

"Are you all right?" Anne asked as I sat beside her, apparently sensing my frustration.

I met her worried gaze. "I broke one of your rules."

She snapped the book closed. "Which one?"

My jaw tightened. "I told the men that I plan to marry you."

"What?" Her voice came out louder than I expected. She rotated to face me. "Why would you do that?" she whispered.

I took several deep breaths. "I had to say it. They doubted my intentions, and they made theirs perfectly clear." My jaw tensed. I rubbed one side of it. "Do you lock your door every night?"

Her eyes rounded. "Yes, of course."

"Good." I shook my head to clear it. I wouldn't repeat the words the men had spoken about Anne, but I needed to ensure she knew the sort of company she was in. "The environment Lady Tottenham has created seems to have given the men leave to behave like swine. I had to defend you."

Anne twisted her fingers together. "Did you tell them we're engaged?"

"No, only that I plan to propose to you." I leaned forward to see her face more fully. "Now you must convince them that you plan to say yes."

She looked down at her hands with a nervous smile. "How do you suggest I do that?"

"A look is all it takes." I nudged her chin up with my finger until her eyes met mine again, hesitant and curious. "Look at me like you adore me," I said with a teasing smile. "Like you trust every word I say, and that you would wait for me, patiently, for years, even if I took that long to propose." I paused. "Pretend I'm Miles."

Her brows drew together, the resolve in her eyes faltering. Her gaze dropped. "I could never do that. You and Miles are far too different." She adjusted her gloves again, staring down at the floor.

I sat back, crossing my legs in front of me. "I will take that as a compliment."

CHAPTER 14

ANNE

Two knocks sounded on my door the next morning. I waited a few seconds before crossing the creaking floorboards and opening the door slowly. The corridor was empty. I had fully expected to find Alexander waiting to help me solve my latest clue. I frowned, taking one step outside the threshold. I gasped in surprise when my calf collided with something solid.

A vase of roses teetered on the floor. I crouched down to steady it, plucking up the note that was nestled amongst the blossoms.

Dear Anne,

I'm sorry you had to eat twenty-three crickets. I wanted to properly congratulate you for your accomplishment. I stole these from the parlor after our chess game. Don't tell Lady Tottenham.

Your counterfeit lover,
Alexander

I read the note again. A laugh rattled in my throat. He was ridiculous. I picked up the bouquet of red roses. Most of them were in full bloom, but a few had wilted already on the edges. Alexander had, evidently, stolen the vase too. The water was running low. I would have to remedy that straight away. I walked back to my room and set the vase on the edge of my window, opening the curtains to allow for more light. The sun had barely finished rising.

With my clue tucked inside my shoe, I made my way out to the corridor, still half-expecting Alexander to be waiting around the corner. How had he escaped to the second floor so quickly? I found the staircase leading up to the study, careful to keep my feet light. With nine other guests still occupying the rooms on the first floor, any creak or stumble from above could wake one of them.

I reached the landing at the top of the stairs, turning right toward the study. The left led to the hexagon room, and the corridor straight ahead would take me to what Lady Tottenham called her 'exercise hall.' The wide and long passage led to a window at one end with cushioned seats and a book-shelf. Portraits hung on nearly every inch of the walls leading up to the lofty ceiling, which was painted with a mural. Statues lurked in every corner, and rugs made of various animal skins flanked the walkway that Lady Tottenham used for exercise.

When I reached the study, I found the door partially open. I gave it a push, stepping tentatively inside. The room was much larger than any study I had ever seen. If I had been the one to name it, I would have called it 'the blue library.' Nearly all the furnishings were the same color. The walls were covered in cream and blue wallpaper, the ceiling was a cornflower blue, and the velvet sofas were a deep navy. The wooden bookshelves, tan book spines, and rosewood desk brought warmth to the space.

Alexander stood by the window. He smiled as I approached. The early morning light softened his features. "Good morning."

I stopped a few feet away from him. "Thank you for the roses...even if they were stolen."

His smile grew. "What is a courtship without flowers?" he asked with one raised eyebrow.

"A fake one?"

He laughed, looking down at the floor as he took a step closer. He interlocked his hands behind his back, his jacket straining over his broad shoulders. "Well, in that case, since I *did* give you flowers, that must mean our courtship is real."

I backed up a step, wagging a finger at him. "That is the sort of logic I refuse to entertain. I made the list of rules for a reason." I could no longer take him seriously, so a laugh burst out of me. He was a relentless tease, that was all. I couldn't allow my thoughts to support the idea that he might mean anything he said. Like the night before, when he told the other men he hoped to marry me. It had been part of the ruse.

He had said it to defend me. My heart skipped.

Alexander was laughing, but I hardly heard him. The emotions in my chest had been sporadic. I couldn't trust them at all. My insides toppled over when his eyes found mine again, a smile still lingering in them. "You do seem to love rules."

I walked to one of the bookshelves as a distraction, running my finger over an old, weathered spine. "And you seem to love breaking them."

His voice came from behind me. "As I said before, only the ones I disagree with."

I sensed his movement across the room. I whirled around before he could reach me. "I'd wager you disagree with most rules."

He leaned one shoulder against the wall. "Why do you suppose I chose law as my profession if I don't have any respect for rules?"

Drat. That was a reasonable question. "Perhaps you enjoy enforcing them, but not following them?"

He shook his head. "Enforcing the law is not my responsibility. My role is to ensure fairness regarding the consequences that occur when rules *are* broken. When I changed my plans for my profession from the church to the law, it was because I wanted to be an advocate for those who were falsely accused. There is no better fulfillment to me than freeing an innocent person from facing punishment they don't deserve—years of imprisonment, or even death."

It was strange to hear Alexander speaking in a serious voice, with passion behind his words. I had come with the sole purpose of sharing my clue with him, but I didn't want this conversation to end. There was more I wanted to know. "You said you couldn't afford a lease in London...where will you go when the house party is over? Have you been able to find many clients?"

He rubbed the back of his neck. "I plan to go back to York. My reputation has grown there better than it ever will in London. I have several connections who will continue to recommend me when I return. At least, I hope they will." He gave a pained smile.

I bit my tongue to stop myself from asking the other question that burned in my mind. If all his clients were in York, then why was he in London at all?

Why was he so eager to greet Miles upon his return?

He had refused to tell me the reason. He had said I wouldn't believe him. In truth, I didn't know what to believe. My head had firm opinions, but my heart had been developing some of its own. The stories Miles had told me about Alexander seemed impossible now.

I pushed my questions aside. Speaking of Miles had only become a point of contention between us. "I'm certain you'll find many clients there," I said with an encouraging smile. I didn't like his somber expression. "And if by any chance you don't, I suppose you could always marry an heiress. Surely you would be capable of charming any lady you wanted."

"Not *any* lady." His eyes met mine.

My throat dried up, and I tried to swallow.

Thankfully, he spoke again, breaking the silence. "You won't find me hunting a fortune. I meant what I said to Octavia. I won't marry for anything but love." He pushed away from the wall, taking a few steps closer to me. "I saw how my parents bickered and avoided one another. Their marriage was arranged because of my father's land and my mother's dowry. To this day, they rarely speak."

My brow furrowed. "Truly? I never knew they were so distant." Miles had never spoken of it, and I had never asked. I had been raised beyond the age of seven without a mother, so I hardly remembered the relationship my father shared with her. I had certainly seen the consequences.

Alexander nodded, his gaze searching my face. "Did your parents marry for love? As I recall, your father raised you alone?"

"Well, I don't know if I would call it that." I walked toward one of the blue velvet sofas, dropping down into the soft cushions. Alexander followed, taking the seat beside me. "My father wasn't involved in my life. He avoided my sister Henrietta entirely." My throat ached. "He loved my mother fiercely. I don't think there was room in his heart for anyone else. When she died giving birth to Henrietta, my father was lost in his grief for so long. He resented Henrietta, blaming her for taking our mother's life. He abandoned both of us by keeping himself distant." I scowled at the floor. "I felt responsible for her. I was the only one left who loved her. Sweet, innocent Henrietta." I blinked hard amid a smile. I missed her. "There wasn't anything I wouldn't do for her. When our father died five years ago, Henrietta and I were sent to live with our aunt and uncle. That arrangement only lasted until Henrietta's first London season."

Alexander's gaze burned against my cheek. I dared a look at his face. "Where is Henrietta now?" he asked.

"Married. Happy." I sniffed. "She deserves it." My eyes burned with tears. I had never shared so much of my upbringing with anyone.

"You practically raised your sister?" His gentle voice disassembled my defenses, block by block.

"She taught me a great deal about patience." I laughed, my throat tight. "It was a challenge looking after her all of the time, but I managed." Keeping my emotions buried was how I had learned to live, but Alexander knew precisely what to say to unravel them.

"Was there anyone looking after you?" he asked.

"No. But I've always had others to look after. I never needed that." I shook my head fast.

"Everyone needs that."

The lump in my throat was difficult to manage. I swallowed hard, reaching under the hem of my skirt for the clue I had tucked in my shoe. This subject was far too uncomfortable. My hands shook as I unfolded the foolscap. "We met to discuss the clue. I nearly forgot." My voice came out too quick.

Alexander stopped me, his fingers wrapping around mine. His grip was soft, just enough to steady my quaking hand. "Anne."

I looked up, shocked my the raw concern in his gaze. He wiped a tear from my cheek with his thumb, but it only made more of them slip down my face. "I promise I will look after you as long as you'll allow me." He looked down for a moment, seeming to gather his words. "No one should fend for themselves at a house party as unpredictable as this one."

I laughed, a choked sound in my throat. "I'm sorry," I said with a groan. "Something is amiss with my composure today."

There wasn't a hint of judgment in his eyes. "Don't apologize. Feelings can be uncomfortable, especially if they're not what you expected."

My heart gave an unexpected thud.

I wiped at my nose, tearing my gaze away from his face. "We are going to run out of time." I dried my cheeks with the back of my glove before holding up the foolscap.

Alexander took it from my hand. "Let us see if we can decipher this riddle. How clever can Lady Tottenham be?"

"Remarkably so." I read along as Alexander spoke the riddle aloud.

. . .

To find the prize which you now seek to claim
  Search for the letters that spell out his name.
  You'll find the key underfoot of the game
  With which you'll unlock her heart in its frame.

Alexander fell silent for a long moment, studying the words again. "His name? Who is *he*?"

I snatched the foolscap from his hand again, squinting down at the clue. "There is also a mention of a *she*." I pointed at the last line. "The two must be associated."

"Yes, that would make sense."

"I have considered the possibility that it could be two other guests here," I said. "Perhaps others who are forming an attachment. Mrs. Pike and Mr. Lymington? I have also wondered if the *he* might be you." I glanced up at him. "Lady Tottenham has observed our attachment, so she might have associated my next clue with the letters of your name."

"Let us hope that isn't true. My name has a lot of letters," he said with a laugh.

I exhaled through tight lips. "'Unlock her heart in its frame' must involve a painting or portrait of some kind. I don't think she could be referring to *my* heart."

"In that case, she likely isn't referring to my name," Alexander added.

"That's true." I tapped my foot on the rug. "Do you think Lady Tottenham could be referring to herself or one of the past ladies of Birch house? There are several portraits of women who once lived here."

Alexander's contemplative expression shifted to realization. "She has romanticized her marriage to Lord Tottenham many times. She mentioned that the entire game was in honor of him. It makes sense that he would be the man she's referring to." He bit his lower lip. "Do you know her late husband's name?"

"Lord Tottenham?" I said with a dull laugh.

He smiled. "If only it were so obvious. Our first item of business shall be to learn her late husband's Christian name. Then we may begin searching for the letters."

"That does seem like a reasonable place to start," I said.

Alexander stretched out his long legs in front of him, crossing his ankles. He leaned back, propping one hand behind his head. "It seems I do have a way with riddles."

I maintained my straight posture, glancing at him over my shoulder. "Perhaps I shouldn't involve you," I said with a grimace. "You're already far too arrogant."

His eyes slid to me with a proud smile that confirmed my words. "You're the one who asked me for help."

I pursed my lips, fighting a smile. "I'm already regretting it."

He sat up, rotating toward me. One of his dark brows lifted. "If your faith in me is so lacking, I'm forced to believe that your true motive was to spend more time alone with me."

I gasped, a surge of laughter in my stomach. "You're ridiculous!"

His eyes softened. "You're beautiful."

"Stop that!" I stood from the sofa, marching a few paces away. At a safe distance, I turned to face him again.

He stood, straightening his jacket before taking two strides toward me. I held my ground, though I was tempted to back away a step. His effect on me was unsettling, and avoiding it was becoming more difficult. Each time he moved close to me, I was torn between two decisions. Tug him closer, or push him violently away. The contradiction was infuriating, and it induced far more anxiety than I could manage. *This is Miles's younger brother*, I reminded myself. Developing any feelings for him would be a disaster. Separating Alexander from Miles would be the worst mistake I could make. Observing their many differences, it was easy to forget that they were brothers. But keeping the two connected was the only way I would be able to remain immune to Alexander's obvious charm and flirtation. I had no wish to betray Miles.

I caught my breath, holding it for a moment as I gathered my composure. Alexander was standing so close, those dark eyes gleaming with...what was it exactly? Amusement? It was deeper than that—more layered and complex.

More serious.

His lips still smiled, but his eyes held a riddle of their own. It was impossible to solve. "Am I not allowed to pay you a compliment?" he asked, his voice deep. "You're beautiful. I want you to know that."

My heart fluttered against my will. I tried to swallow, but my throat was suddenly too parched. "You're already forgetting the very first rule on my list," I said in a weak voice. "Flirtation is only allowed with an audience."

His gaze roamed my face for a long moment. "I disagree with that rule."

Just as I opened my mouth to deliver a retort, he took a step back. The distance silenced me. I was suddenly aware of the heat tingling on my cheeks.

"But not to worry," he said. "I'm only rehearsing for the day ahead of us." His smile lingered. "Lady Tottenham and her guests will be expecting a nauseating display of affection at breakfast, and I intend to deliver a worthy performance." He winked.

The lightness in his voice made my shoulders relax. I was taking everything far too seriously. It was a weakness of mine. I needed to relax. Our courtship was fake as long as I allowed it to remain that way. I was in control of my own heart and mind. His actions, and my own feelings, didn't need to be confusing. Alexander and I were friends, that was all. If I continued to keep him at a safe distance, there would be no harm done. I could leave the house party in a few short weeks and be reunited with Miles, with nothing left to hold me back.

He isn't the man you think he is. Alexander's words echoed in the back of my mind.

I had disregarded his words before, but now they were rising to the surface. I was still too afraid to ask what he meant.

I was too afraid I would believe him.

Believing what Alexander had said about Miles would be just as foolish as believing Alexander's compliments and flirtations.

"Very well." I walked past him, sparing just one short glance as I made my way to the door. "At breakfast, you may flirt all you want." I stopped in the doorway. "But you may wish to avoid displaying too much of that nauseating affection in front of Mrs. Pike. She does tend to have a sensitive stomach."

I caught one quick glimpse of his smile before I hurried into the corridor.

When I returned to my room, I called Jane to come help arrange my hair more properly for breakfast. She tugged on a strand of my hair, pulling it tight toward the crown of my head. I met her gaze in the mirror. "Surely you are too young to have worked for the late Lord Tottenham?"

She nodded, adding a pin to my hair. "I never knew 'im, my lady."

"Do you know his Christian name?"

Jane's eyes widened with surprise, likely at the peculiarity of my question. "Yes."

I cast her a curious look, trying to look as innocent as possible. "What is it? His portrait only refers to him as 'The Earl of Tottenham.'"

She took the rags out of the front half of my hair, leaving behind a set of neat curls. "'is name was Walter. I've 'eard the mistress refer to 'im by that name many times."

I smiled. "A lovely name."

Jane's brow twinged with confusion, but she said nothing more as she placed the last few pins and took her leave.

Walter. Only six letters. That couldn't be so difficult.

I needed to keep my focus on the prize, and not just Lady Tottenham's mysterious one. An engagement to the man I had always loved was finally possible. It was within reach. The house party would carry on with its peculiar activities, I would carry on searching for clues, and Alexander and I would carry on with our fake courtship. Before I knew it, the weeks would be over, Lady Tottenham's prize would be claimed, and Miles would be back in London.

At the end of it, there were only two outcomes. I would win, or I would lose.

Either way, at least I would know that I never gave up.

All I had to do was keep my heart under strict watch for the rest of the house party, especially around Alexander. It had been unpredictable of late.

Even less predictable than Lady Tottenham's dessert menu.

CHAPTER 15

ANNE

I sneaked into the drawing room, closing the door softly behind me. The darkness sent a chill over my spine, so I hurried to draw the curtains. They hadn't yet been opened for the morning.

It had been two days since I had put in a dedicated effort to my search for the letters that spelled *Walter*. Before that, I had spent a week searching and thinking, and I hadn't found a single one. Not a *W*, not an *A*. Nothing. Alexander had been helping me with my search, but he hadn't been successful either. I would have assumed that the name was incorrect, but I hadn't found any obvious letters around the house at all. I had checked all the engravings in the wood in the study, parlor, hexagon room, and vestibule. I had opened most of the books in the study as well, paying attention to the order of the spines and titles on the shelves.

The only room I hadn't searched yet was the drawing room.

The early mornings were my only opportunity to search the house unnoticed, but ever since I had seen Lady Tottenham meeting with her visitor, the man with the spectacles, I had been wary of venturing to the drawing room before breakfast.

Keeping my steps quiet, I crossed the room to the fireplace. The mantle was trimmed with carved wood. I examined every inch, not finding a single letter. I stepped back in frustration. I was looking in the wrong place. Those carvings had been there for more than a century. Even Lady Tottenham wouldn't be wild enough to dig a knife into such a historic part of the house.

It had been nine days since I had been given that blasted clue, and I hadn't made any progress in solving it. I had spent the days of the party adhering to Lady Tottenham's schedule, following her rules, and convincing every guest at the house that Alexander and I were madly in love. The games carried on, but the crickets had been the worst of it. The week before, Lady Tottenham had been feeling unwell and had kept to her room for four days straight. Without a strict schedule or strange games to participate in, we had been free to spend the days at our own leisure.

Victoria and Mrs. Pike embroidered or played the pianoforte in the drawing room most afternoons, and I often joined them. Octavia preferred to be where the men were, outside riding horses, shooting arrows, playing croquet, or some other form of sport. She seemed to have given up on Alexander and had turned her attentions to Mr. Hatcher. He had been previously intrigued by Victoria, but it had only taken Octavia a day to steal his attention from her sister with her constant flirting. Mrs. Pike and Mr. Lymington seemed to be the perfect match, and he often joined her in the drawing room, quietly reading while she played music or stitched.

Alexander rarely associated with the other men of the party, and if he did, it was only with Mr. Amesbury and Mr. Lymington. The three of them often invited me to play whist, though Alexander and I were not a fair team. We won every time. Most afternoons, Alexander joined Mrs. Pike, Victoria, and me in the drawing room while we embroidered. I sat with him on the opposite side of the room, and he even allowed me to teach him how to embroider a simple flower. He only punctured his finger twice, and I felt horrible for laughing.

When Lady Tottenham was well again, she had resumed her games, including the midnight ones. I received four invitations over the course of the week to join the other weary guests in the parlor. Alexander and I were always invited to join on the same evenings, and I noticed that Octavia and Mr. Hatcher had been paired together as well. Mrs. Pike and Mr. Lymington arrived on the same evenings. As did Victoria and Mr. Amesbury, though she didn't seem to be interested in him at all. The other three men—Lord Kirkham included—were only invited on rare occasions.

Lady Tottenham must have lost hope in the possibility of any of them making a match at her party.

Lord Kirkham no longer frightened me. My fake courtship had done its duty in deterring him. But I had developed a new fear over the course of the four midnight parlor games I had attended.

Kissing forfeits.

Victoria had been forced to kiss Mr. Amesbury after failing to write a suitable poem during a game of wit. Mrs. Pike had kissed Mr. Lymington after losing the game the night before. Each time Alexander and I had played a game as partners, we had managed to win. But there were enough evenings remaining at Birch House that I feared my luck would eventually run out.

Our friendship had finally become comfortable. My acting abilities had improved. Pretending to adore Alexander in public felt natural, though I reminded myself every day that it wasn't natural at all. It was fake. We were not courting, we were pretending. Any stolen moments we took in the drawing room during the afternoons were strictly for the purpose of adding credibility to our act. *Of course* we would choose to spend our spare moments together if we had formed an attachment.

We would only confuse everyone if we didn't.

I moved to the bookcase, checking the spines of all the volumes. I only had a few minutes before—

I froze as the door unlatched behind me. I snatched a book from the shelf, pretending to read a page somewhere in the middle.

I looked up as the door opened. I slumped with relief. "I thought you were Lady Tottenham and her secret lover," I said with a breathless laugh.

Alexander grinned. "Not to worry. It's only *your* secret lover."

I had learned to ignore remarks like that. He found my reactions far too entertaining. He had agreed to help me search the drawing room for clues before the other guests awoke and began roaming the house.

I shoved the book back into its place on the shelf before turning around. Alexander strode toward me, hands interlocked behind his back. He stopped to examine the bookshelf. His dark hair was more curled than usual, still slightly damp on the ends. He smelled of fresh soap and leather. His jaw was clean shaven, and I found myself staring at it for far too long.

His eyes met mine.

"You—you shaved," I blurted.

A smile curved the edges of his lips. I stared at that too. "I can't take the credit. The valet did it," he said. "Have you found anything?"

It wasn't fair how handsome he looked so early in the morning. The tan of his waistcoat brought out the warm tones of his eyes, and with his recent shave, a dimple that had never been apparent before made a dent near one side of his mouth.

I snapped my attention back to the bookcase, shaking my head. "I haven't made any progress."

"I'm beginning to think that Lady Tottenham might have sent you on a hopeless quest." He drew my gaze back to his. "Either that, or she hasn't revealed the next piece of the puzzle yet. She could be...testing your patience?"

I sighed. "I feel like I don't know what I'm looking for. Surely it's right in front of my nose, but I'm somehow missing it. Where am I to find the letters of her late husband's name scattered around the house? And what do they mean if I do find them? We're still not even certain Walter is the correct name at all. It could be anything, really."

Alexander wandered toward the tea table as I rambled on about my frustrations. He bent down to examine something on the surface. His nose wrinkled with disgust. "Come and look at this."

I stopped talking, hurrying over to his side. A footed glass bowl rested at the center of the tea table. Inside, slimy black creatures writhed back and forth in an inch of water, as if trying to escape the bowl. "Leeches?" I jerked back.

Alexander grimaced. "Would you eat twenty-three of those for another clue?"

"At the moment, I might consider it."

His eyes rounded before a laugh burst out of him. "You might very well have the opportunity. They could be part of a game planned for today."

My stomach twisted with dread. "I wouldn't be surprised."

He reached toward the bowl, two fingers outstretched.

"What on earth are you doing?" I backed up two steps.

He glanced over his shoulder with a wicked smile. "I thought you might like to greet one of them."

"Don't you dare touch—" I gasped.

He lifted the entire bowl off the tea table, taking a large stride in my direction. His teasing had gone too far on more than one occasion, but this was the worst yet. I ran toward the pianoforte, but he caught up to me in seconds. His arm hooked around my waist, stopping me in my tracks. My terror turned to uncontrolled laughter. I squeezed my eyes shut as I envisioned the entire bowl of leeches capsizing over my head. His laughter rumbled against my back. I wiggled free of his grasp and whirled to face him. "Put that down at once!"

His eyes gleamed with mischief.

If not for the footsteps in the corridor, I doubted he would have put it down.

We exchanged a glance. Was it Lady Tottenham and the man with the spectacles? Alexander and I had been found lurking nearby during one of their meetings before. It would be mortifying to be found alone there again. He rushed back to the tea table to replace the bowl. Without consulting me, my legs carried me behind the pianoforte in the corner. I crouched down, tucking my body against the wall.

Alexander appeared beside me.

"What are you doing?" I whispered in a panic.

"We're hiding partners." He sat on the floor, tucking his knees to his chest.

His body pressed against me. I was stuck between the bench of the pianoforte and the tight corner of the two walls.

"I don't recall agreeing to that," I whispered.

"Well, you're trapped with me now." His breath rustled against my neck. A shiver raced over my shoulders. "Whether you like it or not," he added. I could hear the smile in his voice.

Whether I liked it or not was a very good question.

I held a finger to my lips as the drawing room door opened.

"I've looked in all the other rooms," a female voice said. "It has to be this one." I recognized the whining tone as Octavia's.

"Did you remember to look in the exercise hall?" The second voice was similar to the first, but less grating. It had to be Victoria's.

"I'm not daft! Of course I did," Octavia snapped.

I kept my gaze focused on the legs of the pianoforte. I could see the hem of Octavia's skirt as she passed the center of the room, pausing near the tea table. If she glanced downward in our direction, she would definitely see us. I kept my breathing quiet, though my heart pounded fast and hard against my ribs.

Octavia gasped, and for a moment I thought she had discovered us. "Leeches!" The glee in her voice was concerning. "This must be the clue."

Victoria rustled toward her sister. "They are monstrous."

"How many are there?" Octavia asked eagerly.

"Ten."

"Does that mean ten o' clock?"

"What else could it mean? 'My blood-thirsty friends shall tell you the time at which the key to my heart you might find.'" A squeal of delight followed the words. "We must keep our eyes open at ten o' clock this evening."

They lingered for a moment longer before the rustling of their skirts carried them back to the door. I held my breath until it clicked shut behind them.

"It would seem you have a bit of competition," Alexander said. His voice was close to my ear.

I met his gaze. His face was only inches away. My heart picked up speed. The defenses I had been building over the past week leaped into action. I wriggled away from him, crawling out from behind the pianoforte. I had never felt less graceful in my entire life. I jumped to my feet, brushing off my skirts. "I suspected that others might have received clues as well." I sighed with frustration. "But it would seem the Colborne sisters are closer than I am to finding the key." I scowled at the floor. "Their riddle sounded far less complicated than mine."

Alexander stood, brushing off the back of his trousers. "It must mean Lady Tottenham has more confidence in your intellect. She gave you a riddle she believes you're capable of solving."

I glanced at the bowl of leeches again. "Ten o'clock. Is she going to present them with a key at that time? Could it truly be that easy?"

"I doubt it." Alexander followed me to the tea table. The ten black leeches squirmed in the water.

"Shall we pirate their clue?" I wiggled my eyebrows.

"This is your game." Alexander laughed. "I will do as you wish, captain."

I paced along one edge of the table. "Well I can't possibly ignore what I just heard."

He nodded. "If there's something to be discovered at ten this evening, then you ought to pay attention."

I froze. "What if it isn't this evening? It's only eight-thirty right now." I gestured toward the longcase clock. "It could be ten this morning?"

Alexander's eyes narrowed in thought. "That *is* possible, and less obvious."

A smile tugged on my lips. "Lady Tottenham is never obvious."

CHAPTER 16

ALEXANDER

"We shall meet in the hexagon room for a game in one hour," Lady Tottenham announced over breakfast.

Anne shot me a glance. In one hour, it would be ten o'clock. She sat beside me at the long table as we ate with the other guests. I had given up on feeding her pieces of fruit in front of them. She didn't seem to like it.

She wore a pale yellow morning dress that was dotted with small flowers. Her determined gaze checked the clock nearly every minute as she pushed food around on her plate with a fork. I enjoyed meals with the entire household, only because the ruse permitted me to admire Anne without hiding it. I glanced at her at least as often as she glanced at the clock.

We had avoided the subject of my brother for the entire week. We had spent hours together during the early mornings and afternoons, reading, talking, drawing—and she had even tried to teach me embroidery. That was when I realized how pathetically lost I was. I never would have touched an embroidery needle for anyone but her. I was addicted to making her laugh—to earning that lovely sound, or catching her with one of her secret smiles. I glanced at her face. A smear of jam hovered on the corner of her mouth. I thrived on moments like this.

"Allow me to help you, my dear." I picked up my serviette, raising it to Anne's face.

Her eyes widened as I dabbed the jam away. I put on my most charming smile.

She recovered from her shock with a bashful expression. "Oh! Thank you, Mr. Holland, you are too kind."

I gazed down at her. "Anything for you, my love."

She shot me a warning glance before taking a prolonged sip from her cup. I held back the laugh in my throat. Taking my acting too far was one of my new favorite pastimes.

Over the past week, we had successfully deterred Octavia, as well as Lord Kirkham and Mr. Barnwall. As inseparable as Anne and I had become, the entire party assumed an engagement was imminent. Lord Kirkham and Mr. Barnwall sat across from us at the table that morning. Lord Kirkham stabbed a piece of sausage with his fork. He spoke to Mr. Barnwall, but I could hear every word of their quiet conversation.

"I may tear my hair out if I'm forced to play another ridiculous game," Lord Kirkham said.

"Particularly the evening ones. I already made up my mind on the subject. If I'm invited to another midnight game, I'll be ignoring the letter."

Lord Kirkham nodded. "I'll join you in that protest. The only reason I'm still here is because of my father's connection to the late Lord Tottenham. It would be bad form to disrespect his widow, especially as rich and powerful as she is."

"And mad."

Lord Kirkham chuckled. "That she is."

Mr. Barnwall took a large bite of toast. "The only reason I'm still here is the food."

"And the women," Lord Kirkham added.

"All of them are spoken for."

"Not Victoria Colborne." Lord Kirkham grinned. "Shall we start a friendly competition for her attention?"

Mr. Barnwall sneered. "All she seems interested in are books and embroidery." Both men looked in Victoria's direction.

"Surely one of us could change that."

I didn't doubt Victoria's ability to snub both men, but I wouldn't wish Lord Kirkham's attention upon anyone. I would have to keep an eye on that situation and intervene if necessary. Mrs. Pike was prone to distraction as a chaperone, especially with her blooming romance with Mr. Lymington. Octavia seemed to thrive without supervision, but Victoria was far more innocent.

I hadn't realized Anne had been eavesdropping as well until she leaned toward me. "I shall have to warn Victoria," she whispered.

I nodded, threading my arm over the back of Anne's chair. I studied the side of her face. Her brow creased with worry as she glanced in Victoria's direction. She had grown accustomed to nurturing others, as if it were a sense of duty within her.

My conversation with Anne in the study had repeated through my mind many times over the past week. As a child, she had never had anyone to nurture and care for her. I had grown rather protective of her since that conversation, and since my conversation with the men over port in the dining room. She was capable of fending for herself as she always had, but that didn't mean she should have to.

At the moment, her heart was what I wanted most to protect.

In some way, Miles must have given Anne a sense of security, one that she had been missing her entire life. Did she truly love him, or had she been clinging to that feeling? Her marriage didn't seem to have given her any security at all. I still didn't understand why she had married the baron, but I had seen how she had deflected the subject with Octavia. The question seemed too personal to ask.

I was kept awake every night with dread for the end of the house party. Even that day, my head ached and throbbed. I didn't want to see Anne heartbroken by Miles. I didn't want him to come back to London and erase that beautiful smile of hers. The moment he learned of her financial ruin, he would disappear again. I wanted to be there for Anne, to support her when that happened, but I worried that she still didn't trust me. We had developed a friendship, but there was still a barrier between us. We avoided the subject of Miles for a reason.

If I had learned anything about my brother, it was that he was capable of ruining anything. I didn't want him to ruin my friendship with Anne.

When it came time to gather in the hexagon room, Anne held tight to my arm. She practically dragged me through the corridor. It was ten o'clock. Her hunt for the next clue was underway. We were the first guests to enter the room, followed closely by the Colborne sisters.

The brown velvet chairs were arranged in a circle once again. The last time we had played a game in that room, it had been buffy gruffy. Lord Tottenham's portrait stared down at us from above the fireplace. *Walter.* He must have been a very patient man to have put up with Lady Tottenham's wild nature. Surely he had been a bit wild himself. His hunting prizes lined all the walls, mounted up high, and arranged in glass cases below.

Lady Tottenham brought up the rear of the group, instructing all of us to sit. She stood in the middle of the circle. "Today, I should like to test your ability to decipher truth from lies." My eyes settled on a small stuffed bird that had been nestled amongst her curls, which formed the shape of a nest. I couldn't look away as she finished her speech. "I will choose two of you to think of one story from your life that you wish to tell. You must also think of a story that is entirely false. All of the guests must agree on which story is the true one. Tonight after dinner, we shall all reveal our answers. If your true story was guessed correctly, then you shall have to pay a forfeit." She smiled. "It seems an excellent way for us all to become better acquainted."

Anne's gaze darted around the room, taking in our surroundings.

Mr. Barnwall slumped in his chair, arms crossed. His bored expression mirrored Lord Kirkham's.

"I usually don't participate in my own games, but this time, I should like to go first," Lady Tottenham said. She held up her hands, and I half-expected a key to fall from the ceiling and land in her palm. "As you can see, there are many animals in this room. They are all no longer living, just like my husband." She glanced up at the portrait above the fireplace. "Lord Tottenham's love of hunting was a point of contention between us. He preferred animals dead and on his plate, or on his wall. I preferred to keep them as pets. We met during my first Season. I had a dowry of little significance, and my father had no title—only a small estate that could have been called a cottage. I caught Lord Tottenham's eye despite all that I lacked." A wistful smile climbed her cheeks, but then her mouth snapped back to a grim line. "He was rich and titled, but I did *not* like him. I found him to be an arrogant, pompous scoundrel. When I saw this place, Birch House, particularly this room—I hated him even more." Her nostrils flared. "He disgusted me, in fact.

"Lord Tottenham did all he could to impress me. He was a kind man, but his atrocious hobbies infuriated me. My heart was cold toward him. One day, everything changed. He ceased bringing me flowers and brought me something else instead." She paused, a warm smile on her face. "He brought me a rabbit. A living one," she added. "I had always wanted a pet of my own, but my parents had never allowed it. From that point forward, I allowed our courtship to progress. I saw him for who he truly was. I fell in love slowly, but it was a true and lasting love."

It was difficult to imagine Lady Tottenham in her youth with a tenderness in her heart for animals. Had she become wild and carefree after her husband had died? Or had she always been that way? I paused, remembering the nature of the game. *Her story could be false.*

"Now, for my second story," she said. "It is similar to the first, but with a few differences. You must decide which story is true." She began with a deep breath. "When I came to London for my first Season, I was determined to marry a man of wealth and consequence. I chose Lord Tottenham from the moment I saw him at my first ball. He was tall and handsome, and every lady in Town wanted him. I was raised to hunt alongside my father, though such practices are considered most unladylike." She gave a demure smile. "I discovered that Lord Tottenham also enjoyed hunting. Though I was advised not to mention my own proclivity for the sport, I engaged him in conversation on the subject. I captured his interest that night, and he gifted me with a rifle the next day. It caused quite the scandal." She gestured to the left. "That is the very rifle that hangs on the wall to this day. I fell in love with Lord Tottenham not only for his handsome face, but for his willingness to break the rules of society without a single qualm." She clapped her hands together after a pause. "There you have my two stories. I will allow you to deliberate and provide a unanimous conclusion as to which story is true, and which is false." She took a step away from the circle.

I turned toward Anne. "The second one must be true."

She raised one eyebrow. "Why?"

I lowered my voice, leaning closer. "Does she seem more inclined to shoot an animal or cradle one in her arms?"

Anne covered her mouth to muffle her laughter. "I cannot envision the latter."

After very little deliberation, the group concluded the same. Lady Tottenham wrote the decision on a sheet of foolscap. Her answer wouldn't be revealed until that evening alongside the others.

She examined each face in the circle, stopping in front of Anne. "I should like to hear from the two other widows in the circle. Lady Daventry, I should like to hear your two stories next. Since I have just told the story of how I met my late husband, please tell us two variations of the story of how you met yours. Mrs. Pike will be next."

Anne's eyes rounded. She gave a submissive nod, though I sensed her nervousness. She squared her shoulders and rose to her feet, making her way to the center of the circle. She twisted one edge of her glove. Her yellow dress was like sunshine, but her eyes held a storm.

My back stiffened. I crossed my arms over my chest in an attempt to keep myself seated. She looked terrified, though she hid it behind her confident posture as always. There was little I could do to reassure her from my chair, so I forced myself to be still and listen.

"Four years ago I was in London with my sister Henrietta for her first Season," she began. "My plan was to find her a suitable match, and to ensure that she married for love. She has always been a romantic. My aunt, who was acting as our chaperone, had already deemed me a spinster after I failed to find a match in my previous seasons. Therefore, both our efforts were focused on Henrietta." Anne licked her lips, keeping her gaze fixed on the floor. "I—I met the Baron of Daventry at a ball. He took an interest in me upon our first acquaintance. Because of the words of my aunt, I feared I was running out of time to marry for love. I knew the baron could provide me with a comfortable life, so when he offered his proposal, I accepted." She looked up. Her eyes connected with mine.

Could that have been true? Even then, had she been waiting helplessly for Miles to propose? If she had given up on him then, why was she still waiting for him now? It didn't make sense.

"I shall tell the second story now," Anne said in a quiet voice.

I leaned forward, my elbows on my knees.

"During Henrietta's first season, our aunt was not an attentive chaperone," she began. "I took it upon myself to ensure Henrietta was behaving properly. At a ball one night, I lost sight of her. I went searching for her in the corridors, and I found her with the Baron of Daventry. As naive as she was, she didn't understand his true intentions in leading her away from the party."

Her throat shifted with a swallow, and she wrung her hands together. "When I sent her back to our aunt, the baron soon turned his advances to me. He was strong, and he had been drinking. I couldn't push him away in time. He kissed me just as the Duchess of Thorne and several others came upon us through the nearby entrance. Being caught in such a public place, my reputation was at risk. The next day when his drinks had worn off, he did the honorable thing and proposed. My aunt and uncle gave me little choice in the matter. If I didn't repair my reputation by accepting him, Henrietta and I would no longer be allowed back into their home." She blinked fast, her jaw tight. "So I married him."

My heart stung, and Anne's words about her sister in the study rang through my mind. *There wasn't anything I wouldn't do for her.*

Anne had saved her sister from a dreadful situation, putting her own reputation at risk. A surge of anger rose in my chest. Had the baron been cruel to her during their marriage? She had already expressed that she never loved him, but the thought of anyone hurting her was enough to set my blood boiling. Why hadn't Miles intervened? If he had cared for her at all, he could have married her himself.

Anne returned to her chair. Her cheeks were ruddy, her eyes slightly wet. She didn't seem eager to look at me, or at anyone else. I reached over to her lap and took her hand, interlocking my fingers with hers. She finally met my gaze, her liquid eyes cutting a hole through my chest. I gave her fingers a squeeze. There wasn't a need for words.

I knew which story was true, but the other guests were still deliberating.

"I think the first story is true," Octavia said.

Victoria shook her head. "I disagree. I think it's the second one."

I didn't give my opinion. I didn't want Anne to have to pay a forfeit by having her true story guessed correctly. After a few minutes of discussion, the group settled on an answer.

"The second story is the true one," Mrs. Pike said in a firm voice. "That is our final answer."

Lady Tottenham wrote down the decision with a somber look. She must have sensed the truth in the story as well.

Mrs. Pike took her turn, but I hardly listened. I kept Anne's hand wrapped up in mine, tracing my thumb across the back of her knuckles. She didn't pull her hand away, but I had no way of knowing if she wanted to or not. Anything could be excused as part of our ruse. I wanted her to know that my choice to hold her hand in that moment wasn't an act. But if I told her, I knew she wouldn't allow it. So I held her fingers in mine while I could, my heart aching deep inside my chest—for her pain, and for my own. I didn't know if my show of affection felt real to Anne, but it was real to me.

CHAPTER 17

ANNE

Rain pattered on the window in my bedchamber. I watched the droplets trickle down and drip to the ground below. I rested my elbow on the windowsill, my chin in my hand. After the game that morning, my mood had been somber, so hiding in my room had seemed the best way to spend my free hours of the afternoon. There were very few people I had ever told the story of how my marriage to the baron had come about. It wasn't a subject I enjoyed dwelling on. A dull ache remained in my heart despite the hours I had spent trying to remedy it.

The guests had correctly chosen the true story. That meant that not only would I have to pay a forfeit that evening, but they all were able to see the truth about my past. I felt vulnerable, and that wasn't a feeling I ever enjoyed.

I stared at the rain, counting the droplets on the other side of the glass. It didn't seem to be a heavy rain. My restless legs twitched beneath my skirts. The unrest inside me needed to be expelled somehow, and a walk through the rain seemed to be the perfect thing. Before I could change my mind, I tied my bonnet and hurried down the stairs. I heard voices in the drawing room, so I sneaked past the doorway before making my way down the corridor and out into the courtyard.

The cobblestones were flooded with small puddles. I kept my gaze on the ground to avoid the largest ones. My bonnet protected my face from the rain, but the light droplets were refreshing against my arms and the back of my neck. I breathed in the earthy, fresh air, already feeling the slightest bit stronger than I had a few moments before—more capable of controlling my emotions. What had happened with the baron was a thing of the past. I had buried it long ago. Today, it had been unearthed, yet that wasn't what bothered me the most.

Alexander's face was burned into my mind. His gentle touch on my hand. The warm comfort that had flooded my soul at the gesture was difficult to understand, but it lingered with me. I didn't want it to. I wanted my feelings of closeness to Alexander to go away, right alongside the painful feelings that were associated with the baron. I wanted all of it *gone*. It was all far too unwelcome.

I headed toward the grass. I kept my head low, watching for mud and puddles. As I rounded the corner of the house, a deep voice startled me.

"Anne?"

I jerked my gaze upward, jumping back a pace. Alexander stood a few feet in front of me, hands outstretched as if he had expected me to collide with him. His hair was damp from the rain, his shirtsleeves covered in small, wet dots. "I saw you from the window. I came to see if you were all right."

I drew a deep breath, though my heart was already skittering. It was in search of a hiding place, but there were none. I looked down at the grass again, forcing a smile to my face. "Oh, yes, I'm well. I thought the rain looked inviting so I thought I might take a walk in it."

"May I join you?" Alexander's voice sent a spiral of nervousness through my stomach.

"Of course." I glanced up at him as he offered his arm. We walked in silence for a long moment, our feet soundless across the sodden grass.

"The others wondered where you had gone...and why we were apart," Alexander said.

"And you came outside to appease their concerns," I stated with a nod.

He stopped walking, turning to face me. "I came outside because I was concerned about you."

I swallowed, fiddling with the end of my bonnet ribbon. "There is no cause for concern." I smiled, but he remained serious. I walked away, but he caught up to me.

"Lady Tottenham should not have forced you to publicly speak on the subject of your late husband. She should have seen how that might trouble you."

My lungs were tight. I released a sharp breath. "Truly—I'm not troubled. I married him, and that is in the past. He is gone now."

Alexander's brow furrowed. "You married him to protect your sister." His eyes met mine. "That was the true story, was it not?"

I gave a nod so small I wasn't certain he even caught it.

He walked beside me, but I kept my hands clasped together.

"I've never known anyone to make such a selfless sacrifice," he said.

"I'm glad I did it. I wouldn't have been able to bear seeing Henrietta married to such a horrible man." I clamped my mouth shut.

Alexander's eyes flashed with anger. "Was he a horrible husband? Did he treat you poorly?"

My stomach lurched with dread. "I knew he wasn't a good man from the day he tried to take advantage of Henrietta, and then of me. I was only married to him for half a year before he died, but during that time he treated me in a manner that gave me no cause to mourn him or to have the slightest sense of regret over his departure from my life." My breath shook on the way out. "His head was injured after a fall from his horse. He died a few days later."

Alexander walked in front of me, turning to face me completely. "You never should have had to endure that marriage." His eyes darkened with anger. His features were somber, his mouth a firm line, and he asked the question I dreaded most. "When you were faced with the obligation to marry the baron, where was Miles?"

I didn't want to tell him the rest of the story. I had never told anyone how I had written to Miles to explain the situation, and how desperately I had hoped he would come to my rescue and propose to me instead. The thought must not have crossed his mind. Miles had been hurt by the news, dissuaded from coming back to London. It was my fault for not breaking the rules of propriety just that once. I could have asked him if he would save me. I could have declared my feelings first.

The rain fell faster around us, the droplets growing in size and speed. Alexander's shirt was soaked through on the shoulders, his hair sending droplets down his forehead.

I closed my eyes. "Miles—he wasn't in London. There was nothing he could have done."

Alexander scowled. "He could have come back and married you himself."

A stab of pain struck my chest, and I scrambled to defend him. "He didn't understand the situation. I didn't explain it well enough. I hurt him. Miles and I had discussed our future together many times. I expected him to propose when he came back to London. I—I think he was under the impression that I chose to marry the baron because of his title or money."

Alexander pushed his wet hair off his forehead, his jaw tight. "And Miles would never be as mercenary as that." His sardonic tone struck a chord of frustration in me.

I glared at him. "No, he wouldn't. It isn't in his nature."

"What do *you* know of his nature? You only know what he wants you to know. He hides the rest, and he hides it well." The bitterness in his voice shocked me. "I grew up in the same household as Miles. I would argue that I have a firmer grasp on his character than you claim to."

My fists tightened at my sides. My neck grew hot, tingling across my ears. The rain did little to cool it. "I only know the kindness he showed me. I refuse to form a new opinion of him based on yours. Brothers often do not see eye to eye."

Alexander pinched the bridge of his nose. "I tried to keep my opinion to myself before, but I see now I have no other choice but to share it." He met my gaze. The intensity in his eyes was unnerving. "He is a liar, a cheat, and he cares for no one but himself. Miles will hurt you, Anne. He will hurt you all over again, and I don't want to see that."

My anger seethed within me, but was stopped suddenly by a wave of pain so strong I nearly fell to the ground. "Why must you try to turn me against him?" My voice burst out. I shivered, my wet gown sticking to my skin. My conflicting feelings toward Alexander had been troubling enough, but now his words against Miles were growing more believable. I wanted to push them away. I didn't want to listen.

A lump formed in my throat, and my words fell to a quiet whisper. "He's all I have." I wiped harshly against my cheek as a tear fell. "Miles was my friend for years when I had no one else. He showed me kindness when I felt all alone. I have spent my entire life doing things for other people, but I have come to London for *myself*. For my future. For *my* happiness." Determination surged in my chest, and I took one step closer to Alexander. My anger pulsed strong within me, and my voice grew in strength. "*I* was the one who ruined the chance Miles and I had to be together, and I plan to seize my second chance when it comes. There is nothing you can do to stop me. Seeing your behavior now, I have no doubt that any animosity you claim that Miles has shown you was provoked and well-deserved."

My words hung between us, and the air fell silent. Alexander looked down at the ground, scuffing the sole of his boot against the wet grass. After a long moment, he looked up. Regret tore through my chest at the pain in his eyes—the shattered pieces of his pride. I had been too harsh. Guilt flooded my chest, and I nearly apologized, but my throat was too tight. My skin thrummed with emotion, a mixture that was too volatile to trust or understand. All signs of anger had vanished from Alexander's face, but the passion remained. His forehead creased, his chest rising and falling in one heavy breath. "It was never my intention to stand in the way of your happiness," he said in a hoarse voice. He cleared his throat. "I'm sorry that I have hindered it so greatly."

That's wrong. My heart reared up against his words, sensing the mistruth in them. Alexander was my friend. He had contributed to my happiness over the past fortnight. I wanted to protest, but I couldn't find the words. Why couldn't I tell him that I was sorry, and that I still needed him to be my friend? My heart pounded with dread. Had I just pushed him away? I glanced at his lips, unsmiling, serious.

I needed his teasing smile back.

I realized how long I had been staring at his mouth, so I quickly snapped my gaze away. A wave of unexpected longing crashed through my stomach when I caught his gaze on my lips. His eyes met mine. There was something intangible wedged between us. A barrier of some sort. Whatever it was, it needed to stay there.

"The rain has gotten worse," he said in a curt voice. "You should go back inside."

"Alexander—" My voice cut off as he started walking ahead of me, leaving the house, and me, in the distance. My heart stung. I pressed my hand against the side of Birch House, the rough stone snagging on my gloves. Where was he going?

I watched his back until his disappeared around the front of the house. Perhaps he was taking a different entrance, or perhaps he wanted to stay out in the rain. It was suitable weather for the storm of emotions we had both just displayed. My heart pounded fast, and I cursed myself for being so harsh. Whether I liked to admit it or not, Miles had hurt Alexander somehow. Miles wasn't perfect, I knew that, but I was afraid to accept that he might have once been unkind, or even cruel toward his brother.

I blinked fast against the tears that burned my eyes. The truth settled into my bones, rooting me to the ground. It was possible. Anyone was capable of having dark, uncharacteristic moments.

Including myself.

CHAPTER 18

ANNE

Where was that *blasted* key?

My mind wandered as I sat in the drawing room after dinner that evening. I had focused my attention back on the game, hoping it would distract me from the other events of the day. Since that morning, I had been too preoccupied with the clue Lady Tottenham had given Octavia and Victoria, and not on my own clue. At ten o' clock that morning in the hexagon room, no key had materialized in front of us. I hadn't expected it to be that simple, of course, but I had nothing to work with. Perhaps all Lady Tottenham had done was reveal the location of the key. Was it somewhere in the hexagon room? That *was* where Lord Tottenham's portrait was located, after all.

There was still the matter of those elusive 'letters' I was meant to find. By heeding the clue about the leeches, I was skipping an important part of my own riddle. The verse had read, *You'll find the key underfoot of the game.* Did that refer to the last parlor game of the day? How did Octavia's clue intertwine with my own? My brain hurt from trying to solve the puzzle.

Was it all worth the effort? The mysterious prize was beginning to feel like a sham.

The men were still in the dining room, so I sat exclusively among all the female guests in the drawing room. I picked up a book, but I wasn't actually reading. I couldn't focus. I had failed the game of deceit that morning miserably. Soon enough, I would have to pay a forfeit.

Victoria sat alone on a settee by the bookcase. Her blond curls were tight against her forehead, her intelligent eyes observing the other women in the room. I stood, crossing the rug to join her on the settee. "Good evening, Miss Colborne," I said with a smile.

"Good evening, my lady." She shifted to allow room for me to sit beside her. "How are you faring? I thought it was cruel of Lady Tottenham to force you into sharing such a personal story from your past." She scowled in our hostess's direction. Thankfully, Octavia was playing a jubilant song on the pianoforte, drowning out our voices.

Victoria's kind eyes were so different from her sister's. My heart was touched by her sympathy. "I am well now, thank you," I said. "I thought I should warn you about a conversation I overheard at breakfast this morning. You may want to be wary of Lord Kirkham and Mr. Barnwall. They have agreed upon a competition to win your favor."

Victoria's eyes widened, and then her nose scrunched with disgust. "Thank you for warning me, that is very kind of you. I shall be on my guard. I despise them both."

I laughed. "I must agree with you."

She tipped her head to one side. "I heard a rumor that you kissed Lord Kirkham at the first midnight parlor game."

Would that ever stop haunting me? I grimaced. "I regret that decision deeply," I said with a laugh. "I would never choose him a second time."

Victoria gave a mischievous grin. "Surely you would choose Mr. Holland now."

I swallowed, putting on a smile of my own. "Yes, of course." I thought of that morning, when Alexander had held my hand after I returned to my chair. I could practically still feel his fingers around mine. They had left an impression. It had only been my hand, but no one had ever touched me like that. His touch had spoken to me without words. It had awoken new emotions, and silenced others. Dread, pain, fear— they had all vanished. It was unlike anything I had ever felt before.

But then we had argued outside in the rain. Guilt stabbed at my heart all over again.

Victoria leaned closer, interrupting my thoughts. "I'm very glad you managed to steal Mr. Holland's attention from my sister. She always gets what she wants. It's infuriating." She sat back with a smug grin.

I didn't know how to respond to that. I gave an awkward laugh, casting my gaze toward the door as the men made their entrance.

My heart hammered when I saw Alexander. Our last conversation had been repeating in my mind all evening. I had been trying to formulate an apology, but the right words had evaded me. Was it better to keep distance between us? Our ruse had successfully deterred Octavia and Lord Kirkham. What point was there in continuing it? There was only one week remaining of the party.

My shoulders straightened, my heart in my throat as Alexander's gaze met mine. His dark hair shone in the candlelight, his wary eyes seeming to debate the wisdom of sitting beside me. If he didn't, there would be speculation about the strength of our attachment. If he did, the evening would be painfully awkward.

He started in my direction.

I held my breath and lowered my gaze to the book in my lap.

I felt his weight shift the settee cushion. I gathered the courage to look up. His gaze was already on my face. Before I could say a word, Victoria leaned across me.

"Good evening, Mr. Holland. Lady Daventry and I were just speaking of you." She gave a broad smile.

Alexander cast me a sidelong glance. "Well, I'm sorry to have interrupted such a diverting subject."

She laughed. I tried to join, but it sounded more like a whimper. I cleared my throat. With Victoria sitting close by, it wasn't the proper time to attempt to formulate an apology. We were in public, so it was all we could do to act as if nothing was amiss between us. Alexander seemed to recognize that all too well.

"Was Lady Daventry telling you how much she adores me?" he asked with a charming smile.

Victoria nodded. "Not in such obvious terms, but yes, she was." She threw me a wink.

My face burned. I could feel Alexander's gaze, but I didn't dare look away from the pages of my book. I was not in the mood for acting that night. I didn't trust myself to play my role correctly. My mind was in a thousand different places.

My heart was in a thousand others.

I felt horrible for the words I had spoken to Alexander earlier that day, and for the contention between us. I wanted to erase all of it and go back to being his friend, but I didn't know how. There had been a shift in our relationship, and I was fairly certain it was irreversible. I was overly aware of every movement he made on the settee beside me.

As the minutes rolled on, Octavia played several songs on the pianoforte, Mr. Lymington read several pages of poetry, and I stared at the clock. It was nearly ten. There had been no obvious 'key' revealed that morning, so I could only assume that it would be revealed that evening instead.

On the tenth chime of the clock, Lady Tottenham stood from her chair, calling the room to attention. "The time has come to reveal the answers from our game this morning. Lady Daventry, Mrs. Pike, and I each told two stories, and you were charged with the task of deciding which one was true and which was false. If any of us are caught in our lies, then we must pay a forfeit."

My stomach lurched.

She gave a smug smile. "I regret to inform you that your guess regarding my story was incorrect. I did indeed fall in love with Lord Tottenham after he redeemed himself by gifting me a pet rabbit."

"Drat," I muttered. "I was certain she wasn't fond of animals."

"As was I," Alexander said. "Can you envision her with a pet rabbit?"

"No." I glanced at his face with a smile before remembering

how he must have hated me. He smiled back, and my heart gave a distinct leap. I looked away, embarrassed for no apparent reason. My head was light, my hands perspiring. I would have to reveal my story next.

Lady Tottenham grinned at the dismayed whispers of her guests. She must have known all along we would guess incorrectly. "The rabbit," she said in a slow voice, "as silly as it was, became the key to unlocking my heart."

I sat up straighter.

The key to her heart...was her pet rabbit? Was that the clue?

I scowled at Lady Tottenham's face as I tried to piece together the riddles in my mind. According to the clue given to the Colborne sisters, the key would be revealed at ten o' clock. Lady Tottenham could not have explained it in clearer terms.

Had I just pirated their clue?

I glanced at Octavia, who sat beside Mrs. Pike on the other side of the room. She wore an eager smile. She wasn't a fool. She had heard it just as clearly as I had.

My mind raced. What did it mean? According to my riddle, the key would be found 'underfoot of the game,' and only after I had found the letters that spelled out what I had assumed was Lord Tottenham's christian name, Walter. The two riddles didn't align. Something still seemed to be missing.

"Lady Daventry?"

I blinked, my vision coming into focus. Lady Tottenham stared at me expectantly.

"Y-yes?" I stammered.

"It is your turn." She motioned me forward.

I stood, my legs shaking beneath me as I crossed the room to stand beside her. I steeled myself against the dread in my stomach. "Of my two stories, the second was true," I announced. "You all guessed correctly."

Mrs. Pike applauded for herself, and the others soon followed. I glanced at Lady Tottenham for direction. She stepped forward, a consoling smile on her face. "Unfortunately you were caught in your lie, my dear. That means you must pay a forfeit."

I cringed inwardly at the word, a fresh surge of fear accompanying it. I could eat a hundred crickets before I would kiss Lord Kirkham again—or anyone else for that matter. My heart hammered. Lady Tottenham did love crickets, but she loved forcing her guests to kiss even more.

Lady Tottenham tapped her chin dramatically. "I should like to change the way forfeits are paid. Rather than drawing one out of a hat, I have written the names of all the guests and placed them in this bowl." She turned toward the mantel and took the bowl in her hands. "The person whose name you draw will decide your fate. He or she will choose what your forfeit must be."

I gulped, but gave a nod. I reached into the bowl, taking the first slip of foolscap I touched. As long as I didn't choose Lord Kirkham, Mr. Barnwall, or Mr. St. Vincent, the required forfeit was likely to be something safe and minimally embarrassing. I would be happy to embarrass myself with a dance or song or silly poem. A few days before, Octavia had been forced to perform a mime, pretending she was a dog for five minutes. I could manage something humiliating like that.

Lady Tottenham snatched the slip from my hand before I could unfold it. She read the name I had chosen in a loud voice. "Miss Victoria Colborne."

At first I was relieved, but then I remembered our conversation from earlier that evening. My heart raced as Victoria's lips curled into a sly smile. She cast me a knowing look. I tried to protest with my eyes, but it didn't work.

She stood, joining Lady Tottenham and me by the fireplace. "Lady Daventry has paid me a kindness this evening, and I should like to repay her with a forfeit that she is sure to happily perform." Her blonde curls bounced as she turned toward me with that lingering mischief in her smile. "Lady Daventry, I require you to kiss Mr. Holland."

My lungs refused to expand. My chest was tight, and my head swam.

"On the mouth," Victoria added with a grin.

Mrs. Pike looked like she might faint from chagrin as Victoria practically skipped back to her seat on the other side of the room. I followed her movement with my gaze, all the way back to where Alexander sat.

I met his eyes, and my heart beat even faster. What would happen if I refused to pay the forfeit? I weighed the consequences in my mind. Mrs. Fitzgibbon had already been sent home along with her two cousins. What should stop Lady Tottenham from banishing me from Birch House for not keeping her rules? My pulse thrummed in my neck, and I could already feel heat climbing my cheeks. It could be quick. I could plant a quick kiss on his lips and be done with it. I didn't have a choice this time.

"Come forward, Mr. Holland," Lady Tottenham said in a gleeful voice. "Your affection for Lady Daventry is no secret. You may now display it properly. Or rather improperly, I suppose." She chuckled.

I felt ill. My legs shook beneath me as Alexander stood from the settee. We had hardly spoken since our argument that afternoon, and the tension between us was still tangible. His dark eyes were difficult to read until he came closer. The caution in his gaze was obvious, but perhaps only to me. My heart was fully prepared to spring out of my chest. *This is a game*, I reminded myself. *A harmless game.* Our attachment was fake, so this kiss could be just as fake. But was there such a thing as a fake kiss? Lips touched lips. That was a kiss. A real, inarguable kiss.

One of my rules had clearly stated that there wasn't to be any kissing, even for forfeits, but that rule was about to be broken, just like all the others. It was an obligation. I took a deep breath as Alexander drew a step closer.

With his back to the other guests, he searched my gaze, and I gave a minuscule nod. He was too tall for me to initiate the kiss, so I remained perfectly still until he lifted his hand to my face, his fingertips threading into my hair as he cradled my cheek. Shivers followed his touch, but I tried my best to ignore them. I swallowed, my breath hitching as his eyes lowered to my lips. I wished he would move a little faster to end it quickly, but he seemed intent to take his time.

He leaned his head down slowly. I had never been so nervous for anything, yet my anticipation had transformed from fear to desire in a matter of seconds. I closed my eyes, rising on my toes to close the space between us. His lips captured mine softly.

Although my lungs were full of air, they felt suddenly empty. My head was light. My skin was on fire, and my legs quaked beneath me. Alexander's lips were soft and gentle, not greedy or harsh like others I had kissed before. I didn't dare touch him. My hands hung limp at my sides, the only part of me that remembered we had an audience. But my lips parted with his, just once, stealing a few more seconds of a kiss that I had fully intended to last one, perhaps even less.

I remembered where we were—what we were doing—and pulled away fast. My cheeks burned. Alexander's eyes met mine, shadowed by the dim candlelight of the room. My heart thudded. I didn't dare look at him for long.

"That is what I call a proper kiss," Lady Tottenham said with a clap of her hands. Her eyes gleamed with pride.

I smiled and gave an awkward laugh, but my insides were storming with confusion and a horde of other emotions I couldn't name. My lips tingled as I hurried back to my seat beside Victoria. Alexander was right behind me, joining me back on the settee.

I stared straight ahead, swallowing hard against the sudden dryness in my throat. I had known that kissing Alexander, even as a forfeit, would be a mistake.

I had always known that it wouldn't be a forgettable experience.

Victoria nudged me, her wide smile lighting up her entire face. "When he offers his proposal, remember who to thank," she whispered.

She reminded me of my friend Nora. A little mischievous, too romantic, but kind-hearted. Her efforts were well-intentioned, though misguided. But how could she have known any better? Alexander was far too skilled an actor. Apparently my acting was improving as well. My heart pounded, accusing me of the lies I was telling myself.

After a few minutes, I couldn't bear the awkwardness any longer. I stood, excusing myself with a curtsy. Lady Tottenham didn't protest as I rushed into the corridor and back to my bedchamber. I shut the door and leaned against it, pressing a hand to my chest as I tried to calm my breathing.

My gaze caught on the pile of letters on my writing desk. I hurried toward it, digging frantically through them until I found the one from Miles. I read it again, grasping onto every word. I needed to be reminded of my purpose. My heart was muddled. It had once been clear, like an untouched lake, but Alexander had stomped through it, raising up clouds of mud in the water.

I focused on the last paragraph.

When I learned that you were widowed, I already had plans to go to India. I was afraid my feelings might not have been returned. Now that I am here, I regret my decision to leave. I am coming back to London. I plan to arrive no later than the middle of September of this year in the hopes that we might soon marry. I hope to find you there.

With all of my heart,
   Miles

I hugged the letter to my chest, careful not to crumple it. This was my purpose in being here. I needed to remember that. Miles was coming back for me, and I was at risk of betraying him by growing too close to his brother. What would Miles think if he knew I had kissed Alexander, even as part of a game? Would he change his mind?

I returned the letter to the desk, keeping my palm pressed

on top of it. I breathed deeply. I needed to forget that kiss, but my lips still burned. My stomach fluttered at the thought of it. I pushed the sensation away, searching for a distraction. My gaze caught on the pile of letters from Lady Tottenham—the midnight parlor game invitations. In my search for the letter from Miles, the pile had fallen askew, leaving several letters flipped to the blank side.

Except they weren't blank at all.

My heart picked up speed as I snatched up the first letter. In the top left corner was one small letter.

W

On the bottom right corner was another.

R

I dug through the pile and found all six invitations, flipping them all to the opposite side. Each one had a letter in the top corner, and another in the bottom. How had I never noticed before? I scooped them up and moved them to my bed, placing them in a line with their backs facing me.

Search for the letters that spell out his name.

I stood back a step, a wave of realization crashing over my shoulders. The riddle had told me to search for letters, but there had been two meanings to the clue. The letters of his name were on Lady Tottenham's *letters*: all the dreaded letters that had been slipped under my door. There were six.

I checked the date on each one, arranging them in order from the first to the last. The letters in the top corners aligned, and I gasped with delight.

WALTER

I checked the corresponding letters on the bottom corners, which came together to form one word.

RABBIT

My eyes rounded, and I covered my mouth with one hand. Lady Tottenham had led Octavia and Victoria to the same conclusion, but with a different riddle. The key to her heart was a rabbit according to the clue she had given the Colborne sisters, but according to my riddle, I would find the key 'underfoot of the game.' My mind raced back to that morning at ten when we had gathered for the first half of the story game. We had played the game in the hexagon room.

Could that have been part of the Colborne sisters' clue as well?

Lady Tottenham's lie had been the story about the rifle, which she claimed was the one hanging on the wall in the hexagon room. If the true key to her heart was her pet rabbit... was it also in that room? The six walls flashed through my mind.

The doorway.

The fireplace with Lord Tottenham's portrait.

The rifle with the sofa beneath it.

The ornate wallpaper and wood carvings.

The window.

The large animal heads, and the glass case filled with small animals and birds.

Was her pet rabbit among them?

My mind was going in the right direction. I knew it. I paced across the room, desperate to keep the momentum. I recited my own riddle out loud.

"To find the prize which you now seek to claim
Search for the letters that spell out his name.
You'll find the key underfoot of the game
With which you'll unlock her heart in its frame."

I stopped. There was more than one word with a double meaning in that riddle.

You'll find the key underfoot of the game.

It wasn't referring to the games we played at Birch House. They were a diversion. It must have referred to the term for the wild animals that had been hunted by Lord Tottenham. *Game* animals. Why had I not seen that before? We had played so many other games; I had wrongly assumed that they were what the riddle referred to.

I paused to gather my racing thoughts, walking back to the pile of letters on my bed. It all made sense now. I was closer to the prize than I had ever been before. It was nearly midnight, but it couldn't wait until the next day. I hadn't received an invitation to the midnight parlor game that night. With any luck, Octavia and Victoria *had* been invited, and wouldn't be able to search for their clue until the next morning.

I couldn't waste another moment.

My hand shook as I picked up the candle beside my bed and slipped into the corridor.

CHAPTER 19

ALEXANDER

The painting on the drawing room ceiling was blurry. I had been staring at it for too long. The other guests had all retired for the evening, but I hadn't moved from my place on the settee. The minutes had been passing, but my mind was still frozen at ten o'clock. I had kissed Anne. She had run away.

But what a kiss it had been.

I sat up, stretching my legs out in front of me. I raked a hand over my hair, tugging at my tight cravat until it came loose. The turmoil in my chest made it difficult to sit still. Since my conversation with Anne in the rain that afternoon, I had been certain she would never have feelings for me. She had made her opinion of me clear. But that kiss...it hadn't been one-sided. It hadn't been an act. Surely I hadn't imagined the emotion I had seen in her eyes. She might have still had feelings for Miles, but she might have also had feelings for me, too. The fact of the matter was that I was here, and he was not. I had the upper hand. I already knew I would take much better care of Anne's heart than he ever had. All I had to do was continue to show her.

I had to prove it.

Before that night, I had been sure of my feelings, but that kiss had sealed it. Anne had stolen my heart, and there was no way I would ever reclaim it. I wanted to show her that I could make her happy. I wanted to tell her how I felt, but it still seemed too soon, especially after what had been said earlier that day. If she had even the slightest feelings for me, she needed time to realize them on her own. I couldn't risk scaring her.

The idea that I might never kiss her again was a devastation I could hardly think on. I stood from the settee, striding out into the corridor. The house was quiet, but my thoughts raged louder than ever. I prayed that I wouldn't find an invitation to the parlor in my bedchamber. I was too distracted to play another game. I was tired of games. All of them. I didn't want my courtship with Anne to be fake, or our kiss to be excused as a forfeit. I wanted to kiss her again, and leave her with no question regarding my feelings for her. In time, I would do just that.

I wanted to prove to her that a man who truly cares for her would never leave her behind or leave her waiting. He would fight for her.

When I reached the first floor, I paused outside my bedchamber. A small flame flickered down the corridor—a light from a single candle. It was most likely a maid delivering the parlor game invitations, but I waited until the figure walked closer in the darkness. The candle illuminated her face.

Anne's hazel eyes rounded in surprise as her light bounced in my direction, pulling me out of the shadows. "Alexander!

You frightened me," her breathless whisper was barely audible. Her pale blue gown looked closer to green in the warm light.

"I'm sorry." I took a deep breath. I hadn't expected to see her again so soon. I was worried the thoughts she had interrupted were still written all over my face. "Were you invited to the midnight game?" I asked.

She bit her lower lip, and I had to look away.

"No." She shifted on her feet. "Were you?"

I opened my bedchamber door, taking a quick sweep of the floor inside the doorway. There wasn't a letter in sight. "It appears not," I said, closing the door again. "If you're not going to the parlor, then where are you going?"

She stared up at me, her face flooded with reservation. "It is nothing of concern." She turned toward the staircase that led up to the second floor. "Goodnight."

I laughed under my breath. "Anne—" I strode toward her. "You can't sneak around at midnight and not expect me to be curious."

She turned around on the stair above me. A hint of fear crossed her expression as she realized how close her face was to mine. Elevated on the stair above, her height was close to my own. "If you must know..." her voice lowered to a faint whisper, "I finally solved the riddle."

She turned around again. I followed her up the stairs. "You solved it and you weren't planning to tell me?" I kept my voice light, hoping to dispel the awkwardness between us. It was obvious why she was avoiding me. She had enjoyed our kiss as much as I had, but she was afraid to accept it.

At the top of the stairs, she brushed a curl from her forehead. "Well...I couldn't wait until tomorrow." Her words spilled out fast. "I didn't know you were awake."

"I couldn't sleep."

She met my gaze. Her rosy lips pressed together as she hurried her gaze to the floor again. "Nor could I." She paused, a scowl marking her brow. "I-I feel horrible about our conversation this afternoon. I should not have said you deserved any unkindness, no matter who it came from. Your disputes with Miles are not my business. Despite our...differing opinions of him, I don't see a reason why we shouldn't still be friends." Her voice weakened at the end of the sentence. Her gaze lifted. "I'm sorry. Let us agree to forget all the events of today."

I smiled, unable to help myself. "Not all of them."

Her eyes rounded, but she didn't glare at me like she usually did when I said something flirtatious. Instead, she seemed unsure of whether to throw her candle at me or run back down the stairs. She opened her mouth to speak, but I saved her from the task of a finding a reply.

"So, did you find the letters of Lord Tottenham's name?"

Her shoulders relaxed. "Yes. They were written on the backs of the invitations to the midnight games. Each letter had a corresponding one that spelled 'rabbit.'"

"The key to Lady Tottenham's heart." I gave a slow nod. "I heard her say that this evening."

Anne pointed toward the hexagon room, an eager smile on her lips. "The key is underfoot of the game. The game *animals*. I think there's a rabbit in that glass case, and we are going to find a key under its foot."

My jaw lowered, and a laugh burst out of my chest. Anne put a frantic finger to her lips, reaching forward to tug on my arm. "We mustn't be caught."

"How did we not realize that before?" I asked in a whisper. "Game animals are the only sort of game that have feet."

Her smile grew. She shook her head in bewilderment. "I hope I'm not mistaken."

"There's only one way to find out." I raised one eyebrow. I stepped ahead of her, holding the door to the hexagon room as she walked through with her candle. I closed it gently behind us. The hinge made a slight creak, but it was nothing that would alert the rest of the house. Anne raised her candle, casting the light around the dark room.

"It's quite terrifying in here at night," she whispered. The candlelight reflected off the glass eyes of a deer on the wall. She stopped in front of Lord Tottenham's portrait, and I joined her in her study of it.

"Do you think Lady Tottenham truly loved him?" Anne asked in a skeptical voice. "Or did she only love the rabbit?"

I glanced at the side of her face as she examined the portrait. "I think she loved him all along," I said. "No one falls in love because of a rabbit, not even Lady Tottenham. All the rabbit did was make her see him differently; it helped her *realize* that she loved him. Once she stopped resisting him, her feelings were obvious."

Anne's eyes found mine in the dark. "I suppose that could be true, but Lady Tottenham is clever. Even at her young age when she met him, I'm certain she knew her own mind." She cast her light in the direction of the glass case.

I followed her to the row of animals behind the glass. "Knowing your mind and knowing your heart are two very different things."

Anne seemed intent to ignore that statement. She moved her candle quickly along the length of the glass with a scowl. I recognized the problem before either of us voiced it. Among the many hunting trophies were various species of birds, foxes, squirrels, and...several different rabbits.

We exchanged a glance.

Anne handed me her candle before moving to the end of the case and sliding the latch. Thankfully it wasn't locked. The hinges creaked as she opened the glass door. Her nose wrinkled.

"That does not smell pleasant."

I inhaled the musty air with a matching grimace. Anne laughed, covering her nose with one hand. When the shock subsided, she leaned forward, examining each of the three rabbits. "Do you suppose one of them was her pet? She might have chosen to have it preserved and kept at Birch House." She threw me a mischievous smile. "Which one do you think was her pet?"

"If I guess correctly, what do I win?" I asked with a grin.

She groaned. "Must everything be a game?"

I laughed, crouching down to face the three rabbits. They stood in a row. One was much larger than the other two. All three had light brown fur and glassy eyes. Anne bent down to examine them with me, resting her hands on the edge of the case. I held the candle up to the first rabbit, the smallest of the three. I cringed at the rough stitching that had been done to cover one of its ears. "This one looks far too ragged."

Anne nodded. "Lady Tottenham would have protected her pet rabbit's ears at all costs."

"She likely put him in a bonnet and dress."

Anne tipped her head back with a laugh, a genuine smile spreading across her cheeks. "Perhaps she even employed a maid to fan him."

I laughed, moving the candle closer to the largest one. We both gasped.

Anne burst into giggles. "Why does he look like he could be a pugilist?"

The rabbit's face had been contorted into what appeared to be a scowl, its large frame resting on its back legs, the short arms curved at its sides. "Someone stole this creature's boxing gloves and he wants them back," I whispered.

Anne's laugh was contagious. My laughter subsided, and I watched her as she struggled to compose herself. In truth, she had never been more beautiful. I couldn't look away.

Her eyes shot open. "Alexander!"

I followed her gaze to the rabbit. I smelled the burning fur before I saw it. I jerked the candle back, but it was too late.

The rabbit's face was on fire.

Smoke spiraled up into the air, a tiny orange glow racing across the old, dry fur. I panicked, tugging my cravat off my neck and crumpling it into a ball before smothering the singed right side of its face. The rabbit tipped over, but I fell to my hands and knees, keeping the cravat pressed against it. I peeled it back, releasing a heavy sigh of relief to find the smoke dissipating. A clump of burned fur sprinkled to the ground.

I lost control of my laughter again, glancing back at Anne. She was covering her mouth with one hand. Her entire body shook, her eyes gleaming with amusement. I leaned back on my heels to lift the rabbit back to its feet, my balance faltering. She took my arm to steady me, her own laughter echoing off all six walls of the room. Anne's eyes shone with tears, but not the sad kind. She doubled over, gripping my arm as we crouched in front of the case. She wiped at the corner of her eye, pressing one hand to her stomach. My cheeks ached as my laughter subsided.

She reached across me, snatching the candle from my hand. "You cannot be trusted with this."

"It was an accident." I reached for the base of the candle, throwing her off balance as she tried to keep it far away from me. She cast me a warning look. "Would you like to contend with a flaming grouse? We are going to set the entire case on fire."

I grinned and snatched at the candle again. She tipped forward, but I caught her by the waist, pulling her back to a neutral position. Her smile faltered as her gaze met mine, and she hastily swiped at a curl on her brow. Our very recent kiss plummeted back into my mind. Was she thinking of it too? I held the candle steady in my other hand. If we kissed again I would be distracted enough to set all three rabbits on fire. Perhaps even my own shirt.

It would be worth it.

Anne's eyes flickered away from mine. Her features hardened to a business-like expression again. I released my grip on her waist as we returned our attention to the rabbits.

"My guess would be that this one was her pet." She reached forward to pat the top of the third rabbit's head. "Look at his face. He has a gentle disposition. The taxidermist took great care in making him presentable." She took a deep breath and carefully lifted the rabbit a few inches off the floor.

Beneath its right foot was a tiny gold key.

CHAPTER 20

ANNE

I gasped, a wave of delight seizing my entire body. The head of the key was shaped like a heart. I slowly picked it up before placing the rabbit back on the floor. I wrapped my fingers around the key, enclosing it tightly in my fist. I was already terrified of losing it.

"I can't believe I actually found it." I muttered, throwing Alexander an exhilarated smile.

"You're clever." His eyes creased at the corners with a broad smile. "I knew you would."

I stared at him. My stomach ached from laughing, and my excitement had dulled my senses. The sudden urge to throw my arms around his neck and kiss him senseless struck me as unexpectedly as the flame that had struck that rabbit's face. A different fire spread quickly through my chest, bringing a wave of heat to my cheeks. What the devil was wrong with me? I tore my gaze away from his. In moments like these, I usually stared at his cravat, but it was gone. He had used it to snuff out the flames. His sharp jawline and bare neck made him look casual —recklessly handsome—like the sort of man who started fires but never put them out.

To distract myself from my wayward thoughts, I opened my palm and looked at the key. I scolded my heart back to a normal rhythm. "Now all that remains is finding Lady Totten-ham's heart and unlocking it."

"When I first arrived here, I wasn't certain she had a heart," Alexander said with a laugh.

I stood up, the backs of my knees aching from crouching for so long. "That's what I thought when she warned us all that we might be sent away." My voice lowered to a whisper. "Ever since then I have been overly wary of that possibility."

Alexander's dark eyes captured mine as he stood tall beside me. "You have nothing to be concerned about. You keep the rules."

"Yes, but now we have burned the face of one of her rabbits," I said with a groan. "That seems like grounds for dismissal."

"I'll take the blame if necessary." He gave me a reassuring smile. "I'll ensure she sends me away instead."

"No! I need you." I clamped my mouth shut. "I mean—I want you...to stay." My aimless corrections brought a surge of heat to my face. Thankfully the room was dark.

Alexander's smile softened. "I would never leave you behind. Not to worry."

I twisted my hands together, nearly forgetting about the key in my palm. His words nestled over my heart like a blanket. I tried to kick it off, but it was tangled. I couldn't shake the feeling of security that enveloped me. "Good," I said in a hoarse voice. I cleared my throat, tipping my chin up to look at him. "You have to stay at least long enough to see me win the prize."

"I wouldn't miss it." His eyes searched my face, a wry smile twisting his lips. "Do you suppose the prize could be a pet rabbit of your own? Or perhaps, even your choice of one of the animals in that case?"

I put a hand to my forehead. "Don't say such a thing. I have worked too hard."

My reaction only seemed to encourage him. "A cricket feast all to yourself, perhaps?" He raised one eyebrow. "Or a private moment alone with Lord Kirkham between the drawing room doors?"

I swatted at his arm. "You're ridiculous!" My laughter echoed off the six walls, and I had to cover my mouth to quiet it. I glanced at the door. We had to ensure we were back in our rooms by the end of the midnight game. If any guests saw us roaming the corridors together so late, gossip was sure to spread beyond the house party. Lady Tottenham may have allowed certain liberties amongst her guests, but Mrs. Pike would still frown upon suspicious behavior. As a widow, I had played the role of chaperone many times, but I did not require one myself. That was a dangerous position to be in. It had made me too relaxed.

With the key in hand, I walked toward the door. I turned the handle and pulled. It didn't move. I pulled again and rattled it. My stomach sank. I whirled around just as Alexander approached. "It's locked."

"Again?" He tested the handle himself, prying and pushing against the door. "Who would have known we were in here?" He met my gaze over his shoulder.

I shook my head in bewilderment. Did the household staff

lock all the doors late at night? Perhaps only the hexagon room, with its valuable collections displayed inside, was deemed necessary to lock when the house was filled with strangers. I paced away from the door, my heart thudding in my chest. "We could be trapped here all night." The reality settled into my bones. My stomach twisted.

Alexander pried at the lock one more time, but the effort was futile. The bolt was solid. He turned around, raking a hand over his hair with an exhale through his lips. "I think we are."

"Do you think it was intentional? Could Lady Tottenham have heard us?"

"She would be two floors below in the parlor at this hour." He shook his head. "It must have been a servant who thought the room was empty. The doors are thick. They may not have heard us."

"It also could have been a servant who Lady Tottenham sent to do her bidding." My prevailing suspect was still our hostess. She thrived on impropriety. She was losing her mind, I was certain of it. Not only was she turning a blind eye to improper situations, but she was orchestrating them. She had been doing so the entire house party. Why should locking Alexander and me in a room together a second time be any more scandalous than the first? There were no boundaries Lady Tottenham wouldn't cross.

"I suppose that could be the case," Alexander said. "She has been known to do such a thing before."

I gave a grim nod. He remained by the door as I walked toward one of the brown velvet chairs. I sat down in one swift motion, crossing my arms over my chest. The silence in the room was deafening. My heart pounded. I didn't know whether to laugh or scream in frustration. I could bear spending an entire night in the company of all those horrifying stuffed creatures in the glass case. I could endure every single pair of glass eyes watching me fall asleep.

But Alexander?

He frightened me the most.

"I wonder if our kiss encouraged her," he said as he started in my direction. My spine stiffened. I had hoped the subject of our *forfeit*—which was the only safe word to use in reference to that event in my mind—would not come up. If we discussed what had happened, that made it far too real.

"It was part of a game." My words spilled out fast. "It shouldn't have encouraged anyone." I swallowed, keeping my arms folded tight. After reading my letter from Miles again that evening, I had been reminded of my place. Alexander needed to be reminded of his. There was an understanding between Miles and me, and it would hurt him if he knew that I had become so close to his brother. Creating some sort of distance was necessary.

The locked door, however, had other ideas.

Alexander set the candle on the mantel before sitting in the chair beside me. My eyes had adjusted to the moonlight that came through the window, making the details of the room much clearer than they had been before. His eyes connected with mine. "Lady Tottenham has been invested in our fake courtship since the beginning. Of course it encouraged her."

Hearing him refer to the courtship as fake sent a wave of relief over my shoulders, even if we were still discussing the forfeit. "That is true. We did play our roles well this evening. I suspect it was Lady Tottenham's favorite moment of the entire house party."

"And mine."

My stomach dropped. I shot him a look of dismay, even as my heart raced in my chest. I searched for the teasing look I expected to find on his face, but it was absent. I opened my mouth to speak, but no words came out. How did he expect me to respond?

He smiled, looking down at the floor. "Forgive me. I've broken one of your rules again." His eyes lifted to my face. His smile still remained, but it was weaker than usual—more uncertain.

I took a deep breath. "The rules are vital, especially if we are going to be trapped here all night."

Alexander stretched his legs out in front of him, propping one hand behind his head. "I think we ought to be less concerned about your rules and more concerned about the rabbit pugilist that undoubtedly wants revenge." He nodded toward the glass case, one eyebrow raised.

I almost slapped him. "Don't say that! He might hear you."

His broad smile released the tension in my shoulders instantly, though I was still recovering from what he had said about the kiss. I banished the thought from my mind.

"His ears are quite large," Alexander said with a teasing gleam in his eye. "I suspect he hears everything."

I laughed, grateful that the awkwardness had been dispelled. I lifted my chin. "You may try to frighten me all you like. I am not afraid of a stuffed rabbit."

"What *are* you afraid of?"

The question caught me by surprise. Alexander turned his head to look at me, his dark hair falling over his brow. He looked so comfortable leaning back in his chair. I sat up straight, hands folded in my lap.

"Lady Tottenham," I said with a half-smile.

He chuckled, but didn't relent. "What else? A serious answer. What are you *most* afraid of?"

I had always tried to present myself in a way that was perceived as confident, strong, and unbreakable. I had spent years trying to convince myself that I was all of those things. But it was a facade—a charade—one just as ridiculous as my courtship with Alexander. In many ways, I was weak. I was tired. I was terrified of more things than I cared to admit. I leaned back, no longer caring about propriety. I rested the back of my neck against the top of my chair, turning my gaze upward.

"I'm afraid of everything I can't control." I laughed, because it was so ridiculous, but the truth of that statement settled in my bones. I stared up at the dark hexagonal ceiling and the window at the center. The cloudless night sky left the stars bare. I counted them as I listed all the things that frustrated me. "The financial state of my late husband can't be changed. I can't earn money on my own. I can't leave Birch House. I can't choose to marry Miles unless he chooses me first. I can't make him love me. I can't plan to marry him. I can only hope for it. Of late, I have felt particularly helpless. My fate feels out of my hands, and it terrifies me."

Each thing I had just listed was just as out of reach as those stars above me. I turned to look at Alexander. "I would eat a thousand crickets for breakfast every morning if it meant I could feel some sense of security." My laughter hurt, aching deep in my chest. "To have a home that feels safe and permanent." My throat tightened. "To have a family. To belong somewhere, with someone. I'm afraid I might never have those things. I cannot simply go find that future. I can't control when or how it comes, and no amount of determination can change that. I've been waiting and waiting, yet that still might not be enough." I held my breath. I needed to stop spilling out the contents of my heart to Alexander. My fears and worries about Miles had been festering. It was a relief to speak them aloud, even if it was a mistake. What if he hadn't meant the words in his letter? I hated to face the truth, but he had led me astray before.

Alexander's gaze traced over my face. I felt suddenly ashamed for revealing so much. My cheeks grew hot, my eyes stinging. I looked at the sky again.

"I won't pretend to be wise," he said in a quiet voice. "But I believe the future that is meant for you will find you. There is no need to exhaust yourself in the pursuit of something that is so uncertain. There is peace that comes from letting go of the reins. Think about how much happier you could be if you weren't always focused on steering a wild horse." His mouth spread into a smile. "Let it run. You never know where it will lead you."

"Straight into a tree," I said with one raised eyebrow.

He shrugged. "Perhaps that tree is the best thing you've ever had."

I tipped my head back with a laugh. "I never knew you could be so metaphorical."

He gave a pompous smile. "I'm a poet."

"I would sooner believe you were a vicar."

He laughed softly, crossing his arms over his chest. "That was what I always wanted to be. It was my original plan to have an occupation in the church."

I studied the side of his face. "What happened?"

His throat shifted with a swallow, his forehead creasing. "It didn't go according to plan."

I wanted to ask another question, but he turned to look at me. "I was not accepted in the parish, and had to make other arrangements. Fate sent me on another course, and I am grateful to be a barrister now."

"At least you *could* make other plans. The only choice I have is to marry."

Alexander regarded me seriously. "What will you do if Miles doesn't propose?"

A wave of fear washed over my skin, but when I found his eyes in the dark, it subsided. He looked genuinely curious. "I cannot think of that possibility yet. He has given me reason to believe he will. He wrote me a letter before I came here." I took a deep breath. I hadn't mentioned it to Alexander yet. "It was essentially a proposal."

His brows lowered. "What did it say?"

"He said his travels to India gave him time to reflect...and he declared his intentions of spending his future with me."

Alexander's jaw tightened as he turned his attention to the stars. He said nothing for several seconds. My heart hammered in my chest. Was he...disappointed? I couldn't see him clearly enough in the dimness. He sat up slowly, stretching his arms out in front of him. "Well." He took a deep breath. "I hope he is true to his word." His voice was stiff, lacking the playfulness I had grown accustomed to.

I watched him as he stood from his chair, casting his gaze around the room. "The first order of business is to find you a comfortable place to sleep." He extended his hand to me. I took it, and he tugged me to my feet. He didn't release my fingers, guiding me by the hand toward the one sofa that rested beneath the rifle on the wall.

"But where will you sleep?"

"Don't fret over me." He held tight to my hand. "Go on." He nodded toward the sofa.

"Alexander—" I planted my feet where I stood. "I don't think I'm capable of sleeping. I'm too nervous that the door will open at any moment. You should try to sleep on the sofa, and I will stay in a chair near the door."

He laughed under his breath. "That is not an option. I would never be able to sleep knowing you weren't comfortable."

"I'm not tired."

He gave my fingers a squeeze, a slow smile curving his lips. "Don't lie to me, Anne. Your eyes are practically falling closed."

"They are not." I suppressed a yawn in my throat.

"You've had an eventful evening. You solved the riddle, you found the key, you kissed me in front of all the guests at Birch house..." his smile took on a teasing edge, "that is enough to exhaust a person."

His references to the kiss were enough to make sleep far more appealing. It meant I could ignore him. I dropped down onto the cushions, tugging my hand from his grasp. He chuckled as I lay down and nestled my head onto the arm of the sofa. There were no blankets or pillows to be found throughout the room.

I watched Alexander with concern as he lay down on the rug beside the sofa. He tucked one arm under his head, sprawling out with his chest against the floor. His eyes closed, his dark lashes creating two crescents on his cheeks. A smile tugged on my lips. He looked so endearing. He shifted as he tried to find a comfortable position, and I found myself staring at him for far too long. With his eyes closed, I took the opportunity to slip the heart-shaped key inside the bodice of my dress, keeping it close to my own heart.

I shifted toward the edge, one of my arms hanging off the sofa. "You look terribly uncomfortable," I said.

He opened his eyes, his mouth spreading in a smile. It was strange to be laying beside Alexander, even if I was elevated on the sofa. He patted the floor. "No, I assure you, I am quite comfortable."

"You're lying to *me* now."

His smile was contagious.

"Is there nothing you can use as a pillow?" I cast my gaze around the room.

He shook his head. "My arm is sufficient."

I sighed.

"Sleep well," he said.

"Wait—what are we to do in the morning?" I asked in a hushed voice. "We must leave the moment the servants unlock the doors."

"We will." His eyes settled on my face. "But Lady Tottenham will be disappointed that her trap didn't result in an engagement."

I laughed, my weariness contributing to my delirium. "How could she think that forcing us to be locked in this room for the night would make you propose to me?"

He propped his head up on one elbow. "Had I thought the answer would be favorable, perhaps it would have worked." Before I could process his words, he reached for the hand that I had left hanging off the sofa. He pressed a soft kiss to the back of my fingers before rolling over, hiding his face from view. "Goodnight, Anne."

My head was light for a moment, my stomach twisting. I

rolled over until I faced the inside of the sofa. My pulse raced past my ears. I almost forgot to respond.

"Goodnight," I squeaked. I scowled at the dark fabric in front of me, tucking my hands close to my chest. My thoughts spun. I squeezed my eyes shut in an effort to banish the warm sensation that tingled throughout my every limb. Had Alexander just declared his feelings for me? His words hadn't been straightforward, but that didn't matter.

I had been practicing riddles, and that was an easy one.

I lay in silence for several minutes. I could hear Alexander's light breathing. He wasn't asleep either. I held perfectly still until the weight of my body made my hands and wrists numb. As restless as I was, I didn't dare move. There was a taut rope connecting me to Alexander, and if I shifted, even the slightest bit, I feared he would somehow feel it. I wanted to break the tension, but I didn't know how. The only thing that could break it was dawn, but it was still hours away.

Alexander shifted on the floor. "On second thought," he whispered, "the pugilist might make a more comfortable pillow."

I could name many occasions in my life when I had hidden away in the privacy of my bedchamber, burrowed under my blankets, and cried until I fell asleep. I had never fallen asleep laughing before, but that was the last thing I remembered before my consciousness finally drifted away.

♟♟♟

I rubbed my eyes before opening them. I blinked fast, taking in my surroundings. The hexagon room was bright, the rooftop window letting in enough light to blind me. I covered my face with both hands before sitting up. The events of the night before came crashing back into my mind. I checked the floor beside the sofa.

Alexander was gone.

I smoothed my hands over my sleep-tousled hair as I scrutinized the rest of the room. The three rabbits in the case, one with charred fur on its face, reminded me of the reason I had been there at all. My hand flew to my chest, and I withdrew the tiny key from my bodice. So it hadn't been a dream. I had found the key, and Alexander had been trapped in the room with me overnight. But where was he now? How late was it?

I pinched my cheeks to give them a little color before testing the doorknob. It was unlocked. Why hadn't Alexander awoken me?

I slipped into the corridor, making my way down to my bedchamber. I would need Jane to help make me presentable. Just as I approached the door, Victoria and Octavia rounded the corner.

"Ah, Lady Daventry! Are you on your way to breakfast?" Victoria's wide eyes flitted over me from head to toe. A crease formed in her brow.

"Is it breakfast already?" I brushed a limp curl from my forehead. I could only imagine how ragged I must have looked. How had I slept so long on that stiff sofa?

"Yes." Victoria exchanged a look with her sister, who observed me with a smug smile.

"Were you up late, my lady?" Octavia narrowed her eyes at me. "What were you doing?"

I immediately understood the nature of their suspicions, so

I decided the truth would be best. "I was searching for clues that might lead me to Lady Tottenham's prize."

Octavia's nostrils flared. "I doubt that prize even exists."

"Did you find clues?" Victoria asked.

I swallowed, closing my fist tighter around the key in my palm. "Oh, only something small."

"What did you find?" Octavia stepped closer to me with an eager look.

"It would not be a competition if I told you." I shrugged, taking hold the doorknob.

"You wore that gown yesterday, did you not?" Victoria's searching gaze made me shift on my feet.

"Yes. I fell asleep in the study." I flashed a quick smile. "I lost track of time." I didn't want to lead them to the hexagon room. Even though I did have the key, the final pieces of the clue could have still been in that room. "I will see you at breakfast."

Before they could question me further, I hurried into my bedchamber and closed the door. I called Jane to help me change into a pale yellow morning dress and arrange my hair as quickly as possible, then rushed down to the breakfast room. I wiped the perspiration from my hairline as I made my way to the sideboard. I glanced over my shoulder, expecting to find Alexander at one of the tables.

The crowd was sparse, and he wasn't among them. Mrs. Pike's voice snapped my attention away from the other guests.

"Good morning, Lady Daventry." Her voice was raspy before she cleared her throat. She cast a nervous glance at the door.

"Good morning." I put a smile on my face, though my

insides wriggled with nervousness. Her stare was relentless. "Where is Lady Tottenham?"

"She wasn't feeling well this morning." She paused. "But she isn't the only one who won't be joining us for breakfast."

I frowned. "What do you mean?"

Octavia took a sip from her cup. "You have missed the news."

"News?"

Mrs. Pike exchanged a look with Victoria. "Unfortunately, our party has decreased in numbers again."

My heart plummeted.

"You may have noticed a few people are, well...absent this morning. The housekeeper informed us that Lady Tottenham sent several of the guests away. After the events of yesterday evening, they will no longer be welcome at Birch House."

CHAPTER 21

ALEXANDER

I stopped the coach outside of Martin's, stepping out onto the crowded cobblestones. I lowered the brim of my hat on my forehead and tightened my cravat. I needed to look fashionable if I hoped to obtain a loan from the banker at Martin's. It couldn't come across as a desperate plea, or I would be sent away. All I needed was enough to live on until I could obtain more clients in York. Leaving London at the end of the house party was no longer part of my plan. If I could help it, I would stay long enough to have a fighting chance at Anne's hand in marriage.

I walked quickly, weaving through the crowds that gathered on the streets. I had grown comfortable with the location of Birch House, so far removed from the heart of London society. Lady Tottenham had no rules in place that prevented her guests from venturing into town for business, so I didn't expect she would have a problem with my departure that morning.

I hadn't slept more than an hour or two the night before, and not only because my bed had been the floorboards of the hexagon room. My mind and emotions had been spinning out of control. After learning of the written proposal Miles had sent to Anne, I was no longer certain what his intentions were. He might have assumed she had money from her previous marriage, but perhaps he didn't. He might have truly loved her.

It was hard to imagine Miles loving anyone, but if there was a woman who could soften his heart, it was Anne. It was impossible not to love her.

I had been falling in love with her since the first day of the house party.

I smiled at the thought of her face squished against the sofa cushion, curls falling over her forehead. Her eyes had been twitching with a dream of some sort. I had left her there, sleeping, when I heard the door unlock just after sunrise. My trip to the bank was my last hope of remaining in London after Lady Tottenham's hospitality expired. The money Miles owed me was likely long gone, but that wouldn't stop me from confronting him when he came back to London.

I stopped walking, my gaze catching on a man at the threshold of the gentleman's club, Russell's, across the street. I rubbed my eyes, blinking hard. My lack of sleep must have been causing hallucinations. I looked at the doorway of Russell's a second time, my brow creasing.

The man with the navy blue jacket looked exactly like Miles.

I froze, watching him as he started walking in the opposite direction. I had only caught a short glimpse of his face, but with his back turned, I recognized his height, the shape of his shoulders, and even the saunter in his step. It was my brother. I was sure of it.

My plans at the bank vanished, falling down my list of priorities. I jogged across the street, narrowly dodging a team of horses. The coachman cursed at me as I ran, but I didn't care. What was Miles doing back in London already? I could hardly believe my luck at finding him on the street, but his presence in town was more troubling than it was fortunate. Anger pulsed in my neck as I slowed my approach, taking large strides up the cobblestones behind him. When I came close enough, I stopped walking.

I spoke in a loud voice. "I didn't think I'd see you for another fortnight."

His steps halted.

I had known he would recognize my voice, even amid the noise all around us. He turned around slowly, a lopsided smile on his mouth. "Alexander?" He scoffed with disbelief. His skin was tanner than usual, freckles smattered across his cheeks. He had won the favor of countless people with his blue eyes and wide smile. He had an innocent face no matter what expression he wore. His brown hair had been lightened in the sun, but it was combed and styled neatly. Not a hair was out of place. His cravat was starched and clean, and despite my efforts to intimidate him, he was completely unaffected.

"Was India not to your liking?" I asked, not bothering to hide the venom from my voice. "You spent just as long on the boat as you did in the country."

Miles took a step closer, his smile growing. "You don't have to greet me with such animosity, brother. I plan to repay you in full."

I crossed my arms. "Where have I heard that promise

before?" My voice was hard. "And your confession? I have spent the last four years as a stranger to our family because they still blame me for your mistakes."

He groaned, reaching into his pocket to withdraw a snuff case. "Do relax, brother. I'll tell them the truth eventually, and the money will be back in your pockets. Have patience." He took a pinch of snuff before drawing a deep breath. "I miss the sea air. It smelled much better than London."

My jaw tightened. "Don't change the subject. You will repay me, in full, the two hundred pounds I lent to you by the end of the month."

He laughed. "You have grown far too serious. Two hundred pounds isn't a matter of life or death."

"In my profession, that's nearly half my annual income."

He shrugged, crossing his arms. "At least you're earning more than you would have in the church."

My anger flared. "Are you suggesting I should thank you for ruining the life I had planned for?"

"Yes." He gave an emphatic nod. "You would have never suited the life of a vicar."

I glanced heavenward, my hands fisting at my sides. Miles didn't know how fortunate he was that we were in public. A group of passersby seemed to sense the tension between us. One woman whispered behind her glove to her companion. I stepped into the shade of the nearby shop, hoping it would cool the anger that boiled under my skin.

"I'm surprised to find you in London," Miles said as he stepped up beside me. "I thought your best success was in York."

"It is." I kicked at a twig on the cobblestones. "I came here to reclaim the money you stole."

Miles smiled, his gaze lingering on a group of young ladies as they passed with their chaperones. "I will repay you. I promise. A meager two hundred pounds will be nothing but pocket coins for me soon enough."

His arrogance hadn't always been so apparent as it was now. He had no reason to hide it when there were no observers. "I presume the East India Company was profitable then?" I asked.

He bit the inside of his cheek, shaking his head. "Actually, it wasn't. I was nearly arrested for a number of...fraudulent activities." He waved a hand in front of him. "It's no matter. I realized the life of a nabob isn't for me. I lack the patience for it. There are faster ways to obtain a fortune, and I have plans underway."

I frowned. "Plans? Do you have any money at all?"

"Yes." He scowled. "Not to worry. I will ensure you are paid."

I shook my head, cursing under my breath. I would never see that money. My family would never respect me, and Miles would win, just as he always had. The image of Anne running into his arms flashed through my mind, and a wave of frustration nearly knocked me to the ground. He wouldn't greet her with the arrogant smile he wore now. He would fool her just as he had fooled so many others. Panic set into my bones. If he was scheming something, I needed to find out what it was.

"What are these 'faster ways to obtain a fortune'?" I raised my brows. I was grateful for my extra inch of height as I stepped closer to him. "What are your plans?"

"Marriage." He adjusted the buttons on his silver waistcoat. "I have made arrangements with a widowed baroness. Her late husband had a great deal of land, of which she still shares in the profits."

I glared at him, my jaw tight. "Anne Dixon?"

His eyes widened. "I didn't think you would remember her."

"She is rather unforgettable."

Miles stared at me in confusion for several seconds. "At any rate...there is an understanding between us. I suspect her widowhood has provided her with enough money to live comfortably on. She is a sweet girl, and I am quite fond of her. It would be an agreeable match, to be sure." For a moment, his smile appeared genuine. "If not Anne, I'm certain there are plenty of young ladies with dowries who will be joining the upcoming Season."

I rubbed the back of my neck, trying to steady my breathing. How had a disgusting, fortune-hunting scoundrel like my brother managed to steal Anne's heart? He couldn't even begin to deserve her.

"Are you all right?" Miles's teasing tone grated over my skin. "You could do the same, you know. If you spent less time fixating on the two-hundred pounds, you might be able to focus your attention instead on a beneficial courtship."

I stared at the cobblestones, no longer able to look at his face. It took all I had not to grab him by the neck. If he knew Anne's loyalty, if he had taken a moment to try to understand her heart, he would see that she was worth more than any sum of money. As I had always suspected, he had left her for the chance to go to India without any qualms. When he was unsuccessful, he had convinced her of his devotion through letters to ensure she would wait for him. Once he learned of her destitution, he would surely break her heart. How could someone be so cruel?

I had promised myself I would protect Anne from him. Telling him the truth, and preventing her hopes from escalating further, seemed the best way to do that.

I took a deep breath. "I have become acquainted with Anne during my time in London," I said, looking up from the ground.

Miles reared back in surprise. "How?"

"We have both been guests at a house party hosted by Lady Tottenham at Birch House. I happen to know that Anne's financial state is not what you think. The baron's land has stopped producing. She is destitute."

Miles's face fell.

"If it is your love for her that motivates you, I invite you to honor your proposal." My gaze was hard. "If not, I invite you to leave her alone. Break your ties to her. You have hurt her enough."

Miles exhaled slowly. "That is unfortunate news." He scowled, raking a hand over his hair. He was silent for several seconds. "I have certainly led her to expect an engagement between us."

"Will you keep your word?" I was confident in his answer, but I wanted to hear him admit his folly.

He sighed. "If her situation is as dire as you say, then I cannot. I do feel terrible that she has been awaiting my return, but I have no choice but to pursue a woman with an income or dowry. I did love her once, but we were very young. It was never going to last." His remorse only skimmed the surface of his expression. He met my gaze. "Would you be willing to convey the news to her?"

I scoffed with disbelief. "You cannot be serious. Anne won't take my word for it. She deserves to see your true character so she can understand how little she has truly lost."

Miles's expression darkened. "How do I know you speak the truth about her financial situation? You could be lying in an attempt to ruin my plans."

A surge of anger flooded my chest. "You may ask Anne about her financial state yourself. Unlike you, she is honest. She believes you truly care for her. If that isn't true, you need to tell her. I won't break her heart for you, but I *will* endeavor to make it whole again."

Realization dawned in his features. "You care for her." He tipped his head back with a laugh. "That's even more motivation for you to lie to me. You know she would never choose *you* over me." His sneer pushed my composure over the edge. "Did she already reject you?"

I threw my fist into his nose.

He staggered back, holding his face. He lunged forward without warning, striking me in the cheekbone, then my mouth. I punched blindly at his face, making contact with his jaw. I grabbed his collar, throwing him back until he tripped against a passing gentleman. The gasps of the people on the street brought me back to my senses. I tasted blood in my mouth, and my face throbbed with pain. Miles wiped blood from beneath his nose, his eyes wild with shock.

I had never hit him in my life, but he had never deserved it more. I had wanted to fight him for years, so I felt nothing but satisfaction at the surprise in his expression.

I backed away, eager to escape the onlookers. Our public fight could make the London gossip papers if I wasn't careful. It might have been too late, but I didn't care. I would cherish that moment for the rest of my life. Standing up to Miles and defending Anne all in the same instant was an incomparable victory.

I didn't stop walking for at least ten minutes, making my way as far from Miles as possible. I couldn't visit the banker with blood on my face. I needed to go back to Birch House and warn Anne, but I didn't know how. Was it better if she didn't know Miles was already back in London? It would drive me mad to see her waiting even a second longer for Miles.

I could already feel the swelling on my cheekbone. Knowing I might have broken Miles' nose was my only consolation.

I sat in the coach on the way back to Birch House, debating what to say to Anne when I returned. Ultimately, it would be best if she didn't know Miles was back in London—at least not yet. I would keep it a secret as long as necessary. I needed time to decide what to do. Miles owed Anne an explanation, though I doubted he would give her that.

He had never been one to pay what he owed.

CHAPTER 22

ANNE

My blue embroidery threads formed a knot so large I didn't even try to untangle it. I stabbed the needle through the fabric and set the hoop aside, picking up my teacup instead. My stomach had been in an even greater knot since breakfast.

I could hardly sit still, a heavy sense of dread hovering over me like a storm cloud. Lady Tottenham was still keeping to her room, but the rumors about the gentlemen who had been sent home were still circling the drawing room.

"I can understand why Lord Kirkham, Mr. St. Vincent, and Mr. Barnwall were sent away," Victoria said as she worked on her own embroidery across from me. "All three of them are complete boors. They must have broken one of Lady Tottenham's rules. But it astonishes me that Mr. Holland would be banished from the house. Lady Tottenham seemed to favor him greatly." Her eyes slid in my direction. "I cannot understand why she would interrupt your courtship."

I glanced out the window. A fresh wave of confusion and disappointment made my heart sting. Mr. Lymington, Mr. Hatcher, and Mr. Amesbury rode horses on the back lawn while Mrs. Pike and Octavia watched them at a nearby table. Besides those five, all that remained of the party were Victoria and myself. "I don't understand it either," I muttered before taking a gulp of tea. My throat burned.

A slew of questions had been racing through my mind all morning. Had Alexander been blamed for burning the rabbit? Or had he been discovered in the hexagon room with me and sent away for reasons of impropriety? That didn't seem likely, but I could think of no other explanation. He had disappeared so suddenly, just like the other three men. Just like Mrs. Fitzgibbon and her cousins. I hadn't even had the chance to say goodbye, and with Lady Tottenham ill in her room, I couldn't even ask for an explanation.

I should have been the one sent away.

The only reason Alexander had gone to the hexagon room had been to help me.

I thought of how my stomach had ached from laughter the night before, and now it ached with dread. Without Alexander at the house, the days would be long and dreary.

A pang of longing struck me squarely in the chest. I scratched at my collarbone, trying to make the feeling go away, but it only grew stronger. I already missed him.

Victoria reached forward and placed a gentle hand on my knee, pulling me from my thoughts. "Remember, this is only a house party. A strange one, yes, but you will see Mr. Holland again when it is over." She gave a soft smile. "He will find you."

I nodded, though I wasn't as certain as Victoria. Once I was reunited with Miles, everything would change. If the two brothers never reconciled, then I might never be allowed to be Alexander's friend again. My chest felt hollow as I took a deep breath. "You're right. Thank you, Victoria."

She set her embroidery down on the table before stretching her back. "Now I am going to venture outside for a walk. Would you like to join me?"

What I truly wanted was to be alone. I had far too many emotions and thoughts to sort through. I shook my head. "I'm afraid I lack the energy today." I gave a rueful smile.

"That is quite all right." She made her way to the door, waving her lace-gloved hand. "I hope to find your spirits improved when I return."

I waved, keeping my posture straight until she disappeared into the corridor. The moment she was gone, I slumped my back against the settee. After my victory of finding the key the night before, I would have expected to carry that triumphant feeling with me for days. Instead, I felt utterly defeated. Tears stung the back of my eyes. I never would have thought my friendship with Alexander would leave behind such a void, but I was drowning in it. My neck heated with anger at Lady Tottenham. Why on earth would she send him away? It didn't make sense.

I stood up in one determined motion. There was no use in wasting the day. Even if Alexander was gone—especially if he was gone—I needed to finish Lady Tottenham's game. He might have been sent away because he had helped me find the key. I couldn't waste the opportunity to finish solving the riddle. There was nothing on the schedule for the day, so I had all the time I needed to search for the final pieces of the puzzle.

There was nothing I could do to find out where Alexander was until Lady Tottenham returned to the party. The one thing I could control was my effort to win the game. With all the other guests outside, I would have the freedom to roam and search the house. It was the perfect opportunity.

I hurried to my bedchamber to retrieve the tiny gold key before taking the stairs to the second floor. It was unlikely that Lady Tottenham would place multiple clues in the same room, so I began my search in the study.

Starting on the left side of the room, I examined every inch of the blue walls and ornate portraits. I paid close attention to the plasterwork and wood carvings, moved books on the shelves, and checked behind each one. My meticulous search lasted half an hour. When I was confident I had scoured every inch of the room, I made my way out to the corridor.

The wide and long passage on the second floor was my next task, but it was daunting. Lady Tottenham's 'exercise hall' might as well have been an art gallery. Countless portraits and other paintings striped the walls that led to a window, cushioned bench, and a bookshelf. The tables and sideboards that flanked the corridor were topped with vases and busts. A tiger skin rug, with the head still attached, stared at me from underneath the nearest table. The exhibition was crowded enough to overwhelm me, yet wide and vast enough to almost justify such excessive decoration. Lady Tottenham was nothing if not excessive. She took great pride in this part of the house.

I walked forward, uncertain of the best place to start. The air was surprisingly cold. I wrapped my arms around myself as gooseflesh erupted over my skin. My footfalls echoed as I made my way to the opposite end, taking a brief glance at each item I passed. I gripped the key in my palm hard enough to leave an impression. I unfolded my fingers. "What do you unlock?" I whispered, casting my gaze across the many frames on the walls. Oval frames, landscapes, and portraits stretched all the way up to the ceiling.

I walked slowly as I scrutinized each one on the left side. After several minutes, I paused on a small portrait of a young woman with ginger curls. Her sharp green eyes were familiar. The painting was not as well done as some of the others, but it was still clearly Lady Tottenham. She could not have been older than twenty when it was commissioned. Her pursed lips and vibrant eyes revealed her impish disposition, even all those decades ago. Her larger portrait was at the center of the wall. The likeness must have been taken after her marriage to Lord Tottenham. I gasped when I noticed the small tan rabbit tucked under her arm.

A pang of grief struck my chest at the reminder that Alexander wasn't here to see it. He would have laughed.

I checked both portraits of Lady Tottenham closely, but there were no keyholes hidden in the paint strokes. I took a deep breath as my frustration rose. I hardly knew what I was looking for. A heart in its frame. Lady Tottenham's heart.

The key to her heart was the rabbit, but there was an actual key beneath its foot.

Finding her heart in its frame might only be another clue that would lead me to the true location of the keyhole. My head hurt as I examined the portraits again. There must have been something I was missing.

My gaze froze on the small portrait of her younger likeness. She wore a delicate chain with a large locket resting over her chest. The brush strokes were smudged together, the paint flaking off. It didn't seem to match the rest of the portrait, as if it had been added years after the original work had been done.

I knew I was alone, but I still glanced over my shoulder before scratching lightly at the paint. Tiny flecks stuck to my fingertips. Was the locket significant? Was it some sort of clue? I couldn't look away from that particular portrait. My instincts told me that I was close to discovering something.

I took hold of the gilded frame, jostling it slightly. It was less than two feet tall, and was attached to the wall at both upper corners. I lifted it away from the striped wallpaper, peering behind it.

I nearly dropped the frame on my toes.

The same locket that had been painted over the portrait hung from a nail behind the frame.

My hands shook as I set the portrait down on the floor and unhooked the locket from the wall.

The heavy gold locket was the size of half my palm. The details were much clearer than they had been in the portrait. It was engraved with a small depiction of cupid on one side, with his bow drawn. On the other side was a border in the shape of a heart. At the center, was a tiny keyhole.

My pulse raced. I hadn't expected to find the next clue so quickly. Luck had been on my side. I held up the key to the corresponding hole on the locket. It was a perfect match. Was the locket the prize? Or was there something else inside? I hardly knew what to expect as I wiggled the key into the hole and turned it. My heart leaped as the locket sprung open. A tiny slip of parchment fluttered to the floor.

I snatched it up, nearly dropping the locket in the process. Was it only another clue? I thought I had reached the end of the game, but I should have known better. There was still a week remaining of the house party. I read the short message written on the parchment.

18 Archard Street

"What?" I whispered. I hadn't expected the clues to lead me away from Birch House, but that seemed to be what Lady Tottenham intended. Was it a London address?

Urgency rose up in my throat, making it difficult to draw a breath. I lacked the patience to wait another day to discover what that address meant. With Lady Tottenham feeling unwell, today was my best opportunity to leave the house unnoticed. I was familiar with London, but not with the address inside the locket. The day was young, and my next clue was waiting for me.

I had to find it.

A wild excitement thrummed through my veins as I hastily hung up the portrait, taking the locket and key with me as I made my way back down the stairs. I found a straw bonnet that matched my lavender gown, a shawl, and my reticule before sneaking out into the courtyard. I slipped the locket inside the reticule, counting my shillings as I started in the direction of the square. I needed to find a coachman willing to convey me to 18 Archard Street with very little money. It wouldn't be an easy task, to be sure.

"Ma'am?" A young man emerged from the stables, waving one arm high above his head. He doffed his hat in greeting as he approached. "Where're you off to?"

"Oh—" I froze, unsure of how much I should reveal. "I

have business in Town. I hoped to find a coach to convey me to my destination."

"That is my responsibility, ma'am." He gave a polite smile. "The mistress instructed me to provide the needed conveyance for her guests. I'll have a coach prepared straight away."

I gave a small nod, though the situation made me slightly uneasy. Had he been watching for me? He had jumped out of the stables so quickly.

I waited as he assembled the team of horses and led the coach out to the middle of the courtyard. He opened the door, motioning me inside. I took his hand as I stepped up and sat on the velvet cushions. The tassels that hung from the ceiling matched the blue cushions. "What is your destination?" the coachman asked.

I hesitated. I hadn't the slightest idea where the locket was leading me. I didn't know how far it was from Birch House, or if the coachman would even be willing to convey me there. "The address is in an area I'm unfamiliar with." I gave an apologetic smile. "Do you know where to find Archard Street?"

He smiled. "Oh, yes. Would it be Eighteen Archard Street, perchance?"

My stomach twisted. "Y-yes."

He gave a brisk nod. "A short journey. You shall be there in no time at all." He threw the door shut before clambering into his seat and setting the horses in motion.

I stared out the window. As nervous as I was, I was also painfully curious. I bounced my leg, struggling to sit still. I wanted to tell Alexander about what I had discovered. Where was he? He must have still been in London somewhere. He could not have gone far, especially not since Miles's return was what had brought him to Town in the first place. It surprised me that he hadn't left me with a note explaining what had happened or where he had gone. My heart ached, dampening the thrill I had been feeling only moments before.

As the coachman had promised, it was a short journey. Archard Street was just outside London, at the center of a small village east of Birch House. That explained why I hadn't recognized the name. The coach stopped in front of a row of shops and businesses. The cream stone appeared old and grey under the cloudy sky. My stomach fluttered when I noticed the number at the top of one door.

18

The coachman opened my door, and my legs shook as I stepped out onto the uneven cobblestones. A breeze nearly stole my bonnet as I walked up to the front steps. Did someone live here? Or was it a shop of some sort? I took a deep breath to calm my nerves as I knocked three times on the cracked white paint of the door. I didn't even know what I would say when the door opened. *Good day, I'm sorry to intrude, but I found your address in a locket hidden behind a portrait.*

My shoulders tightened when the door swung open. A short, stout man with grey hair stood just beyond it. He wore a pair of spectacles on his nose. I recognized him instantly. It was the man Lady Tottenham had met with in the drawing room when Alexander and I had been hiding between the doors. The words I had planned to say evaded me for several seconds.

"Good day, sir." I cleared my throat. "My name is Lady Daventry. This may sound peculiar, but—" I searched for a proper explanation, but he stopped me.

"Congratulations, my lady." His face spread into a smile. "You must have found the locket."

I blinked, trying not to appear as perplexed as I felt. "Y-yes. I did." My head swam with confusion.

He gave a deep bow. "Mr. Burrowes, at your service. Please, do come inside." He stepped out of the doorway, waving me forward. The old floorboards creaked under my feet as I stepped into the entryway. Mr. Burrowes led me toward the room to our left. Bookshelves lined the walls, and two leather chairs faced a desk.

"Have a seat, my lady." Mr. Burrowes moved to the opposite side of the desk, waiting for me to sit in one of the leather chairs.

When we were both settled, he clasped his hands atop the desk with a smile. "Do you have the locket? I must verify that you are indeed the winner of Lady Tottenham's game."

A sense of accomplishment jolted through me. Winner? I hardly had time to process his words. "Yes, it's here." I reached inside my reticule, fumbling for the locket before sliding it across the desk. "I-I confess I'm quite confused." I gave a nervous laugh. "I'm not certain why I'm here."

Mr. Burrowes pushed his spectacles farther up the bridge of his nose, lifting the locket in front of his gaze with a satisfied smile. "That is for me to explain."

I nodded, watching his every move with misgiving. I had assumed this man was Lady Tottenham's secret lover, though I would never tell him that. He slid the locket back to me before unlocking a cupboard behind him. The silence was excruciating as he thumbed through a stack of documents, finally settling on one and withdrawing it from the pile.

He turned to face me in his chair. "Lady Tottenham is one of my most creative clients. I was the only solicitor in the county who would agree to carry out her...*unique* arrangements." He chuckled. "I know nothing about you, Lady Daventry, but I can make the assumption that you must be quite clever, and quite determined."

He set the document down on the desk, sliding it forward. I didn't have time to read a single word of it before Mr. Burrowes spoke again.

"Today, according to Lady Tottenham's instruction, we shall name you the sole beneficiary of her property, possessions, and fortune...which amounts to approximately fifty thousand pounds."

CHAPTER 23

ANNE

I must have misheard him. The knot in my stomach tightened, my vision blurring at the edges. My mouth hung open in shock. I found myself shaking my head. The entire room seemed to be drifting away from me, Mr. Burrowes's face and congratulatory smile fading farther and farther into the distance.

I gripped the sides of my chair, feeling dangerously close to drifting away with the rest of the room. "Her—her fortune? Me?" My words didn't make any sense.

Mr. Burrowes chuckled. "It will be yours. Earlier this year, she received grave news from her physician regarding her health and longevity. So she organized her house party with the purpose of finding an heir or heiress in a timely manner. She has no children of her own, and no relatives she had any desire to bestow the honor upon."

My mind reeled. "But—I hardly know her. I'm still not even certain why I was invited to her party."

"She has a tender place in her heart for widows like yourself. She understands how fortunate she has been to remain unmarried, to have wealth to sustain her. She was open to the possibility of any of her guests obtaining her fortune, but I do believe she always hoped one of the widows would solve her riddles first."

I stared blankly at him. I could hardly comprehend what was happening. It couldn't have possibly been true. Fifty-thousand pounds was a much larger fortune than I had even imagined Lady Tottenham possessed. Was this all a sham? Could it have been a test of some sort?

"Would you like a glass of water?" Mr. Burrowes's amused smile brought me back to my senses.

"No, that is all right." I blinked fast. "I am overwhelmed. I don't know what to think." I exhaled slowly in an attempt to relax the turmoil inside my chest.

"Well then, I will tell you what you should think." He leaned forward with a gentle smile. "You should be overjoyed. Your life is forever changed." He picked up a quill and wrote my name in one of the blank spaces near the top of the will.

I sat back against my chair. My emotions were numb, suppressed by an overwhelming feeling of raw astonishment.

Mr. Burrowes tucked the will back into the cabinet, locking the door behind it. "I would suggest you address any further questions to Lady Tottenham as soon as possible. She will confirm what I have explained to you. You are soon to be one of the wealthiest women in all of England."

♟♟♟

Birch House was quiet when I stepped into the vestibule. I stopped on the first row of checkered tiles. I was still in a daze. I took in the ceiling, the walls, all the furnishings and grandeur. Would it really be all mine one day? My stomach fluttered with disbelief. How could it be possible? I needed to speak with Lady Tottenham to ensure it wasn't a trick of some sort— another element to her many games. My lack of trust in her sense of reality was completely plausible.

I pressed a hand to my stomach, feeling suddenly ill. Was Lady Tottenham truly dying? All those days during the house party that she had felt unwell and kept to her room made sense now. Her coughing fits, her pale skin and excessive rouge, even the bowl of leeches. The other man I had seen frequently visiting the house must have been her physician. The pieces fit together in my mind like yet another puzzle. Her complete lack of regard for propriety must have been due to the lack of time she had left to live. She had nothing to lose, and everything to give away.

The list of questions I had for Lady Tottenham grew longer by the second. Besides all my questions about her will, I needed to know why she had sent Alexander away from Birch House. So much had occurred in one morning, I could hardly keep track of it all.

I had almost reached the base of the staircase when I heard my name.

"Anne?"

A jolt of shock shot through me. I looked toward the top

of the stairs. "Alexander?" My voice was a weak whisper. I remained planted where I stood in complete bafflement as he walked down the stairs toward me. He stopped on the checkered tiles just a few feet away. His brown irises looked lighter than usual as he took me in. "Did you sleep well in the hexagon room? I haven't seen you all day."

My voice was buried under a massive pile of emotions. I managed to dig it out after a few seconds. "Where have you been?" I snapped. "I have spent the entire day thinking Lady Tottenham sent you away." I searched his face with concern. His cheekbone was red with hints of purple, and it was swelling. "What happened to you?" I asked amid a gasp.

A muscle jumped in his jaw. He shook his head. "It's nothing." He smiled, as if that would excuse the fact that he had been injured.

"Did you fight Lord Kirkham? Or—or one of the other men that Lady Tottenham banished from the house?"

His eyebrows lifted. "They're gone? It seems I've missed a great deal of news this morning."

"Lord Kirkham, Mr. Barnwall, and Mr. St. Vincent were all sent home. I thought you were too. Lady Tottenham has been ill in her room all day and hasn't confirmed the rumors, so I assumed you were among the guests banished from the house." My voice trailed off as my gaze found his bruises again. I released an anxious breath. "Who did this?" I reached up and skimmed my fingertips over his swelling cheekbone. He flinched, but didn't pull away. His heavy eyes connected with mine. He was silent for several seconds.

"I'll explain later." He caught my fingertips in his hand as I lowered it from his face.

I scowled. "You can't walk through the door with a bruise on your face and expect me to disregard it."

"Please." He leaned down to look in my eyes. "Trust me."

"If it was Lord Kirkham who hurt you, I will go fight him myself." I widened my eyes with sincerity.

Alexander laughed.

"You're staying for the remainder of the house party, then?" I asked.

"I assure you, I haven't been banished. I'm not leaving. I told you I wouldn't."

I gave a quick nod, all my panic from the day slowly deflating from my back and shoulders. I practically forgot about the life-changing piece of news I had received from Mr. Burrowes. All I could think about was the smile creeping over Alexander's lips. "Were you that worried?" he asked—with far too much satisfaction.

My defenses rose instinctively. "I just—I didn't think it would be fair if you were sent away. You did nothing wrong. I disagreed with the...*justice* of the situation." I cringed.

Alexander's smile only grew wider. "You would make an excellent barrister."

I exhaled in a failed attempt at a laugh, putting one hand to my forehead with embarrassment. "I confess I was quite distraught, actually. I didn't have the opportunity to say good-bye. I wouldn't like it if our parting was so sudden."

"I wouldn't either."

My stomach gave a violent flutter when he met my eyes. I fought the confusion that raged in my chest. My mind was alert, but my heart was muddled. Alexander still held onto my fingers, which didn't help my sense of clarity.

The front door opened behind us, and I quickly tugged my

hand away from Alexander's, stepping away from him. Mrs. Pike stood in the doorway, eyes round. If we had been acting, I would have happily clung to Alexander's hand in front of Mrs. Pike. Instead we had jumped apart like we had been caught committing a crime.

"Mr. Holland?" Mrs. Pike pressed a hand to her bosom. "What happened to your face?"

He hesitated before addressing her with a smile. "A disagreement was settled...perhaps not in the most cordial way."

Mrs. Pike was obviously brimming with as many questions as I was. She made no move to exit the vestibule. I couldn't finish my conversation with Alexander with Mrs. Pike hovering nearby. I hadn't even had the chance to tell him what had happened that morning. Perhaps it wasn't wise to spread the news yet. He could have his secrets, and I could have mine.

Mrs. Pike's gaze darted between Alexander and me. The door opened again. Victoria, Mr. Hatcher, and Octavia stepped inside, their loud voices and laughter echoing.

Alexander gave a bow in Mrs. Pike's direction. "Please excuse me." He met my gaze before starting up the stairs again.

I wanted to stop him, but he turned around too quickly. I watched his back as he disappeared around the corner and his footfalls faded into the distance. I glared in his direction. Why wouldn't he tell me what had happened? He was being far too mysterious. My relief at seeing him again hadn't lasted long. Now I was worried for other reasons.

"Lady Daventry, would you like to join us in the drawing room for a game of whist?" Victoria's voice came from behind me. "Mrs. Pike doesn't wish to play, and I need a partner."

What I truly wanted to do was run to my room and hide

under my blankets. I could still feel the weight of the locket in my reticule. I wouldn't be able to focus on anything until I spoke with Lady Tottenham face to face.

"I don't feel well. I'm sorry." I cast Victoria an apologetic glance before starting up the stairs. I held tight to the bannister. My heart pounded as I walked up to the first floor and turned right. All the guest bedchambers were on the left. I had never had a reason to turn toward Lady Tottenham's wing of the house.

I was likely forbidden to do so.

The silence in the corridor was eerie. My spine tingled with fear. Was it wise to intrude on her solitude? I could wait until she joined the party again, but I doubted I would keep my sanity in the process. My curiosity raged inside me, forcing my feet forward. I didn't even know which room was hers. I almost turned around when a maid stepped out of the first door to my left.

Her dark brown eyes widened when she saw me. She carried a bowl of water, and it sloshed over one of her arms.

"I'm sorry!" I reached forward to steady it. "I didn't mean to startle you."

She curtsied, holding the bowl tight against her body.

"Is this Lady Tottenham's bedchamber? I heard she was unwell today and thought I might pay her a visit."

"Indeed, ma'am. She just awoke." She curtsied again before passing to my right, leaving me alone in the corridor.

I pressed down my nervousness, taking a shaky breath. And then I knocked on the door. "My lady?" I spoke in a loud, clear voice. "This is Lady Daventry. May I enter?"

"You may." Her raspy voice sent my heart pounding. I had never been as intimidated by her as I was now. I opened the door. The curtains were partially closed, so my eyes took a moment to adjust to the dimness. The four poster bed looked tiny compared to the vastness of the room. The furnishings showcased her wealth just as heartily as the other rooms of the house. Lady Tottenham's ginger curls spilled out over her white pillows, her eyes no less sharp than usual as she watched me step into the room.

I gave a deep curtsy. "I am very sorry to intrude, my lady. I heard you were unwell."

"I have had better days." She sat up against her headboard with a groan. The ruffles of her night dress consumed her entire neck. "I suspect your day has been a bit more riveting than mine." She raised one eyebrow.

I reached inside my reticule and withdrew the locket. "Are you referring to this?" I cast her a nervous look.

Her wrinkles deepened with a gleeful smile. "I knew you were clever enough to find it. You were my first choice from the beginning. Octavia showed promise, but she ultimately failed." In a matter of seconds, Lady Tottenham had transformed away from the feeble woman I had seen lying in the bed. She grinned. "I am most eager to hear your thoughts on the matter. I trust you spoke with Mr. Burrowes?"

I moved to stand by her bedside, searching for the right words. "I did—but, my lady, I find it difficult to accept such an undeserved inheritance. All I did was solve a riddle."

"You may not like games, my dear, but you are good at them." Her eyes gleamed with delight. "You did more than solve a riddle. You showed a determined spirit, wit, and independence. I have watched your heart open during the course of my party. Nothing has brought me greater entertainment than watching you fall in love with Mr. Holland despite your initial resistance. I told you there would be many different opportunities to secure your future comfort."

I felt a pang of guilt. She didn't know the courtship had been fake. Accepting her inheritance would haunt me forever if she didn't know the truth. I lowered my gaze to the floor. "My lady, you are too generous. I must confess something." I took a deep breath. "When you arranged the midnight parlor game between Mr. Holland and me, his victory in our chess game led us to the agreement that we would pretend to form an attachment in order to prevent the attentions of the other guests—Lord Kirkham and Octavia in particular." My words rushed out. "We are not actually courting."

Lady Tottenham's expression didn't falter. "I knew that. I'm not as easily fooled as the others. I have a keen sense for truth and falsehood." She shrugged. "Besides that, my footman heard your conversation that night and relayed it to me."

"You knew all along?" My face burned.

"Yes, but that is no matter. As the days have gone on, I have seen your attachment become real. I will not retract my words from before, in fact, I will reaffirm them. It has been a joy watching you fall in love with Mr. Alexander Holland."

I opened my mouth, but no words came out. I wasn't in love with Alexander—he was my friend. He was *only* my friend. I repeated the words in my mind. I had told myself that exact thing countless times, yet it was becoming difficult to believe. I thought of him more than I thought of anyone else... even Miles. It vexed me. My chest flooded with frustration.

Lady Tottenham continued speaking. "I admit that I was wrong to try to match you with Lord Kirkham. If I had known he was such a bother to you, I would have sent him away much sooner."

I gathered my thoughts. "Why *did* you send him away?" I needed to discover if he had been the cause of Alexander's injuries. Had they argued? Had Lord Kirkham challenged him to fisticuffs? It wouldn't have been surprising.

Lady Tottenham's upper lip pursed with distaste. "When he declined my invitation to the midnight game yesterday evening, I was forced to retract my hospitality. Mr. Barnwall and Mr. St. Vincent ignored my invitations as well. It vexed me greatly." Her nostrils flared. "With little time left to live, I no longer have any reason to endure company I don't enjoy."

I had been guilty of not enjoying Lady Tottenham's company on multiple occasions, but looking at her now, I admired her. She had been dealt a difficult hand of cards in life. She didn't seem to care for her money nearly as much as she cared for her late husband. I would wager that she would have traded it all at any moment for one more day with him. She didn't care what anyone thought of her, yet she still formed a strong opinion of everyone else. Somehow, she liked me. She liked me enough to leave me with fifty thousand pounds. A grim feeling enveloped my heart.

"I was very sorry to hear of the state of your health," I said.

She smirked. "Oh, posh. The sooner I die, the sooner you become rich."

I gasped. "My lady—"

She gave a hooting laugh. It turned into a cough. "My physician says I have a month or two left, but I intend on living at least another year," she said in a raspy voice. "I will have plenty of time to prepare you for the role you will undertake as mistress of Birch House. I will make an announcement to all the guests at breakfast tomorrow morning that you have won my prize and will be my heiress. I will use my connections to ensure the news is spread amongst the *ton*. I will also send invitations to my closest friends in town to attend a ball in your honor tomorrow evening. The arrangements have already been underway."

I felt the color drain from my face. "Is it truly necessary to inform so many people at once? I feel as though most of Town doesn't even know who I am."

"But they will." She smiled. "You, Lady Daventry, are about to be quite famous."

I pressed my lips together, a mixture of fear and excitement battling inside me. My financial worries were dormant, saved by this unexpected stroke of good fortune. I no longer had to wonder if I would have a place to live, or a future beyond my dreams of marrying Miles. I was not trapped anymore. If Miles failed to return to London and keep his promise to me, I would not be forced to find a husband elsewhere. For the first time, I had a choice. I had power of my own in a society that made me feel helpless.

"I would ask you not to reveal anything to the other guests here until after I make my announcement tomorrow. I should like to be the one to introduce you as my heiress."

"Of course." I swallowed hard.

She slumped down onto her pillows again with a dramatic sigh, closing her eyes. "Let us hope I have the strength to leave my bed tomorrow. Now go. I am tired."

"Thank you," I blurted. "That doesn't feel like enough to say, but thank you for the opportunity you have given me. My gratitude is truly beyond words."

One of her eyes opened. She stared at me with her left eye, her expression frozen in a perpetual wink. "Thank *you* for playing my game so well."

A second pang of guilt forced another confession out of my mouth. "There is another incident for which I must apologize. One of the rabbits in the hexagon room—"

Her other eye opened. "I will be more inclined to forgive the charring of that poor creature's face if I see an engagement transpire between you and Mr. Holland. I have done all I can to help you recognize the passionate love you have for one another, and I am growing impatient."

My ears tingled with heat. How did she know about the rabbit already? Her servants must have reported everything to her. I wrung my hands together. "My lady, I think you have mistook the nature of our relationship. Mr. Holland and I are friends."

"I have seen the way he looks at you, child. That is not how a man looks at his friend." Her eyelids drooped, but she still grinned. "He has marriage on his mind, to be sure."

My stomach flopped. His words from the night before came rushing back to my mind, about how he might have proposed had he thought the answer would be favorable. A question had been prying at my mind all day, and now it finally slipped through the cracks: If I had never known Miles, what would my answer be? I pushed the thought from my mind, a sickening feeling spreading in my stomach. Developing feelings for Alexander would complicate everything. It would be a disaster.

But was it too late?

Now was not the time to argue with Lady Tottenham, so I gave a submissive nod. She could still change her mind about making me her heiress. I half-expected her to at any moment. I needed to ensure she still enjoyed my company, or I would be cast out to the streets just like Lord Kirkham.

"Leave me now. I must rest." Her eyes closed, ending the conversation in an instant.

"Good day, my lady. I hope you feel better soon."

She grunted in response.

I walked out of the room, my steps burdened with the heavy secret I carried on my back.

CHAPTER 24

ALEXANDER

The leeches and toads in the pond didn't bother me nearly as much as the true leech I had encountered on the street that morning.

I tugged off my boots, tossing them into the pile with my jacket, waistcoat, and cravat. I rolled up my shirtsleeves and dove into the pond on the west lawn of Birch House. The cold water awoke my senses, causing chills to burst over my skin.

I came up for air, stroking my arms through the water as I floated on my back. The sky was gold and orange as the sun slowly disappeared behind the treeline. The cold water soothed the bruise on my cheek, so I dipped my head under again. I broke the surface, shaking the excess water from my hair.

I had spent the afternoon in my room thinking about my conversation with Miles. My anger had been spreading like a fire inside me. He didn't even have the decency to break his connection with Anne properly. He planned to disappear and leave her waiting as he had already done so many times before. He had no honor, no sense of obligation, and no dignity. He had never been true to his word, and he wouldn't start now. I couldn't believe he had written such a straightforward letter to Anne. It made sense why she had been holding out hope for so long. She viewed the letter as a proposal. He viewed it as disposable.

The worst part was that until Anne knew that Miles was back in London, and that he had changed his mind, she would be loyal to him.

My course of action was unclear, and I couldn't seem to make a decision. Miles had made it obvious to me that he was no longer interested in marrying her. If Anne knew that I had told him about her financial situation, she would be angry with me. If I spoke ill of his character and motives, she would blame me for trying to turn her against him. I wanted to believe that I had gained her trust, but perhaps I hadn't. Miles was years ahead of me.

I had been avoiding Anne all day because I knew she would ask again about my bruises. I hadn't yet decided how I would explain what had happened. At dinner, everyone had been curious, but I had managed to deflect their questions. When the ladies withdrew to the drawing room, I had left my port at the table with the other men to come outside alone. With Lady Tottenham ill in her room and unable to dictate my actions, I had escaped the party for the evening. There was nothing on the schedule, so I expected the other guests would dissolve from the drawing room early as well.

It was clear that we were all growing weary of one another's company.

The only person I cared to see was Anne, but I couldn't

risk her asking too many questions that I didn't know if I should answer.

I wiped the water off my face, pushing it back into my hairline. Crickets chirped loudly in the tall grass around the pond. Apparently Lady Tottenham's groundskeeper hadn't caught them all. The noise only added to my disagreeable mood.

I blinked the droplets from my eyelids, my vision adjusting to the fading light. The warmth and beauty of the sunset stretched out over the entire lawn and all the gardens surrounding it. The other guests were likely still gathered in the drawing room. The men would be lazily reading poetry in an attempt to entertain themselves. Octavia was surely playing her third piece on the pianoforte by now, not giving her sister the opportunity to display her talents. Anne must have been sitting on her usual place on the settee, looking beautiful, observing every conversation, but being too sweet and witty to take part in any of them, though being humble enough not to realize that.

I held my breath and closed my eyes, sinking under the water again. Darkness enveloped me as I swam to the opposite side of the pond. Everyone would think I had gone mad if they saw me out here. I no longer cared. I should have come to this pond weeks ago. It was refreshing and peaceful. Besides the crickets.

"What on earth are you doing?"

I blinked the water from my eyes at the sight of Anne traipsing through the grass in her champagne evening gown. She stopped at the water's edge. She held her skirts up with delicate fingers, dark brows drawn together.

As shocked as I was to see her, my spirits instantly lifted at her horrified expression. She was far too endearing not to tease.

"Swimming." I sank down until just my neck and head floated above the water. "Would you like to join me?"

She exhaled with disbelief. "No, thank you."

I laughed, floating on my back. "Are you certain? The water is quite refreshing."

"I have never been more certain of anything."

I glanced up to see her appalled expression. "Well, if you're simply going to watch me swim, would you do me a service and eat a few of those crickets? They are far too loud."

A laugh burst out of her. "Alexander. Come out of that water at once. There are toads and fish in there."

"Are you telling me there aren't toads in there?" I pointed toward the house.

Her smile broadened, and she turned her face away in an effort to hide it. She shook her head at me. "If you are referring to Mr. Lymington—"

"You're the one who pointed out the similarity."

Her laugh was delightful, and I would have bottled the sound if I could. She leaned forward. "You're atrocious."

In the glow of sunset, she looked nothing short of a goddess. I stared up at her, momentarily caught off-guard. My heart was in my throat at the thought of losing her. It was likely in my eyes too, and for a moment I was struck with the fear that she could read my thoughts. I had never known the vulnerability of loving someone who didn't love me in return. The pain was a thousand times worse when I remembered that it was my brother she loved instead.

"How did you know where to find me?" I asked.

"Mr. Hatcher mentioned that you wanted to take a walk outside." Her brows drew together again. "A walk sounded much better than sitting in that drawing room all evening."

"I will tell you what's even better than a walk."

She raised her brows. "Hmm...a swim?"

I chuckled. "I know I won't convince you. You are quite stubborn at times."

She scoffed. "Refusing to jump into a pond full of toads fully clothed in my evening gown does not make me stubborn. It makes me sensible."

I stood up in the shallow water, trudging toward her.

A wave of satisfaction passed through me as I watched her gaze lower to my chest and shoulders. My shirt was soaked through, leaving little to the imagination. The first time we had met, she had seen me without a shirt, so she shouldn't have been as scandalized as she appeared. "Are you calling me insensible?" I asked.

She averted her eyes after several seconds, staring down at the water. She brushed hastily at a curl on her forehead. "Yes, I am."

My confidence grew as I stepped out of the water, joining her on the grass. "I suppose it *would* have been more sensible not to wear my clothes."

The setting sun reflected off her irises, bringing out the dark green hues. "Need I call you atrocious a second time?"

I sensed her nervousness as I took a step closer. "Only if you mean it."

She smelled of roses. Her skin glowed. "You are wicked for not telling me what happened to you this morning. Why did you return looking like you had lost a fight?" Her eyes flickered to my cheekbone.

"I certainly didn't lose."

She frowned, planting her hands on her hips. "So you did fight someone."

I bent over to pick up my jacket, shaking the loose blades of grass from it. "Would you believe me if I told you it was the rabbit pugilist? He has a powerful lead hook."

Her frown didn't falter. "Please be serious for one moment."

I stood up with a solemn expression.

Anne was shivering. She wrapped her arms around herself. "I have been worried about you. You disappeared all morning and I thought you were never coming back, you refused to tell me why you were injured, and then proceeded to hide away in your room all afternoon. I thought something horrible had happened." She caught her breath. "All I want to know is who did this to you."

I draped my jacket around her back and shoulders, holding tight to the lapels on both sides. Her eyes searched my face, taking a stab at my resolve. I couldn't stop myself from telling her the truth.

"Miles." I pressed my lips together, my jaw clenching of its own accord. I didn't want to see her reaction, but I couldn't look away from her face.

Her eyes widened. "What?"

I gave a grim nod.

"He's in London already?" Her voice weakened. "When did he arrive?"

"I'm not certain. I happened upon him by chance outside Martin's bank."

She scowled in confusion. "Why did he strike you?"

"Because I did it first."

Her round eyes flooded with apprehension.

"Our conversation resulted in a disagreement. I found it prudent to knock a little sense into him."

She looked so small, tucked inside my jacket. I held it tight around her. She had stopped shivering, but the disapproval on her face was just as cold. "How could you greet your own brother in that manner after such a long time apart?"

"He deserved it." I leaned down to look in her eyes, moving my hands to her shoulders. "Anne—he is not coming for you." I took a deep breath. "He lied. I'm sorry. He told me that he has changed his mind."

Her eyes flashed with hurt, and she took a step back, shaking her head. "That doesn't make sense. He wrote me a letter. He left India because of me."

"Why did he go to India at all?" My words came out harsher than I intended. I tried to steady my frustration with a deep breath. "If I had been in love with you all those years ago, I would have behaved much differently. If I had learned that you were widowed, and that you had any desire to see me again, I would have never run to the first ship that could take me all the way across the world." I stepped toward her, my heart racing with sudden determination. I cradled her face in my hands. "I would have run to you, and I would have made *you* my world. I would have married you before I could lose you again."

She stared up at me in shock, a sheen of tears clouding her eyes.

I traced my thumb over her cheek, grazing the edge of her lower lip. Before I could lose my nerve, I leaned down and kissed her. It might not have been wise, but my wisdom had been evading me all day. I waited for any sign of protest, but she gave none. I thought she would stop me, but she did far more than that. She kissed me back.

She melted forward, taking a handful of my sodden shirt,

her lips pressing hard against mine. I took it as encouragement, wrapping my arms around her waist and pulling her against me. Her hands unfolded against my chest, and I felt the warmth of her palms through my damp shirt. A shiver followed her touch, racing over the length of my spine. My mouth moved against hers with all the passion I had been restraining. I needed to leave her with no question that I adored her. That I loved her.

All at once, her hands pushed against my chest, breaking us apart. My jacket slipped off her shoulders, falling to the ground. Her frantic gaze flickered over my face, her fingers lifting to her lips. Her hand shook.

Regret washed over me. "Anne—" I reached for her arm, but she retreated another step. I couldn't imagine the conflicting emotions she must have felt. I cursed myself for kissing her in such a vulnerable moment. I hadn't given her time to process my words about Miles before I essentially confessed my feelings for her. It was clear that I had over-whelmed her.

She turned toward the house, her face in her hands.

I strode forward. "Anne, wait—"

She walked faster, apparently eager to escape me. I let her go, kicking at a puddle of water in the grass. I rubbed the back of my neck, cursing under my breath. Despite his unworthi-ness, she needed to grieve Miles if I ever hoped to win her heart.

My impatience might have cost me the opportunity.

CHAPTER 25

ANNE

I didn't stop walking until I reached my bedchamber. My heart pounded so hard it hurt. My lips still burned from Alexander's kiss. I burst through the door, closing it firmly behind me. I paced across the room, wiping at a tear on my cheek. I stopped in front of the looking glass, catching sight of my wild eyes and flushed lips.

What had I done?

That kiss had not been part of a game. It hadn't been a forfeit. I had no excuse. Though Alexander had started it, I had been a willing participant. Butterflies still raged in my stomach. I should have pushed him away from the first touch of his lips, but I was weak. Pain radiated around my heart, spreading through my arms and fingers. I pressed a hand to my chest as a lump formed in my throat. A sob rattled my body, and I leaned over the vanity table to steady myself.

Was it true? Had Miles changed his mind?

How could he change his mind before seeing me one last time? It wasn't fair.

The day had been exhausting and confusing enough already before Alexander had all but proposed to me. He had left me with no question about his feelings. My heart had never been more conflicted. How could I trust what Alexander told me about Miles? He had initiated the brawl with Miles on the street that day.

Was it his jealousy that caused it?

What if Miles did plan to be true to his word, but Alexander was simply making one last attempt to turn me against him? He could have lied about his conversation with Miles. I needed to find him to learn for myself what his intentions were.

I wiped the last of my tears from my cheeks. For the moment, it would be wise to bury my conflicting emotions. I had nothing to cry about. Today should have been the most thrilling, happy day of my life. I was the heiress of Birch House and Lady Tottenham's fortune. That needed to be at the front of my mind. Her announcement would be made in the morning. I needed to rest.

But as I fell asleep, all I could think of was Alexander. His dark eyes, his wet hair, his white shirt clinging to his chest, his sweet words, his kiss, his arms around me...it all played out in a never-ending circle. I couldn't turn back time. That moment would haunt me forever.

My eyes were puffy as Jane arranged my hair in the morning. I chose my brown floral morning dress before making my way downstairs. I was more restless than usual, jumping at every sound behind me on the staircase. I didn't know what I would do if I encountered Alexander before reaching the safety of the room full of guests. I didn't know what I would say to him or how to behave.

I stopped at the breakfast room door with a forceful breath. *Relax,* I demanded. My nerves had multiple causes, one of which was about to unfold. If Lady Tottenham was well enough to join us at breakfast, she had promised to make an announcement to the household about my victory in her game. I squared my shoulders before entering the room.

Lady Tottenham sat at the head of the long table. Victoria, Octavia, and Mrs. Pike stood at the sideboard. All the men had already assembled their plates and were sitting at the round table.

Alexander wasn't there yet.

Relief streamed over me. I released the breath in my lungs. Upon noticing my entrance, Lady Tottenham waved me forward, gesturing at the open chair nearest her place at the head of the table. I gave a gracious smile, crossing the room to join her.

"You look well," I said. "Are you feeling much improved?"

Her thin brows lifted. "Oh, yes. I couldn't miss the opportunity to make my announcement this morning."

My stomach twisted. Octavia was listening. She set her plate down at the table, tipping her head to one side as she observed my position beside Lady Tottenham. I usually sat at the round table beside Alexander, but that would not be happening today.

Where was he? Was he still avoiding the party? I dared a look at the doorway, my heart beating a shallow rhythm. I didn't know whether I wanted to see him or not. What would he think when he heard Lady Tottenham's announcement? I wanted to explain everything to him—how I had found the locket, gone to London, and dared to knock on Lady Tottenham's bedchamber door.

But how could I face him?

How could we ever interact the way we used to?

That kiss had changed everything.

"Are you all right, my dear?" Lady Tottenham's round green eyes tugged me out of my thoughts. I had been staring at the door for too long.

"Yes, of course." I forced a smile.

"What would you like? Eggs? Toast? Nectarines?" She snapped her fingers, apparently signaling the nearest footman to pick up a plate.

"Oh—the fruit would be sufficient."

"You must never serve yourself from this day forward. The wonderful thing about my efficient staff is that you shall never have to lift a finger."

I cast my gaze around the table as the footman lowered my plate to the table in front of me. I wasn't certain my stomach could hold any food at the moment. Victoria's fork paused, her jaw hanging open. Before that morning, Lady Tottenham had only ever utilized servants for her own benefit. She seemed to enjoy stirring up gossip prior to her announcement. I could tell by the smirk on her lips.

"Eat, child. You look like a ghost."

I glanced at her from the corner of my eye. Lady Tottenham was the one who had practically matched her white sheets the day before. How had she managed to regain so much energy?

I stabbed at a slice of nectarine with my fork. My grip loosened when I looked up at the doorway. Alexander strode into the room. He wore a light blue waistcoat with a navy jacket— the same jacket he had draped over my shoulders the night before. I stared down at my plate before he could meet my eyes, my pulse picking up speed. Lady Tottenham knew that our ruse was over, but what would the other guests think if Alexander and I began ignoring one another?

They might not even notice. They would soon have a much larger piece of gossip to chew on.

Lady Tottenham perked up in her chair, watchful eyes examining the entire room. I didn't dare look up from the table. I could feel Alexander's gaze on me as he passed. He must have taken a seat, because Lady Tottenham spoke in a loud voice. "Now that you are all present, there is a very important announcement I should like to make."

Taking a gulp from my glass of water, I prepared for the scrutiny I was soon to be under. I straightened my spine. I offered my hand when Lady Tottenham rose shakily to her feet.

"On your first day at Birch House, I offered all of you one vital piece of information. Not only would we play many games during the course of the party, but the entire party itself has been a game. I watched for those among you who showed the most wit, the most independence, and determination. Some of you received clues and riddles. Some of those riddles went unsolved or ignored, but Lady Daventry played my game to the end. She showed that she was dedicated enough to win my prize."

I met Octavia's gaze. She did not look pleased.

"Lord Tottenham and I were never blessed with children of our own, but our wealth has multiplied fruitfully enough, given my wise investments in the past decades. But my physician has recently informed me that my health is in rapid decline, so I was forced to face the question of whom to name as the sole beneficiary of my will. Lord Tottenham's fondness for games led me to the idea of organizing a competition amongst my acquaintances, with the prize unbeknownst to any of you. If you had known what you were competing for, there would have been bloodshed." She laughed, placing one hand on my shoulder. "Alas, Lady Daventry was the only one to solve my puzzle, and so I have named her the heiress of Birch House and my fifty thousand pounds. Let us all give her a congratulatory round of applause."

The shock in the room was palpable. The air was too thick to inhale. Mrs. Pike gasped, and Victoria choked on her water.

Mr. Lymington was the first one to applaud. The others joined him one at a time. The scattered, bewildered clapping made me want to sink into my chair and disappear. The overall reaction was shock, but I sensed the immediate regret of all the women at my table. Mr. Lymington was the only person smiling. Mr. Hatcher put his head in his hands.

I accidentally looked at Alexander. His shock was written all over his face.

Lady Tottenham continued, "Lady Daventry solved my puzzle much more quickly than I expected. Nevertheless, we shall not dissolve the house party just yet. You are all welcome for the remainder of the week as promised, so long as you keep the rules and offer your full participation. You may have noticed that Lord Kirkham, Mr. St. Vincent, and Mr. Barnwall were...*eliminated*, if you will. They declined my invitation to a midnight game." She sighed. "At any rate, we shall carry on with another diverting day. The game is over, but the party continues. Tonight I will hold a ball celebrating my new heiress. You are all welcome to attend, of course."

She settled into her chair. She appeared completely unaffected by the sense of dismay in the room. She knew that none of the guests dared question her. I aspired to her level of confidence. She spread a large dollop of orange marmalade on her toast before taking a bite.

"Congratulations, my lady." Mrs. Pike's voice was kind, but her eyes shone with envy. Her modest living could have benefitted from such a fortune, to be sure. I was not more deserving than Mrs. Pike, or Victoria, or anyone else. The inheritance felt like nothing short of charity, and I had never been comfortable with receiving that from anyone.

"How did you solve the riddle?" Victoria asked with an awed expression. "Octavia and I had clues of our own, but we never finished."

"The key was the most difficult bit," I said. "It was hidden in the hexagon room."

"I thought so!" Victoria stabbed at her plate with frustration. "We must have been close to finding it ourselves. Tell us more."

I told them the entire story. I was overly aware of Alexander from the corner of my eye, observing the conversation. I felt guilty for being the sole beneficiary when he had accompanied me on so many of my quests for the riddles. I wanted to discuss all the details with him and to hear his thoughts on the matter. He must have been eager to speak with me, but I was surrounded.

The attention from the others was just as suffocating.

Finally, Lady Tottenham excused everyone but me from the breakfast room without any manner of subtlety. The prattle seemed to be overburdening her as well.

My stomach sank when Alexander stood from his seat at the table. I nearly jumped out of my chair to follow him. The awkwardness between us had to be resolved somehow. I was slowly drowning in it.

When the room was empty, Lady Tottenham leaned toward me. "One of my connections has made a publication this morning that might interest you." She waved a footman forward, whispering an intelligible request. Less than a minute later, he returned to the room with a silver salver. A document rested on top.

Lady Tottenham gestured for me to take it. My eyes widened when I read the name of the column.

BEHIND

THE FAN

By *Lady Teignmouth*

September 10, 1818

A widow nearing the age of thirty would be a subject of pity if she were to enter the marriage mart this Season. However, one such widow could prove to be the greatest competition to any young debutante with or without a sizeable dowry. It has come to my attention that the widow of the late Baron of Daventry has been named heiress of Birch House of Lockhart Square. Prepare, my dear reader, to be further astonished. Lady Daventry will also inherit the respectable widow Lady Tottenham's entire fortune of fifty thousand pounds.

During the course of a house party hosted by Lady Tottenham herself, fourteen guests were presented with the challenge of playing a series of games, solving riddles, and remaining in Lady Tottenham's favor. I, and many others, will surely find the method quite peculiar, though the outcome cannot be argued with. In the end, Lady Daventry prevailed. Will she join the marriage mart this season? A fine beauty, an accomplished mind, and fifty thousand will make her an incomparable this Season. She has won a life-altering prize. Now the true question remains: Who will win her hand?

My sources have informed me that this very fortunate woman will not settle for less than true love. Has someone already stolen her heart? Or is it available for the taking? Mr. Alexander Holland, a fellow guest at Birch House, has already been in steady pursuit of Lady Daventry. I suspect he is soon to have a great deal of competition.

For an article written by Lady Teignmouth, I was surprised by the lack of insults. The final lines brought a wave of heat to my cheeks. My fake courtship with Alexander was never meant to spread outside of Birch House, but now all of London would learn of it. I exhaled through my lips. "How did Lady Teignmouth discover the news so quickly?" I whispered.

Lady Tottenham smiled. "We are well-acquainted."

"You know her?" As far as I knew, there was no woman in London called 'Lady Teignmouth.' It was a *nom de plume*. After years of writing hateful gossip about the people of London, I doubted she would ever reveal her true identity.

Lady Tottenham gave a deep chuckle, lowering her voice. "I thought you were more clever than that."

I raised my eyebrows. The mischievous smile on her face made my jaw drop. "You?"

She touched one of her ginger curls, a gleam of pride lighting up her face. "It will be our secret."

I gasped. "You wrote about my sister and Lord Bampton? About Leonora and Mr. Ball?"

"The incident with Lord Bampton was what first brought you and your sister to my attention. Ever since then, I have been intrigued by you—a respectable widow with a wild younger sister and a very dismal future. I invited you here for a reason. I always hoped you would win."

All the new information I had gathered over the past day made my head hurt. A laugh escaped my throat. "I want to be angry with you for writing those articles, but how can I? You have improved my life forever."

She laughed, patting my arm. "It's the least I can do." She winked. "Now, since I am feeling well today, we must take advantage of it. Come with me to the study. We shall begin your training. You have a natural grace and elegance about you, but the mistress of Birch House must be *incomparable*."

I helped her to her feet with a nod. "I will never live up to you," I said with a nervous laugh.

"No, you will not." She looped her arm through my elbow with a pompous smile. "But I should like to see you try."

She led me out of the room with a chuckle.

I never would have expected it, but it seemed Lady Tottenham was now my only friend at Birch House.

In the study, she spent the entire morning showing me all the ledgers, listing all the servants that had been most loyal, and explaining all the positions of the household. She showed me the menu of her cook's most successful dishes, the housekeeper's schedule, the contact address for her steward, solicitor, and physician, and countless other items of business that would surely flee my mind after a night's rest. It would take more than one morning for me to memorize all of it. Lady Tottenham's high spirits gave me hope that she would live longer than expected. I had much to learn.

My head spun as I left the study two hours later. Perhaps I could write a letter to Henrietta. She would be positively bewildered to hear about all that had transpired in my life. I desperately craved her advice and good humor. I needed it now more than ever.

I held up my skirts to keep from tripping as I made my way down both flights of stairs toward the ground floor of the house. I doubted there was anyone amongst the guests who wanted to see me. They must have all been enjoying their time gossiping about me. I would ruin their conversation if I walked into the drawing room now.

Was Alexander in his room? Was he outside? I doubted he was in the mood for socializing. My heart pounded at the thought of facing him. I had to eventually. The recent memory of our kiss galloped through my mind.

A knock echoed at the front door as I passed through the vestibule. I paused, stepping behind the bannister to watch as the butler opened the door.

I felt the blood drain from my face as I heard the voice beyond the doorway.

"Yes, come in," The butler said as he stepped aside, giving me a clear view of the man crossing the threshold of Birch House.

It was Miles.

CHAPTER 26

ANNE

Miles took two steps forward, casting his gaze all the way up to the lofty ceiling.

He held a bouquet of blue hydrangeas.

I cowered behind the bannister, my heart in my throat as I observed him. It had been four years, but he had hardly changed. His skin was tanner, but his blue eyes were still the same. His light brown hair was combed neatly, and his ever-present smile flooded my heart with familiarity.

My throat dried up like an autumn leaf, but I managed to choke out his name. "Miles?"

His eyes found me instantly, a wide smile splitting his face. "Anne Dixon, is that truly you?"

I was frozen where I stood, but my head nodded. I didn't dare make a move toward him. He was a stranger at the same time that he was familiar. I had imagined our reunion so many times—I would run into his arms, he would hold me tight, promising to never let go again. But in my imaginary scenario, I hadn't felt shy or afraid like I did now. My feet rooted me to the checkered tiles, a nervous smile tugging on my mouth. My heart pounded as he strode toward me.

He snatched up my hand, pressing a kiss to the back of it. "You are..." he shook his head in awe. "You are beautiful. I had nearly forgotten your face."

I seemed to have forgotten how to speak. I stared up at him. I would have been less shocked to have seen a ghost. My legs shook beneath my skirts, but there was nothing I could do to steady myself. Miles was here. He was standing right in front of me. He looked even more handsome than I remembered. He extended the blue hydrangeas with a charming smile. I took them, laughing with disbelief.

"How long have you been back in London?" I asked in a breathless voice.

He held tight to my fingers. "Only a few days."

"How did you manage to find me?"

He sighed, pressing his lips together. "I encountered my brother, Alexander, yesterday, and he mentioned that you were also a guest at Birch House. I came as quickly as I could." His adoring gaze traced every inch of my face. I struggled to compose my thoughts.

"I heard that your meeting with him was less than amicable." At the reminder of their brawl, I noticed a hint of bruising on Miles's nose, one side more swollen than the other.

"Yes, unfortunately Alexander has always resorted to violence to resolve his conflicts." He shook his head with a frown. "He tried his hardest to prevent me from seeing you again, but I would not allow it. I've missed you so very much, Anne." He pulled me into an embrace, tugging me close to his chest. He smelled of pipe smoke with a hint of blue hydrangeas. I wanted to enjoy the closeness I had been waiting so long for, but his words had struck an unpleasant chord in my mind.

I pulled back with a scowl, my heart sinking. "How did Alexander try to prevent you from seeing me?"

His brow creased, and he looked down at the floor. "He threatened me against coming here. He said you didn't care to see me again."

"That isn't true!" I shook my head fast. "He told *me* that you had changed your mind about the letter you wrote to me from India."

Miles's eyes widened. "No." He shook his head, taking both my hands in his. "I meant every word. I don't know why my brother would tell such horrible lies to keep us apart." His jaw tightened. "I should have known that his word couldn't be trusted."

My heart ached, sending waves of dread through my chest. I thought of the night before, when Alexander told me that Miles had changed his mind. Alexander had admitted to starting the fight between them, and then that very night, he had kissed me and made his feelings obvious. Had it been his last attempt to win me over before Miles arrived? A sense of betrayal crept through my heart. Why would he lie so blatantly?

"Have I upset you?" Miles leaned down to look at my eyes.

I shook my head in an effort to clear it. "No. Forgive me, I'm a little confused, that is all." I gave a shaky smile.

"I hope there is no confusion regarding my feelings for you."

I met his gaze. I wanted to say there wasn't, but that

would be a lie. Alexander had pointed out the vital truth that Miles had chosen India over me, even if he did regret his decision. I had tried to justify it over the years, but my heart had protested. Miles was a rope I clung to in order to survive the trials of life, but he had left me swinging helplessly off the edge of a cliff for two years. I had forgiven him over time, continuing to romanticize all the emotions I felt for him. But now, as familiar as his face was, I felt like I was looking at a stranger.

His arrival had overwhelmed me. The flowers, the embrace, his hands wrapped so tightly around mine. My fingers were cold and limp. We couldn't return instantly to our relationship from nearly four years prior. Time had severed our bond, and I felt keenly the distance that had grown between us. We needed time to become acquainted again.

The joy I had felt upon seeing him walk through the door had been dampened by the suspicion that Alexander had lied to me. A fresh stab of pain struck my heart.

"We have been apart for a very long time." My voice was weak. I stared at his cravat instead of his face. "I—I hardly know what to think."

He nudged one finger under my chin, bringing my gaze back to his. "Time cannot steal what we have. The bond we share has carried me through many long months at sea. After you married, I thought I would never see you again. It tortured me." He gave a soft smile. "I would be the most fortunate man in the world to be granted a second chance to win your heart."

I had been yearning to hear those words for so long. My delight only lasted a few seconds before it was replaced with unease. What would he think if he knew I had kissed Alexander not once, but twice? How would he react if he learned that

Alexander had practically handed me his heart the night before? I swallowed the tightness in my throat.

Had Alexander truly lied to me?

I took a deep breath. I didn't know how to respond. I couldn't think clearly with Miles standing so close. He may not have run to me before leaving for India, but he had run to me now. That must have meant something. I had to believe he was genuine, or the last four years of dreaming would have been for nothing. This was the moment I had longed for. I had to seize it without fear, or I might lose my opportunity all over again.

"The—the flowers are lovely," I stammered, burying my nose in the tiny blue petals. I sniffed back my sudden emotion. "They remind me of my childhood."

Miles grinned. "I knew you would like them. I always imagined you with a bouquet of blue hydrangeas at our wedding."

The words, *our wedding,* sent a spiral of nervous butterflies through my stomach. My gaze flew to his.

Miles laughed. "Forgive my boldness, but I want you to know for certain that my intentions have not altered with time. I fully intend to honor the proposal I offered you in my letter."

I gave a quick nod, my breath shaking on the way out.

"You don't need to answer me now, but I invite you to think on it." Miles gave me a reassuring smile.

"It has been an eventful two days. Forgive me if I do not seem like myself."

He raised his brows with a curious look. "What has been so eventful?"

I cursed my mind for instantly jumping to the kiss from the night before. My new inheritance was the most eventful part of the day, but somehow that kiss and Alexander's words had felt just as significant. Just as world-shaking.

"Did you read anything about me in the papers this morning?" I asked.

Miles shook his head with a frown. "No."

I wrung my hands together in front of me. "Not the gossip issue from Lady Teignmouth?"

"I haven't read anything." His brow creased with concern. "What did she write about you?"

I almost told him, but Lady Tottenham's voice from the staircase made me jump.

"Who might this young man be?"

I whirled around. She held tight to the bannister as she descended the final few stairs. Miles stepped forward to assist her, extending his hand with a bow. "Mr. Miles Holland at your service, my lady."

Lady Tottenham pressed a hand to the bosom of her vibrant yellow gown. "Holland? A relation of our dear Alexander?"

Miles nodded with one of his charming smiles. "Ah, yes. I am his elder brother."

Lady Tottenham cast me a delighted glance. "Where is he now? Has he not come to greet you?"

Miles stepped closer to me. "I came to call upon Lady Daventry first and foremost."

A crease formed in Lady Tottenham's brow, but it quickly faded away. "Oh, you must have come to congratulate her on her inheritance." She eyed the bouquet of flowers. "I will send a servant to fetch Alexander from outside."

Panic set into my limbs. "That will not be necessary."

"Why not? Mr. Holland ought to congratulate Alexander as well." Lady Tottenham cast a smile in Miles's direction. "Surely you must know that Lady Daventry has been courting

Alexander throughout this entire house party. It is my hope that they will soon be engaged."

She bustled to the nearest footman. My heart sank through the floor. I had already told her that the courtship had been fake. Why was she pretending otherwise?

Miles's shoulders stiffened. His brow set in a deep crease, his mouth a firm line. I wanted to explain, but Lady Tottenham had already returned to my side. Her large green eyes never left Miles's face. "Would you like to attend Anne's congratulatory ball this evening? I have made arrangements for the finest food and music to celebrate my future heiress."

Miles shook the confusion from his expression, replacing it with a polite smile. "I would be honored, my lady."

CHAPTER 27

ALEXANDER

"You must read this," Victoria said, running across the lawn toward her sister. She held a sheet of foolscap in one hand.

I had been shooting targets with the other men while Octavia and Mrs. Pike observed at the table near the rose bushes. Victoria slapped the foolscap down on the table beside them. No one had expected the announcement that morning. The guests hadn't stopped gossiping about it for the past two hours. If I hadn't been so interested in the subject, I would have retreated to a room in the house where I could be alone. But instead, I tried to eavesdrop as Mrs. Pike and Octavia read the sheet of foolscap at the table. They read in silence, but I awaited their reaction.

I hadn't seen Anne since breakfast. Lady Tottenham had pulled her away, treating her like her new pet. I was desperate to speak with her about what had happened, not only about the shocking news of her inheritance, but the events of the night before. Kissing her had been a mistake, and so had telling her about Miles. I should have known she wouldn't believe me about his intentions. Aggravation scratched at every surface of my skin.

I raised my bow and released an arrow. It flew past the target.

I dropped the bow, surrendering to my curiosity. I walked casually toward the table. "What is it?"

The women looked up from the foolscap. Victoria wore a devious smile. "The latest issue of Behind the Fan. You are mentioned."

I pulled out a chair and sat down. My stomach sank as I read the article from start to finish, pausing on the final lines about the competition for Anne's hand.

"Devil take it," I muttered, forgetting about the ladies present.

Mrs. Pike gasped.

Octavia had hardly spoken to me since the fake courtship had begun. Her lips curled with a smug grin. "Are you actually afraid you might find competition?"

Victoria laughed. "The two of you have been inseparable. There is no man who could steal Lady Daventry's heart now. It is already yours." She grimaced. "Although, she could easily choose to seek a man with a title if that is her ambition."

I pinched the bridge of my nose, reading the entire passage again. I had always known I had competition. It wasn't the final lines that troubled me.

It was the fact that the news about Anne's fortune had already been made public.

I looked up to see a footman approaching the table. His white powdered wig and the tassels on his livery bounced with his exuberant strides. "Mr. Holland, Lady Tottenham requests your presence."

I nodded, pushing myself away from the table. What could Lady Tottenham want? She had never sent for me before. I followed the footman across the lawn and through the house until we rounded the corner to the vestibule.

My strides halted at the scene in front of me. Miles stood beside Anne, with Lady Tottenham facing both of them. Miles caught my gaze, his eyes flashing with a challenge. My worst fears were confirmed. My heart dropped to the floor.

My attention shifted to Anne, searching her face for any sign of her emotions. Was she overjoyed to see Miles? Did she resent me for kissing her? She was impossible to read. All I saw was the horror in her gaze as it darted between Miles and me.

"Ah, there you are, Mr. Holland," Lady Tottenham said with a smile. "Where have you been hiding this charming brother of yours?"

I was about to be the opposite of charming. I composed myself with a deep breath. Miles had always excelled at winning the favor of others because he had a much firmer grasp on his emotions. If he was angry, he rarely showed it in front of spectators. If he was going to be malicious, he did it in secret. Any move I made was being observed by Anne, and if I wanted to have any hope of her believing me, I needed to behave like a gentleman. "He recently returned from India, my lady." I was proud of how calm I sounded.

"Is that so?" Lady Tottenham turned toward Miles. "What brought you back to England?"

Miles cleared his throat. "A prior engagement." His gaze slid in Anne's direction.

I bit the inside of my cheek. "Brother, may I have a word outside?" My efforts to contain my vexation hadn't lasted as long as I hoped.

For a brief moment, Miles revealed a hint of smugness in his expression. "Gladly."

I started toward the door, waiting at the threshold.

"Please excuse me, my lady," Miles said to Lady Tottenham. "It was an honor to make your acquaintance, and it will be a delight to speak with you more this evening at the ball." He took Anne by the hand, pressing his lips to her fingers before starting in my direction. I held her gaze for several seconds until Miles blocked it.

The moment the door closed behind us, the smile fell from Miles's face. His nostrils flared as he followed me down the steps and out to the cobblestones. There wasn't another person in sight throughout the square. Fallen leaves stirred up from the ground with the breeze. "Did you come to tell Anne that you have revoked your proposal?" I asked.

Miles scoffed. "That is what you hope, isn't it? So you can continue courting her behind my back?"

I took one stride toward him, thoroughly tempted to finish the fight we had started the day before. "I fell in love with her, and you were not here to stop me."

"Well, I am here now, and I am not leaving until she's my wife."

I matched his sneer, my blood boiling. "Why the sudden change of heart? Could it have something to do with the news of her inheritance?"

He threw his hands in the air. "What inheritance? Everyone is speaking of it. Please do enlighten me."

I glared at him. "You read about it in the papers and rushed straight here to try to secure her hand. Don't deny it."

His face slowly betrayed him with a smile. "I didn't rush *straight* here. I did stop to purchase flowers on the way." He shook his head in disbelief. "Fifty thousand? All the young ladies of the ton combined could not offer such a sum. I had to read it twice to believe it."

"Does she know that you were aware of the news before coming here?"

"She will never know. And if you try to explain, she will not believe you. She trusts me completely." He loosened his cravat. "There is no point in having you here to complicate matters. You should leave as soon as possible."

His eyes lifted to mine in a casual manner, but I saw through the act. He must have felt some measure of fear that I was a threat to his plans. I had promised myself that I would do everything I could to protect Anne's heart, and that I would never leave her. Nothing could make me break that promise. "No." I crossed my arms. "I'm staying here."

Miles's jaw clenched.

The door to the house opened, making us both turn around.

Anne stood in the doorway. She hurried down the steps, a gust of wind taking hold of her hair. She stopped between us, her brows pulled tight with a scowl. "I cannot bear the thought of the two of you fighting again. You have enough bruises already." Her eyes darted to my face. She released a huffed breath. "Tonight is meant for celebration. Please do not ruin it.

There is archery on the back lawn. If you can behave yourselves, that would be a better use of your time than arguing."

Miles shot me a cold glance before extending his arm toward Anne. "Archery sounds diverting," he said with a smile, his voice taking on a tone far more pleasant than it had been moments before. "I wouldn't dream of ruining your celebration." He paused. "What are we celebrating, exactly?"

She took his arm, but I didn't miss the hesitancy in her movement. He started pulling her away, walking toward the side of the house, but her eyes flickered to my face. "Are you coming too?"

I felt a wave of satisfaction at the vexation on Miles's face. She had ignored his question. As much as I dreaded the thought of watching Miles fawn over her, my answer slipped out of my mouth. "Of course."

She held my gaze as Miles began walking. I caught pieces of their conversation. She explained the details of the game, her victory, and her inheritance. Miles was a far better actor than I had ever been. I almost believed his display of surprise and congratulations, as if he were only just learning of her new fortune.

The two targets were still set up on the back lawn. Mr. Hatcher held one of the bows, squinting across the lawn at the sight of the three of us approaching. The ladies at the table would have even more fresh gossip to keep them occupied after seeing Anne on another man's arm.

Introductions were made, and I could see the intrigue building behind Octavia's gaze. She whispered something to her sister behind her glove.

Miles picked up the available bow, swinging it at his side as he approached his position. He prepared his arrow and shot, missing the target by at least five feet. "It would seem I am out of practice!" he said with a boisterous laugh.

Anne's smile made my stomach sink.

He picked up the bow and proceeded to shoot six more arrows, missing the target each time.

That served as sufficient motivation. Mr. Hatcher had stepped away from the other target, so I claimed his place, choosing an arrow from the pile on the grass. I narrowed my eyes in concentration before letting it fly. It struck the second ring from the center with a solid thud.

I grinned. Miles swiftly picked up another arrow, his brow furrowed.

Anne stood directly between Miles and me, but took one step in my direction. "That was nearly perfect." She gave me an encouraging smile. Her features were shy—more reserved than usual. Perhaps she wanted to mend the awkwardness between us as much as I did.

"Would you like to try?" I held out the bow. "It's easier than you think." I made sure to speak loud enough for Miles to hear.

He lowered his bow, watching as Anne walked tentatively in my direction. Her cheeks were flushed, the curls around her face tossing in the light breeze. As she drew closer, the sunlight caught her irises, revealing the caution in her eyes.

I handed her the bow, lowering my voice to a whisper. "I'd wager you can shoot straighter than my brother." I gave a half-smile, testing her capability to endure any level of teasing.

Her lips twitched. "I'd wager I can shoot straighter than you as well."

I laughed. "Have you shot a bow before?"

"No." She lifted it with a scrutinizing look at the target. "I may require a little direction."

There was nothing stopping me from flirting with her while I had the chance. "Turn toward me." I placed one hand lightly on the small of her back. She met my gaze. "You will draw the arrow with your dominant hand. Hold the bow with the opposite." I guided her left hand to the center of the bow. "Keep a relaxed grip."

She nodded, her throat shifting with a swallow. I handed her an arrow. "Nock the end on the bow string here, and hold it steady between your index and middle fingers. Then draw it back." I stood behind her, adjusting the height of her elbow. My hand lingered on her upper arm. I touched the bare skin at the back of her shoulder, leaning close to her ear. "Relax your posture, aim, and shoot."

She released the arrow instantly. It struck the outside edge of the target. She turned to face me with a smile.

"Well done."

She raised the bow to try again. She lowered her voice. "Lady Tottenham knows about the ruse. She knew all along. There's no longer any reason to continue it, especially not if it causes more hostility between you and Miles."

I handed her an arrow. "It isn't a ruse to me. It never was."

Her wide eyes reminded me of her expression after I had kissed her. I leaned closer, keeping my voice as low as possible. "If there's anyone here who is putting on a ruse, it's Miles. He read the paper this morning. That's the only reason he's here."

Her expression flashed with hurt.

"That was an excellent shot, Anne." Miles jogged across the grass toward her. "You have bested me on your very first attempt. You must try the other target now." He waved her toward his side of the lawn.

I turned around to hide my vexation. I wasn't going to participate in Miles's game of tug-of-war with Anne. She looked conflicted enough already. I could see the signs of unrest in her features as she followed Miles to his target.

I had said my piece. There was nothing more I could do at the moment.

It was Anne's choice who to believe.

CHAPTER 28

ANNE

The green satin on my slippers matched my evening gown. I turned in a circle in front of the looking glass in my bedchamber. Jane had already left the room, leaving me alone with my reflection. My hair was piled high on the crown of my head, with a thin cream satin ribbon threaded throughout the curls. Lady Tottenham had given me a pair of emerald earrings and a necklace to wear. They were beautiful. I had never worn anything so expensive, but she had insisted that I look like a wealthy heiress for the celebration that evening. She claimed it would be a small gathering, consisting of the house party guests as well as her closest friends from London. Somehow I doubted her definition of 'small gathering.'

I was far less concerned with the other invitations that had been sent than I was with the one Lady Tottenham had extended to Miles that afternoon. He had lingered at the house for a few hours that afternoon, shooting arrows and walking the grounds with me, but he would soon be returning for the ball. He and Alexander would be in the same room once again.

During my walk with Miles that afternoon, he had told about his time in India. He claimed to have been successful in his trade, and that he had earned a great deal of money. If he had truly returned to England for me, even after finding success in India, then how could I doubt his devotion? How could I do anything but marry him after he had come on such a long journey? He had made his intentions clear, and now all he waited for was my answer.

But the thought of giving an answer brought on a swell of anxiety. I never would have questioned what I wanted a few weeks before. I had waited years for this, yet now I felt rushed and pressured and...

Terrified.

I did feel a sense of obligation toward him. If I didn't accept his proposal soon, he might grow impatient and leave me again. If I did accept soon, I would lose Alexander forever. That thought was enough to drive a dagger of grief through my chest.

I had no idea what to do.

All I knew, after my conversations with both brothers, was that one of them was lying.

I adjusted the gold bracelet that rested over my glove, meeting my own gaze in the mirror. Determination flashed in my eyes. I was going to find out who it was.

I arrived early in the hexagon room, standing near the door beside Lady Tottenham. Her rouge was a shade darker than usual for the occasion, her lips painted a deep burgundy. She wore a silk gold turban to match her gown with a white feather sticking out the top. "I don't expect a very large crowd, considering that the invitations were sent only yesterday. We will host another celebration next month when the news has spread further."

A flutter of excitement replaced my nerves for a brief moment. I had written a letter to my sister and her husband, as well as my dear friend Nora. The news would reach them in time for the second celebration. I missed them all terribly, and I was eager to see their reaction to my new circumstances. Lady Tottenham was helping me through the adjustment, but I still felt alone.

Victoria and Octavia had been avoiding me since the news had come out the day before.

For all I knew, Miles only wanted to marry me for the fortune.

Alexander and I had barely spoken since he kissed me by the pond. I had so many emotions swirling around my heart I could hardly keep track of them. I had no outlet; no friend to talk to.

I cast my gaze around the room. I had never seen it bathed in candlelight as it was. The rooftop window provided a view of the stars that was sure to impress the guests. The brown velvet chairs and the sofa had been moved against the wall, leaving the floor completely open for dancing. A refreshment table had been set up in the exercise hall, and the musicians gathered near the fireplace, tuning their instruments.

Lord Tottenham's many hunting prizes would serve as spectators for the ball that evening. I winced when I noticed the charred rabbit's face.

The guests arrived slowly over the following ten minutes. Lady Tottenham's estimation was quickly proven wrong. There were at least thirty people, besides the house party guests, who passed the threshold of the hexagon room. Lady Tottenham introduced me to each one. Most of her friends were couples, but there were also a number of young men and women with their chaperones who entered the room. I couldn't begin to memorize all of their names, but they were sure to remember mine. They had come solely to make my acquaintance—and to cast their envious stares in my direction.

I was swept away in a conversation with a tall gentleman and his wife, when I saw Miles enter the room. He cast his gaze across all six walls with a look of approval. He wore a formal dark grey jacket and white cravat, his hair golden in the candle-light. His presence made me straighten my shoulders. His eyes found me across the room, and a smile lit up his face. He made his way to my side.

I tried to focus on his approach, but Alexander had just stepped into the room. My heart leaped. His gaze met mine. His jaw was clean and smooth, and his dark hair fell in soft waves around his face. I never would have described Alexander as elegant, but his black jacket on his broad shoulders and white cravat made him look more proper and refined than any man in the room. But I knew appearances could be deceiving. For example, Lady Tottenham was proper and refined around her visitors, her eccentricities hidden flawlessly. No one would have guessed that she had been encouraging improper meetings between her young guests, forcing them to eat crickets, and locking them in rooms overnight.

Alexander could have been using his handsome face and teasing smiles to turn me against Miles. Likewise, Miles could have been using his charms to secure my fortune.

I tore my gaze away from Alexander as Miles reached me.

"You have never looked more ravishing." His wide smile put me at ease for a short moment.

"Thank you." I lifted my chin, trying to accept his compliment with confidence. Miles had never been so forward with his remarks in the past, nor with his displays of affection. He scooped up my hand and kissed it.

"This is such a peculiar room," he said with a look at the ceiling. "I find it fascinating."

"It's one of my favorite rooms in the house." I had already made a very distinct memory in that room. I almost smiled at the thought of Alexander using the pugilist as a pillow, but then a pang of sadness stole my humor.

"It does seem a peculiar choice for a ballroom," Miles whispered. "I would sooner host balls on the ground level in the parlor. That would be more easily accessible to guests of any age and physical capability." He examined the walls. "This room, however, would serve as an excellent withdrawing area during a party for drinking and cards, especially with the hunting prizes and rifles displayed."

I eyed his eager expression. "You seem to have given it a great deal of thought."

He laughed. "I am simply pointing out the obvious." He turned to face me. "May I beg the honor of your first dance this evening? You are sure to be a popular partner, so I must take my opportunity while I can."

"Of course." My gaze flickered over his shoulder. Alexander was approaching. I fiddled with the bracelet on my wrist, feigning deep interest in it.

"Good evening, Anne. Good evening, Miles." Alexander's voice was polite, which shocked me considering the discord between the two brothers.

Miles did not appear pleased to have him join us, but Alexander didn't seem to care.

Alexander regarded me with a smile. "I came to claim one of your dances, if I may."

My heart fluttered deep inside my chest. "My second dance is available."

He nodded, his dark eyes roaming my face. "I look forward to it."

Miles's expression remained stoic as he observed our conversation. Every word from Alexander's mouth, every expression on his face, confirmed what he had said to me that afternoon. *It isn't a ruse to me. It never was.* He took my hand, pressing his lips to my knuckles.

A wave of heat climbed my neck as Alexander walked away, and I prayed it didn't show on my face. Miles's gaze was hard as he watched his brother retreat into the crowd. "That was bold of him," Miles muttered.

"Why?" The word burst out before I thought better of it.

"He knows that you and I have been unofficially engaged for months. He already lied to try to keep us apart, and now he is flirting with you with the sole purpose of upsetting me." He shook his head with a sad smile. "It's almost as if he's trying to...convince you to withdraw from the arrangements we made before I arrived—as if he thinks you wouldn't be true to your word. He doesn't understand as I do what a loyal and true woman you are." His warm blue eyes had comforted me on many occasions, but now they induced a fresh wave of anxiousness. "It will serve us best to ignore him. We mustn't allow anything *or* anyone to come between us again."

I nodded, but my stomach was in knots.

After giving her guests a few more minutes to mingle, Lady

Tottenham signaled the musicians to begin the first dance. Miles led me to the center of the room, joining the line of dancers. I looked in his eyes as the steps began. His smile was as warm as it had always been, but it didn't have any effect on me. I felt hollow. Disappointment sank through my chest as we danced. I had dreamed of a moment like this for years, yet I felt nothing but apprehension as Miles stood across from me. His hand on my waist, our fingers intertwined, his intense gaze...it all fit the dream I had invented, but my reaction was not what I had expected. I felt like I was dancing with a ghost. Dread enveloped me as I realized that the time we had spent apart might have been the death of my connection to him. He was a stranger with a familiar face. That was all.

As we moved through the steps of the dance, I tried to calm the turmoil in my heart, but it raged on. The shield between us was caused by a hint of resentment. I had always assumed I would run into Miles's arms and marry him the moment he found me again, but perhaps I hadn't given myself enough credit. I was not as malleable as he thought.

Perhaps I wasn't quite as forgiving as *I* thought.

He hadn't even tried to save me from marrying the baron, and I had been excusing his actions as heartbreak ever since. Then he had left me waiting for another two years. He had returned with remorse, but not with an apology. His assumption that we could resume our courtship and become engaged as if nothing had happened—as if *I* had not grown or changed —had been silently irking me since he arrived that afternoon. I had been too afraid to admit it to myself.

When the dance ended, Miles led me to the wall with the glass case full of birds. It was the wall farthest from where Alexander stood. He was in the middle of a conversation with a pretty young woman and a couple who must have been her parents. I resisted a pang of jealousy. My skin was hot, and I couldn't manage to cool it down.

The room was overly crowded and the dance had drained my energy. I had always done well at large parties and social gatherings, but today was different. My stays felt too tight, my hair was heavy, and my gloves made my arms itch. I took a shaky breath.

"Are you all right?" Miles cast me a look of concern, pulling my gaze away from Alexander.

"Yes," I lied.

His brow furrowed deeper. "I'll fetch you a glass of water."

I thanked him with a look as he weaved through the crowd toward the door.

The moment he was gone, a woman similar in age to Lady Tottenham swooped in to begin a conversation with me. I was as polite as possible, offering smiles and thoughtful responses, and inquiring after her life and situation. I wondered if she could see the painstaking effort behind it. Nothing I did or said felt natural, not after the realization that my connection to Miles might have been damaged. Could it be mended? Who was I without my hope for him? How had I allowed myself to become so dependent on a dream? I felt like an imposter in my own skin, the room slowly shrinking in around me.

Miles returned to my side with a glass, and I drank it quickly enough to draw a look of surprise from his face. As soon as the woman I had been conversing with walked away, I turned to face him. "I have a question for you, and I beg you to answer honestly."

Miles's brows lifted. "I have always been honest with you, Anne."

"I know—I just..." I paused. Did I actually know? I scowled at the floor before lifting my chin. "When you called upon me here this afternoon, were you already aware of my inheritance?"

He shook his head immediately. "No. I already told you that. I was as surprised as anyone when you told me the news."

I searched his face, scrutinizing every detail.

His eyes flashed with hurt. "Do you doubt me?"

"No, I—" My chest tightened with guilt.

"Has my brother been planting ideas in your head? I trust you are mature enough to know your own mind." Miles took my empty glass from my hand, cradling my elbow gently. "What more can I do to prove my devotion to you?"

I didn't have a chance to answer before the music began, signaling the start of the second dance. I searched the crowd for Alexander. My heart picked up speed when I saw that he was only a few feet away. I stepped forward, grateful to avoid the question Miles had asked me, even though my insides twisted with nervousness at the thought of dancing with Alexander.

Dancing had never troubled me before. But for some reason, I envisioned myself tripping over my feet if he was touching me.

CHAPTER 29

ANNE

Alexander led me to the dance floor, one hand on the small of my back. The dance opened with a pirouette. He took my hand, wrapping the other around my waist. We turned in a circle, his eyes locked on mine. The bruise on his cheek had lightened already, but it had spread into the side of his hairline. I wanted to take the opportunity to speak with him, but my voice felt useless as I focused on keeping my feet in motion.

"I haven't had a chance to properly congratulate you," he said, a soft smile on his lips. His eyebrows lifted. "I was shocked beyond words to learn what the prize was. I imagine your reaction was the same?" His breath brushed against my neck as the steps brought us closer, sending a shiver across my shoulder blades.

I took a moment to gather my thoughts. I had been

expecting him to open the dance with an argument about how I shouldn't trust Miles.

"I thought it was some sort of trick Lady Tottenham was playing on me." I gave a quiet laugh. "I can hardly believe it's true."

His smile eased my nerves. "How do you feel? Are you happy? Overwhelmed?"

"Both."

We stepped apart, then together, our hands and arms crossing in the air between us. He released one of my hands, and I turned slowly beneath his arm.

"It's difficult to comprehend that this entire house will be mine one day." I shook my head, sharing in his look of bewilderment. "I have been struggling to envision such a future for myself. I feel like it's all a dream, and I might awake at any moment. I might be just like Lady Tottenham one day, hosting house parties and playing games in the parlor...it seems absurd."

Alexander laughed. He lowered his voice, a teasing glint in his eyes. "And surely you will boast of your extensive taxidermy collection at every opportunity."

A laugh bubbled out of my throat. "I confess that is my least favorite part of the inheritance."

"Truly?" His brows shot upward. "Might I assume then that you would have no objection giving it to me?"

The music had built to a lively tempo. My smile felt uncontrollable as I took both Alexander's hands for a rigadoon. "I would, but I'm afraid I cannot trust you to take proper care of the poor creatures. The pugilist can attest to my hesitation."

He chuckled, his hand wrapping around my waist again. I

felt the pressure of every finger. "That was an accident, of which you are just as much to blame," he said in a low voice.

I scoffed. "How was I to blame?"

His eyes settled on my face. "Your smile is far too beautiful, and I was distracted."

My heart leaped. My feet refused to finish the final steps of the dance. The final note of the violin rang out. Alexander bowed, and I curtsied. I felt the weight of many gazes on us. If the guests had read Lady Teignmouth's, or rather—Lady Tottenham's article, they would soon discover that Alexander was the man who was mentioned at the end of the narrative.

Before we had taken three steps away from the dance floor, a gentleman approached me, requesting my next dance. The same pattern continued until the start of the next, and the next, until all my dances were claimed. Somehow Miles ended up at my side between every set. He fetched me punch and water and anything he perceived that I needed. His constant presence at my side was sure to cause confusion among the visitors who assumed, because of the gossip article, that I was courting Alexander.

When I finished my last dance, I returned to my place on the outskirts of the floor. I fanned my face with one hand. Miles stepped up beside me. "Would you take a walk in the corridor with me? The temperature is much more tolerable there."

I gave a quick nod, eager to escape the heat of the room. He extended his arm, leading me out the door. I told myself we wouldn't venture past the refreshment table in order to remain well within sight of any passing guests. This was no longer Lady Tottenham's house party. There wasn't a lack of regard for common rules and propriety in the air tonight. If Miles and I were seen, the consequences could be dire.

"Where are we going?" I asked in a nervous whisper. He was leading me in the direction of the blue library. I practically dug my heels into the floor, stopping him as we turned the corner.

He moved to face me, his chest rising and falling with a deep breath. "I wanted to be alone with you."

"I only needed a breath of fresh air." I swallowed, glancing nervously over my shoulder. The corridor was empty. "I feel much improved. Let us return to the hexagon room."

I started to turn, but Miles grabbed my wrist. "Wait— Anne. It hurt me to witness your uncertainty regarding me."

The despair in his eyes stabbed at my heart. My pulse quickened. "I'm sorry if I have seemed uncertain, but my life has changed drastically in a matter of days. I have much to contend with. Your arrival was sudden and unexpected, and I haven't had time to understand my feelings."

He released my wrist, running his finger up and down my arm. His striking blue eyes captured mine. "That does make sense. However, I still want you to understand *my* feelings. I want you to understand how I adore you. I have traveled thousands of miles to be here with you." His eyes traced over my features one by one, settling on my lips. "If that alone does not prove my devotion, I hope this will." He took me by the waist with one hand, nudging my chin up with the other. I hardly had time to think before he was kissing me.

I froze, trapped between him and the wall behind me. My dreams of kissing Miles, of hearing him profess his love, had never felt like *this*. His lips, eager and harsh, reminded me of the baron's. Panic set into my bones. I squirmed away, breaking the seal of our lips. My heart pounded against my ribs. "Miles!" I scolded in a breathless voice. I glanced over his shoulder. "Someone could have seen that."

"I'm sorry." He caressed my cheek. "I couldn't help myself."

I didn't know how to respond. His gaze was light and dark at the same time. I didn't feel safe. The incident that had forced me into my horrible marriage had started just like this.

A kiss in a dark corridor. Cold panic scratching over my spine. A man who wouldn't take no for an answer.

He leaned down to kiss me again. I turned my face at the last second, and his kiss landed on my cheek. I struggled to move away as he trailed three forceful kisses down my neck. He backed me closer to the wall. "You are so beautiful." He traced one finger over my collarbone before dipping his head down to kiss it.

"Miles, stop," I demanded. I pushed against his chest, but he persisted, as if he thought I would eventually succumb to his advances. Anger surged inside me, but it was accompanied by a fresh wave of fear. I had experienced first-hand the damage that could come to one's reputation by being kissed by a man in a dark corridor during a ball. I had taken the fall for Henrietta last time, but no one had saved me. I was on my own again. I gritted my teeth, pushing against him with all my might.

He flew backward, and for a moment, I thought my own strength had caused him to stumble. But then I saw Alexander with two handfuls of the back of Miles's jacket.

"Did you not hear her?" he barked. "She told you to stop."

Miles caught his balance before shoving hard against

Alexander's shoulders. He lunged forward. "What I do with Anne is none of your business," he growled close to Alexander's face.

"I've made it my business."

Miles wore an amused smile, but anger still flashed behind his eyes. "You didn't even know her a month ago, yet you have been acting like you have some possession over her! Try all you like to take what is mine. You've never succeeded." He shoved Alexander hard in the chest.

A woman's gasp came from near the refreshment table behind them. Alexander lowered his voice to a harsh whisper. "Leave before you cause a greater scene."

"I'm not going anywhere." Miles's jaw tightened.

"Anne's reputation is at stake. She has never had more attention on her, and people are searching for anything to scrutinize."

"Perhaps *you* should leave," Miles said.

Alexander shook his head, standing his ground with folded arms.

Miles glanced at me. I stood by the wall, too stunned to move. My heart pounded fast. "Do you want me to leave?" he asked in a soft voice.

I gave a minuscule nod, a surge of emotion rising in my throat.

His gaze darkened, and he looked down at the floor. "Very well," he said in an abrupt voice. "But I will return tomorrow. We will sort this out." He cast me a reassuring look before turning his back on Alexander.

I held my breath as he walked away, listening to every footstep as he moved down the staircase. When I could no longer hear him, I rushed around the corner, covering my face with my hands. I didn't stop walking until I reached the doors of the blue library. Tears streamed down my cheeks despite my effort to contain them. They soaked into my gloves.

"Anne—" Alexander's voice made me stop. He stepped around me. I peeked at him through my fingers before lowering my hands.

"That was mortifying." I took a shaky breath. "Did anyone else see?"

Alexander shook his head. His eyes were toffee brown in the candlelight, and the mere sight of him reined in my fears.

"I have never seen Miles behave in such a way. It frightened me." I swatted at the tears on my cheeks. The raw concern on Alexander's face was like a balm to my heart, even though it still raced uncontrollably. My legs shook.

He took a step toward me, gathering me close to his chest. He smelled of spices and leather. I melted against him, tucking my elbows against my sides as his arms wrapped all the way around me. "You're safe."

I knew it. I felt it deep in my bones. Alexander would never do anything to hurt or frighten me. I nodded, but my face was still buried in his jacket. I looked up, and his arms loosened around me. I didn't want them to.

"Do you think you can make one more appearance at the party?" he asked. He swiped a tear off my cheek with his thumb. "Or would you rather go to your room? I can deliver your excuses for you if you'd like. I can say that you felt unwell and needed to retire early. It's reasonable that you would feel out of sorts in such a hot room...I could even say that you faint-ed." His quick solutions continued spilling out, but all I could do was stare up at his face and the goodness in his eyes. My heart hammered, demanding that for once, I listen.

I was in love with him.

"What would you like me to do?" he asked when I didn't respond. His sincere eyes gazed into mine. What I wanted was for him to pull me close again and hold me until the party was over, but I didn't dare make such a request.

"I-I think I will return to my room. My watery face will not go unnoticed." I laughed, rubbing the tip of my nose.

Alexander smiled, and I saw the adoration in his gaze. He closed his hands around my heart with that one look. "Your watery face is lovely, but I much prefer to see it without tears." He paused. "Will you be all right?"

I nodded, but a hint of worry crossed my mind. What if Miles hadn't left the house? What if he was downstairs waiting for me? He hadn't seemed like himself that night, and I dreaded the thought of encountering him again. Fear scratched at my skin.

Alexander seemed to read my mind. His brow furrowed. "Would you feel comfortable in the study? If it wouldn't put you under scrutiny, I would walk you to your room, but it may be best to wait until the party is over."

I gave a quick nod. "That would be wise."

I unfurled myself from his arms, taking a step back. My legs still shook, but my pulse had returned to normal. Before he could leave, a question burst out of my mouth, completely unbidden. "Will you tell me what happened between you and Miles?"

He stopped, his mouth a firm line.

"Tell me everything." My voice broke. "I am prepared to hear it. I want to know how he has hurt you and I want to know all the lies he has told." I sniffed. "I am through with hiding from the truth simply because it scares me."

Alexander took a heavy breath, glancing behind him. "I will try to be brief."

I nodded my agreement.

He began in a quiet voice. "I was mischievous as a child, but I grew out of it. Miles seemed to have an opposite trajectory."

I stopped him. "You didn't grow out of it completely."

"I'm not speaking of harmless mischief and teasing. In his adolescence, Miles disregarded every rule my parents tried to enforce. There was once a time he stole a family heirloom—our grandmother's necklace—and sold it, keeping the money for himself. When the investigation was underway, he convinced our elder brother that I was the one who stole it, and with their combined efforts, they convinced my parents of the same. He once wounded one of our horses by riding too recklessly. Because of the reputation I had accrued from his lies, he easily put the blame on me. I was his scapegoat. That is why I was sent away to school rather than being educated at home as my brothers had."

My heart sank. "That is horribly unfair."

"You haven't heard the worst of it." His jaw tightened. He seemed hesitant to continue.

"Please tell me," I whispered.

His hesitant eyes met mine, but he nodded. "Four years ago, I had just finished my education at Oxford. I was working with the local parish near my family estate to become part of the clergy. During that spring and summer, Miles lived at the house as well."

That was the summer I lived with my aunt and uncle. It was just before my fateful Season with Henrietta, when I had become engaged to the baron.

"University, and his time in London, had made Miles a rake," Alexander continued. "I had seen him flirting with maids in the household on many occasions, promising a future he could never give them. In the months that we both lived at our family estate, it was discovered that one of the scullery maids was with child. Miles had already left for London, but he returned to pay the young woman to claim that I was the one who had romanced her. No matter how I denied it, her claims were firm against me. My local parish learned of the disgrace, and my plans for a profession in the church became impossible."

I covered my mouth with one hand. My stomach turned.

Alexander's brow furrowed as he watched my signs of alarm. "I was forced to change my course. I was eventually accepted at an inn of court to study the law. After my studies there were complete, I moved to York, where I was able to use the connections I had made in school to obtain enough work to pay off my educational debts. I finally came ahead and began making a respectable living. I still hoped to regain the respect of my parents, but without a confession from Miles, I doubted it was possible."

He crossed his arms over his chest, looking down at the floor. "Two years ago, just before his embarkation, Miles found me in York. He didn't have enough money for his passage and settlement in India. Like a fool, I made a bargain with him. I would lend him money for his passage and lodging if he would repay me upon his return, and confess the truth to our parents of what had happened two years before. He agreed, took my money, and boarded the next ship. But he didn't confess."

I swallowed hard against the lump in my throat. The summer Miles had romanced the maid...he had been writing me love letters. He had courted me in London at the start of the season before returning home for a time. Now that I knew the story, I felt ill. When I had written to him about my plight with the baron, he had been too preoccupied with paying the maid to blame Alexander to come to my rescue. I had assumed he was heartbroken. I had pitied him. I had felt guilty for years.

Hot anger pulsed through my veins, the heat growing as embarrassment bloomed in my chest. How could I have not seen through his act? His charms hadn't only affected *me*. He used them to his advantage with everyone he met.

I looked up at Alexander's face and the raw concern in his eyes. He hadn't enjoyed telling the story; he knew how it would hurt me. My skin burned with mortification. He had tried to warn me so many times, but I had been blind. Alexander's entire family and parish had turned against him because of what Miles had done. He was owed money that Miles still withheld from him, refusing to take responsibility for his own actions.

I still tasted Miles's uninvited kiss on my lips. In all aspects of his character, he was just as awful, if not even worse, than the baron. The realization made my heart sting.

"That is detestable," I finally choked out. "I'm sorry." My throat tightened around any additional words. My eyes stung.

Alexander drew closer, a hint of frustration in his gaze. "I wanted you to know, but I didn't want the information to hurt you." He searched my eyes. "It's a lot to bear. I'm sorry if I have overwhelmed you."

Footsteps beyond the corridor made me jump back. People were still visiting the refreshment table. If anyone turned the corner, we would no longer be hidden. It wasn't wise to continue our conversation. Alexander looked over his shoulder before taking my hand softly in his. "I will explain your absence to Lady Tottenham. You will be safe in the study."

I nodded. He gave my fingers a squeeze before stepping away. I felt his gaze on me until I was safely behind the door of the blue library.

CHAPTER 30

ALEXANDER

Anne didn't stir as I opened the study door. A light snore escaped her nose as I approached. I smiled. She would murder me if she knew I had even heard the sound. She lay on the blue sofa, one arm tucked under her head. Her dark lashes were like crescents on her cheeks where the last of her tears had dried. I hated to wake her out of such a beautiful slumber, but I also hated to think of her sleeping the entire night on a stiff sofa. The room was dim, lit only by a single candle. The wick had almost burned out.

"Anne," I whispered.

Her eyes fluttered open with a dazed look.

"You're an heiress now, you mustn't ever sleep on a sofa again."

The party had ended several minutes before. Lady Tottenham had been concerned about Anne's whereabouts, but I had explained that she was feeling unwell in her room.

Thankfully Lady Tottenham seemed to be taking a break from her midnight parlor games, so the house was quiet. All the remaining house guests had gone to bed.

Anne stretched her arms, brushing her hair off her face with an embarrassed smile. Her eyes were still half-closed.

"You look exhausted."

"I'm not." She tried to sit up.

I hid my amusement the best I could, but it was to no avail. "I'll carry you." I slipped one arm behind her knees and the other around her back, lifting her off the sofa.

She laughed. Her eyes were wide open now. "You are going to drop me."

"Are you underestimating my strength?"

Her laugh rustled the hair at the nape of my neck, sending a thrill racing across my skin. She squeezed her eyes shut as I descended the stairs, clinging tight to my collar. I could easily envision a future where we stayed up late together and she fell asleep on the sofa. I would carry her to her room every night if it made her smile the way she was now. Eventually she would trust me not to drop her.

I struggled to open the door to Anne's bedchamber, which only made her laugh harder. She helped turn the knob, and I used her legs to push the door open. By the time I reached her bed, we were both laughing. I dropped her softly on top of the blankets.

She blinked up at me. I would never kiss her again unless I knew it was welcome, and her eyes were tugging me forward. I fought the temptation. My sense of propriety had been tainted by Lady Tottenham's house party. I was still a gentleman.

"Sleep well," I said.

"Alexander." She sat up, curls askew. "Thank you."

My hand was on the doorknob. I found the strength to turn it. "Goodnight."

She returned my smile. "Goodnight."

I closed the door behind me with a deep breath. She couldn't possibly be more beautiful and enchanting, especially with her wild curls and drooping eyes. If I had taken any part in drying her tears, I would sleep soundly.

I walked down the corridor to my bedchamber. When I opened the door, I found a folded note just inside the room. "What the devil?" I muttered. I had assumed the midnight parlor games were over.

I unfolded it, scanning the page.

Alexander,

I have in my possession a banknote for two hundred pounds. It is yours if you leave Birch House and stop meddling in my affairs. Meet me outside Russell's at nine o'clock tomorrow morning to receive your payment. In addition, I offer you two thousand pounds after Anne and I are married and the old crone dies. If you require further incentive, I will personally arrange for your transportation to York.

Miles

ANNE

"Toads cannot hurt me," I told myself as I waded into the cold pond water. The early morning air held a slight chill, but I wouldn't allow it to change my mind. I didn't stop walking until my dress was completely submerged. In one fast motion, I ducked my head under the water. A delighted laugh escaped me as I broke the surface.

I never would have admitted it to Alexander, but I had been tempted to test the water ever since I had seen him swimming in it. My sole purpose was to prove to myself that I could do something that seemed completely opposite of my nature. In the past, I would have scolded any young lady who did something so untamed as swimming in a murky pond at dawn.

In the past, I would have never been able to let go of Miles.

All the years I had spent desperately trying to grasp at some sort of control over my future had left my hands raw. I had clung to Miles without noticing the damage he caused, and the true character he possessed. My own sense of worth had changed, and it had nothing to do with the fifty thousand pounds. I deserved someone who wanted me before I had anything but my heart to offer.

I trudged out of the pond, stepping on the wet hem of my dress. I tripped, landing on my belly in a puddle of mud. Scrambling to my feet, I picked up my skirts and walked back to the house. I had informed Jane of my plan, so she awaited me outside the door with a linen towel. She didn't question my actions, but I saw the hidden dismay in her eyes.

Ever since the announcement about Lady Tottenham's will, the servants at Birch House had been particularly attentive to me. They knew that I would one day be responsible for their employment.

I took a hot bath, leaving my hair time to dry in rags before Jane arranged it for breakfast. My anticipation over seeing Alexander was a mixture of nervousness and excitement.

Somehow, I had to make my feelings known to him.

I had never been so bold in my entire life, but Lady Tottenham seemed to have influenced me. Nothing good came from waiting and wishing. If I knew that I loved Alexander, I had to tell him. With the house party winding down to its final days, Lady Tottenham was sure to have a full schedule. It would be difficult to find a moment alone with him.

There was also the matter of breaking my ties with Miles. My heart ached, resisting the idea. He had etched himself on my heart long ago, leaving behind an open wound. But now, that love was like a scar. It had grown over and healed, and nearly disappeared, but it would always be there to remind me of him. The memory of him was dear to me, but the truth of his character had tainted it. I had fallen in love with his facade, and now that the layers were peeled back, my feelings were gone.

I took a deep breath, preparing for what was sure to be another eventful day. My heart fluttered with nerves as I walked into the breakfast room.

Alexander wasn't there. I sat beside Victoria instead. She was the only woman besides Lady Tottenham who didn't seem to despise me after learning of my prize.

"You look lovely," I told her as I glanced yet again at the empty doorway.

"As do you." She smiled, touching one of her blonde curls. "You must be so very excited to form your new wardrobe. You will be able to afford the most fashionable fabrics and trims." She sighed. "You must allow me to come with you to the modiste when you plan your new evening gowns."

I hadn't even thought about building a new wardrobe, but I supposed it would be essential if I planned to attend events in London. Given the public knowledge of my wealth, dressing the part would be expected of me. I hated to speak of the money that was not yet mine, especially with a living, breathing Lady Tottenham sitting in the same room. "Of course," I said in in a quiet voice. "If I can, I will buy you a gown as well."

Her eyes lit up.

Victoria prattled on about her favorite fashions of the year, and I listened, taking note of her observations. I kept one eye on the door.

Alexander never came to breakfast. A walk around the square was planned for the later hours of the morning, but he didn't join us for that either. A seed of worry planted itself in my stomach. Where was he?

I matched my pace with Lady Tottenham's. She had informed me at breakfast that she had further training required of me that afternoon in the study, but I hadn't spoken to her since. The day was cold enough that she didn't require a maid to follow her with a fan, but she did have one holding her parasol. Her pace was slow, her cheekbones appearing more prominent than I remembered. Her mood indicated that she was feeling well, but her appearance contradicted it.

"I wonder where Alexander is this morning," I said, wringing my fingers together. "Have you seen him at all?"

She glanced at me with one eyebrow raised. "I haven't. Perhaps he feels disregarded after your constant attention to his brother yesterday." Her unmasked disapproval made my steps falter.

"There is a long history between Miles and me." I searched for the words to explain what I meant.

"I suspected as much. Tell me more."

I explained as much of the history as I could without boring her. "Yesterday was the first time I had seen him before marrying the baron. He claims to have noble intentions, but...I have lost trust in him."

Lady Tottenham's nose wrinkled. "The moment I met him I smelled a fortune hunter. I have cast away a multitude of such men in the decades since my husband's death. I have quite a sense for it. Mr. Miles Holland is charming, but marrying him will not result in your happiness. I strongly advise you against it. I do not like him. Not one bit. My endorsement will be for dear Alexander until my dying breath." She shot me a stern look.

I straightened my shoulders. "I assure you. My decision became clear yesterday evening." I took a deep breath. "You were right. I do love Alexander."

"Good." She pursed her lips. "If you had married his brother, I fully planned to retract my inheritance."

I hid the shock from my face.

"Has Alexander proposed?" she asked.

I shook my head. "Not...officially. I am worried about why he isn't here today. He and Miles have fought before, and I dread what will happen if they do so again. I cannot bear the thought of a duel." My heart sank. Would it come to pistols or swords? Terror shot up my spine. What if they had met at dawn?

Lady Tottenham sighed. "With Mr. Miles Holland's inept

ability at archery, I would wager my entire fortune on Alexander's success were they to duel."

I scowled at the ground as we walked, my mind racing.

"Oh, stop fretting, child. Alexander will return soon enough, I am certain of it. When he does, I will provide you with an opportunity to speak with him alone." She winked. "I have proven my competency at the task before, have I not?"

She most certainly had.

Her devious smile left me with no question that she had been responsible for the locked door of the hexagon room the night I discovered the key.

My stomach still twisted with dread at the notion that Alexander might have dueled Miles. Their argument hadn't been completely settled the night before, and Miles was undoubtedly angry about how Alexander had intervened. If their quarrel over me put either of them in danger, I would never forgive myself.

The day carried us into the afternoon, and Victoria took me to her room to show me her favorite fashion plates. I enjoyed her company, but a sinking feeling followed me everywhere I went. At dinner, Alexander's chair was still empty.

Lady Tottenham took a bite of roasted pigeon. "Mr. Miles Holland attempted to call upon you this afternoon," she said to me with a look of distaste. "I told him you were not accepting visitors."

My eyes flew to her face. "Did he mention Alexander?"

Lady Tottenham shook her head. "I'm afraid not. His location is still a mystery."

I wanted to thank her for sending Miles away, but I couldn't find the words. I wasn't ready to face him again, though it would have been helpful to ask him if he had seen

Alexander. This was the second time he had disappeared without warning, and it troubled me even more than the first. How dangerous *was* Miles? Had he done something to harm Alexander? The thought made me ill. I set down my fork.

When the meal was over, the ladies withdrew to the drawing room. Octavia's continuous notes on the pianoforte clunked soundlessly. Lady Tottenham arranged a game of hunt the slipper. I tried to enjoy myself, but my worries consumed me. My distrust of Miles had been building all day, flooding my mind with paranoia.

I stared out the dark window and the raindrops that fell on the glass until Octavia finally abandoned the bench of the pianoforte.

CHAPTER 31

ALEXANDER

Dim candlelight glowed in the windows of Birch House as I approached the front door. Waiting until nightfall to return had been essential in order to prevent any suspicion from Miles. After collecting my two hundred pounds from him at Russell's, I had agreed to leave Birch House by the next morning.

But that didn't mean I would leave London completely.

With the money I had secured, I had spent the day searching for a lease on an apartment near Lockhart square so I could court Anne properly and begin building my professional connections in Town. If Anne remained here, I couldn't possibly leave her to go to York.

I could hardly believe that Miles had searched the bedchambers the night before to discover which one was mine and left a note inside my door. He was desperate, and he viewed me as his greatest threat. I had almost crumpled the note, but I had stopped myself. In his desperation, Miles had made a fatal mistake. I could show his note to Anne at any moment as proof of his character and intentions...if that hadn't been made clear enough to her already.

I was no longer afraid that Miles would win. I had felt a sense of peace the night before with Anne. She might have finally trusted me completely. Perhaps after thirty-one years, Miles's lies had caught up to him. I needed to see her, to explain why I had been gone the entire day, but the house was quiet when the butler ushered me into the vestibule. Had everyone already gone to bed?

I passed Anne's room on my way to my own. Her door was closed, but candlelight still flickered through the crack under the door. I was too late to speak with her tonight. I would have to wait until the morning.

Inside my bedchamber, I removed my jacket, loosening my cravat before falling back onto my bed. I released a tense breath, staring up at the ceiling. My confidence regarding Anne's feelings had grown, but Miles had a power I couldn't explain. He was an expert at deceit. What if I hadn't done enough to win Anne's trust? I was fairly certain Miles had come to Birch House that day. He could have fed Anne an abundance of lies while I was finding an apartment.

A scratching sound came from behind me. I rolled over just as a folded note passed under the door, skittering across the floor until it came to a halt near the edge of the rug.

I crossed the room to pick it up, reading the words scrawled across it.

Dear Mr. Holland,

. . .

You have been selected from amongst my guests to participate in this evening's secret parlor game. Please meet in the parlor at midnight.

Your hostess,
  Lady Tottenham

ANNE

Would Lady Tottenham change her will if I didn't attend the midnight game?

Considering how quickly she had sent Lord Kirkham and the others out of the house after they had ignored her invitations, it did seem quite possible.

And after what she had said that day about taking me out of her will if I chose to marry Miles, it seemed quite *probable*, actually.

I replaced my shoes on my feet, adjusting my pink gown in the mirror before slipping out my bedchamber door with a candle in hand. I couldn't guess what to expect as I approached the parlor. The numbers of the party had diminished. We were all weary of so many games. I opened the door, the hinges creaking in the silence. There was already light coming from inside.

My heart thudded in my chest.

Alexander stood on the other side of the room. He looked up at my entrance. A hint of surprise crossed his expression. "Anne."

I couldn't blink as I took in the sight of him.

"We don't have a chess board this time." He flashed a smile, gesturing at the table.

I stayed by the door, my grip tightening on my candlestick. "Where have you been? I thought—I thought Miles had dueled you. I assumed something horrible had happened."

He raised his eyebrows, taking a few steps in my direction. "Did you assume that I would have lost the duel? That would be the second time you have doubted my strength within a day."

"I'm serious." I scowled at him. "I have been fretting about it all evening."

He looked unjustly handsome with his rolled shirtsleeves and tan waistcoat. He stopped several paces away, his soft gaze drinking me in. My heart beat a wild rhythm. This was my opportunity to speak with him alone. Lady Tottenham had provided it, just as she promised. But how could I find the words when he was looking at me like that?

His intense eyes held me captive for a long moment. "I won't pretend not to like when you fret about me," he said with a sideways smile, "but I assure you, there was no duel. I was away for a matter of great importance."

"Did it involve Miles?" I asked in a tentative voice.

He nodded. "He offered to finally repay his debt to me on the condition that I leave Birch House by tomorrow. As added incentive, he offered to contribute two thousand pounds from your fortune. I refused, of course."

My jaw dropped. "That is ridiculous! And presumptuous.

He already owed you money. He doesn't have any right to it. How could he offer it in exchange for something when he hasn't even fulfilled his end of the bargain he made two years ago." Alexander's smile grew as he watched my fit of rage. I took a deep breath. "What?"

"The money he owed is mine now. I took it back."

My anger faded. "You did?" I squeaked. I twisted a loose thread on my skirts. "Are you leaving, then?"

"I am leaving Birch House tomorrow as promised."

My heart sank. I scrambled for the right words. "I'm glad you obtained the money he owed you, but what about his confession to your family and the parish? How will they ever know the truth?"

Alexander's eyes dimmed. "They may never know, but I will do all I can to convince them. Perhaps you can help me."

I nodded. "I will do whatever I can." A nervous flutter rose in my chest. "I-I also want you to know that I plan to reject Miles's proposal. I will write him a letter with my decision, just as he wrote a letter to propose to me. I don't think I owe him more than that."

Alexander took a moment to absorb my words, his face dazed. Was he surprised that I had made my decision already? I had never been more certain. He cleared his throat. "You're right. You don't owe him anything."

I nodded, but I fought a pang of grief in my heart at the idea of Alexander leaving. "When you leave the house tomorrow, where will you go?"

A faint smile touched his lips. "I spent the day finding an apartment near Lockhart square."

My eyes flew open wide. "I thought you were going back to York."

"There is one problem with York that I cannot seem to disregard." He passed the tea table, his steps casual as he approached me. "*You* are not in York."

My heart devoured his words, and I didn't dare breathe or blink for fear of missing them. He finished crossing the room, stopping just in front of me. "I told you before that if I was in love with you, I would have never run in the opposite direction —that I would have married you if I was given the chance. I *am* in love with you, Anne." His eyes roamed my face. "Madly." He touched my cheek, brushing softly at the hair by my ear. "If your feelings allow, I would be honored to be your husband. I give you my heart. It is all yours. I promise to return your loyalty, to remain by your side forever, and to do everything in my power to give you the happiness you deserve. If you'll have me." His eyes were nervous, as if he feared I might crush him with one word.

I had meant to confess my feelings first, but he had beat me to it. Tears sprung to my eyes. My thoughts spun, leaving a large gap following his words. He still waited for my reply. "Why did your parents have to send you away to school?" A smile broke over my face. "I could have known you and fallen in love with you much sooner."

A slow smile tugged on his lips, a crease forming in his cheek. I wanted to kiss it all.

"But that *is* what happened," I said just above a whisper. "I did fall in love with you." I felt nervous and shy, but never more certain of anything. "You have made me feel safe, and loved, and happier than I have ever known. You saved me." My voice cracked as a tear slipped down my cheek. "You saved me from a bleak future and have offered me one that I never thought I would find. I don't care that I am an heiress." I laughed, a choked sound. "There is nothing I would rather be than your wife. I love you." I shook my head as desire overwhelmed me.

His hands caught my face, and before I drew another breath, we were kissing. His lips were soft but insistent. His short stubble rubbed my face but I didn't care. Not at all. My body dissolved against his, wild tremors racing through my veins, reminding me again that every other man I had kissed in my life had been wrong.

He broke away for a moment, his chest rising and falling against mine. His eyes gleamed with amusement. "You are going to set me on fire." He took the candle from my hand, turning to set it on the nearby sideboard. The flame still flickered strong on the wick.

"I'm sorry! You distracted me."

His mouth broke into a smile. I could hardly believe I had just been kissing him, until he closed the distance between us with two large strides. His hands encircled my jaw as he kissed me again, sending a spiral of butterflies through my stomach.

I buried my fingers in his hair. He smelled of fresh rain and the other scent that was uniquely his. His fervent mouth parted my lips again and again. His hands were all over my back and waist and hair, gathering every inch of me forward. He couldn't possibly be closer, yet I needed him to be. I needed it more than I had ever needed anything.

That wild, frantic feeling grew like a flame. I took two handfuls of his shirt, pulling him harder against me. A soft groan came from low in his throat, and he kissed me deeply, until my head spun. The swift succession of intensity brought a lightness to my head, but I had never felt anything more perfect.

He cupped my face in his hands softly, as if it were the most fragile thing he had ever held. "I love you," he whispered. And I knew he meant it. He dipped his head down, leaving a trail of kisses on my neck. Shivers exploded across my skin. He felt like the accumulation of every happy moment of my life. Every smile, every laugh, everything that made my life worth living. He evoked sensations I hadn't known I was capable of feeling. His mouth found mine again. His kiss was slow and gentle, until it faded into a soft brush against my lips.

I felt his mouth curve into a smile the same moment mine did.

"What game did Lady Tottenham intend for us to play?" Alexander asked, pulling back just enough to look in my eyes.

"She has always only cared about the kissing part of her games. I think she will be content."

He laughed, pressing a kiss to my forehead, then my nose, and cheek, all in quick succession. "The real question is whether or not she has locked the door behind us."

My eyes widened. I followed him toward the door, testing the handle. It turned. A flood of relief washed over me. I felt Alexander's hand on my waist as I faced the door. He turned me swiftly toward him, a playful smile on his face as he leaned his other hand against the door, trapping me. I was still rather shy, but my boldness surprised me. I rose on my toes to kiss his grinning lips again. His smile was as delicious as I'd hoped.

I wouldn't have thought it possible, but I experienced every sensation all over again. We laughed between each touch of our lips, until we both became lost in the kiss entirely. My giddiness spun me in circles until I nearly lost my balance. Alexander pressed me against the door, keeping me steady as we kissed and kissed. I wasn't aware of the time that had passed, only that tonight, a locked door would have been far too dangerous.

I took hold of the doorknob, turning it with a click. Alexander pulled back, and I slid around him, laughing. "We should return to our rooms," I said in a breathless voice. My happiness alone could have carried me there weightlessly, but before I knew what was happening, Alexander had scooped me up into his arms.

I clung to his neck as he opened the door, my laughter verging on uncontrollable. As soon as we were in the corridor, I lowered my voice to a whisper. "You don't have to carry me," I protested, even though I adored every second of it.

He smiled. "I plan to make a habit of this."

My head whirled with dreams of living at Birch House with him. I could hardly wait to invite Henrietta here to show her how my life had changed. Marrying Alexander was unexpected, but it didn't scare me. My dreams had never felt more secure. He wasn't going to run away or change his mind or keep me waiting. He valued me and my heart and my time more than anyone ever had.

I tried to imagine the years of laughter and difficulties and adventures ahead of us, but it was all blurred by my happiness. I didn't need to look ahead to things that were unwritten. I had this moment. I had him.

There couldn't be a greater prize.

CHAPTER 32

EPILOGUE

BEHIND

THE FAN

By *Lady Teignmouth*

December 14th, 1818

I t has come to my attention that there is a fortune hunter in our midst. All you dowry-bearing debutantes would do well to guard your reticules as carefully as your hearts in the presence of Mr. Miles Holland. He is the brother of the recently famed Alexander Holland, whose agreeable nature has won the hand of Lady Daventry, granting him a share of Birch House and her future fortune. I find it a suitable victory for a man who has been discredited by his brother all his life.

What is this disputatious history between the Holland brothers? Mr. Miles Holland romanced a scullery maid and left her with child before leaving for London several years ago, paying her a small sum to blame his younger brother for the wrongdoing. The truth, however, has now been brought to light. After receiving a much larger sum from the heiress of Birch House, the anonymous maid has confirmed these accusations against Miles to his family, friends, and parish.

We must conclude that Mr. Miles Holland is not only a fortune hunter, but he is much worse than that. He is a liar, and a rake. Be warned, my dear reader. His charming smiles have been known to capture even the most clever of ladies. He may boast of his riches, but he hasn't a sixpence to scratch with.

On a related, though much more pleasant subject, Lady Daventry and Mr. Alexander Holland were married last month. After their wedding trip in Brighton, they have settled at Birch House with the still vibrant Lady Tottenham, who is sure to persist much longer than her physician's estimations. I have heard she is quite pleased with her choice of heiress, and her subsequent choice of a husband.

Even with my critical eye, I have yet to find anything lacking in Mr. and Mrs. Holland's happily-ever-after.

START THE SERIES FROM THE BEGINNING

Thank you for reading! I hope Anne and Alexander made you smile. Start the series from the beginning with The Earl Next Door!

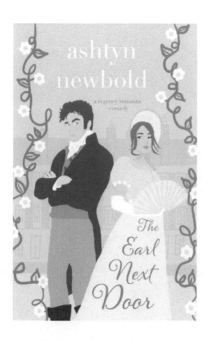

One available house. One pesky Earl. One month to drive him out.

OTHER BOOKS IN THE NOBLE CHARADES SERIES

1. The Earl Next Door

2. The Duke's Diary

Follow the author on social media to stay in the loop about future books!
Instagram - @ashtyn_newbold_author
Facebook
Newsletter

ALSO BY ASHTYN NEWBOLD

Larkhall Letters Series
The Ace of Hearts
The Captain's Confidant
With Love, Louisa
The Matchmaker's Request
Lord Blackwell's Promise

Brides of Brighton Series
A Convenient Engagement
Marrying Miss Milton
Romancing Lord Ramsbury
Miss Weston's Wager
An Unexpected Bride

Standalone novels
To Marry is Madness
In Pursuit of the Painter
The Last Eligible Bachelor
An Unwelcome Suitor
The Earl's Mistletoe Match
Her Silent Knight
A Heart to Keep

ABOUT THE AUTHOR

Ashtyn Newbold grew up with a love of stories. When she discovered Jane Austen books as a teen, she learned she was a sucker for romantic ones. Her first novel was published shortly after high school and she never looked back. When not indulging in sweet romantic comedies and regency period novels (and cookies), she writes romantic stories of her own. Ashtyn also dearly loves to laugh, bake, sing, and do anything that involves creativity and imagination.

Connect with Ashtyn Newbold on these platforms!
  INSTAGRAM: @ashtyn_newbold_author
  FACEBOOK: Author Ashtyn Newbold
  TIKTOK: @ashtynnewboldauthor
  ashtynnewbold.com

Made in United States
Troutdale, OR
09/18/2024

22940586R00217